Ash had been on the market for only a few weeks before we'd gotten it taken off the streets, but in that time it had devastating effects. All because some stupid flower, the Bleeding Soul, *Sangurne N'ashu*, an extremely rare, bioluminescent flower from Charbydon that had the ability to win the war for the nobles in ancient times, and to kill humans or make them addicts for life.

Now the person responsible for putting *ash* on the market was right here. In my city. And he was about to get a visit from a very pissed-off, potentially divine ITF officer.

"Charlie Madigan is an awesome character. . . . I could not put this book down."

—Fallen Angel Reviews

"A strong debut . . . dark and gritty, with plenty of mystery and treachery thrown in. . . . An excellent start to an electrifying new series!"

—*Romantic Times* (4 stars)

"Solid, action-packed with a kick-ass heroine. . . . Kelly Gay knows her craft!"

—Lilith Saintcrow

"Charlie Madigan is the epitome of the modern kick-butt heroine, with a sassy demeanor and a heart of gold."

—Jenna Black

"Kelly Gay's sprawling tour of Underground Atlanta puts me in mind of an estrogen-driven *Blade Runner*, with an imaginative otherworldly population . . . and a heroine who doesn't take crap from any of them. Her dark urban setting is so gritty, vivid, and original that it flaunts one of the greatest qualities of good fantasy: utter believability. . . . Kelly Gay whisked me into a dangerous world and made me want to stick around. . . . I can't wait to spend more time with Charlie Madigan."

—Vicki Pettersson

THE
HOUR
OF
DUST
AND
ASHES

KELLY GAY

POCKET BOOKS

New York   London   Toronto   Sydney   New Delhi

Pocket Books
A Division of Simon & Schuster, Inc.
1230 Avenue of the Americas
New York, NY 10020

This book is a work of fiction. Names, characters, places, and incidents either are products of the author's imagination or are used fictitiously. Any resemblance to actual events or locales or persons, living or dead, is entirely coincidental.

First Pocket Books paperback edition September 2011

POCKET and colophon are registered trademarks of Simon & Schuster, Inc.

For information about special discounts for bulk purchases, please contact Simon & Schuster Special Sales at 1-866-506-1949 or business@simonandschuster.com.

The Simon & Schuster Speakers Bureau can bring authors to your live event. For more information or to book an event, contact the Simon & Schuster Speakers Bureau at 1-866-248-3049 or visit our website at www.simonspeakers.com.

Cover design by John Vairo Jr.
Cover illustration by Chris McGrath

Manufactured in the United States of America

10 9 8 7 6 5 4 3 2 1

ISBN 978-1-4516-2547-9
ISBN 978-1-4516-2549-3 (ebook)

This one's for my sister,
Kameryn Long

(Cont. Sec.1102.07 pg. 620)

- Drug diminishes the will of the human spirit, causing weaker disembodied spirits to easily gain control.
- *Ash* has a honeysuckle aroma. Do not inhale. Once ingested, fatal overdose may occur. Survivors must maintain routine dosage in order to prevent fatal withdraw. No known cure.
- Manufactured using Charbydon flower, *Sangurne N'ashu*. Colloquial term: Bleeding Soul.

Sons of Dawn: A cult created by the biblical King Solomon (son of the human woman Bathsheba and the jinn High Chief Malek Murr). Said to have discovered some truth behind the legend of the **First Ones**. Purpose: to liberate Charbydon from the nobles and return control back to the jinn.

Known Members:

- **Grigori Tennin.** Jinn tribal boss. Resides in Underground Atlanta. Stands to become the next High Chief should the jinn regain control of Charbydon.
- **Llyran.** Adonai. Level Ten felon. Stole the Old Lore from the Hall of Records in Elysia and used the cult to foster his own bid for supreme power. Deceased.
- **Mynogan.** Charbydon noble. High Elder of the royal House of Abaddon. Manufactured the off-world drug *ash* along with Grigori Tennin and Cassius Mott. Orchestrated the ritual to bring darkness over Earth. Deceased.

The First Ones: Divine beings mentioned in the Old Lore of the Elysians. Myth claims that from them, the three noble races descended: the Elysian Adonai, the Charbydon nobles, and humans. The myth also claims that the nobles once ruled in Elysia, but were later cast out into Charbydon.

Noteworthy:

- **The Sons of Dawn's** mission is to find physical proof of the First Ones' existence and prove to the nobles that their true home is in Elysia. This will lead to the nobles waging war for Elysian territory.
- **Ahkneri.** One of the First Ones. Called the Star, and later the instrument of vengeance, retribution, and punishment. Holder of the named weapon, Urzenemelech. (The remains of this being were supposedly discovered by King Solomon and used during the Winter Solstice ritual on top of Helios Tower by Llyran and the Sons of Dawn, but no evidence of such a discovery has been found.)

Darkest Part of Night

IN THE YEAR 1979, the Psy race made the decision to embrace Silence and condition all emotion out of their young; to become without hope or despair, anger or fear, sorrow or joy.

Mothers and fathers sentenced their children to lives of icy control out of a soul-deep love those children would never feel in return. They told their babies that Silence was a precious gift, that it would save them from the madness and violence that so often came intertwined with the staggering beauty of their psychic abilities.

Without Silence, said a leading philosopher of the day, *we will cannibalize ourselves in a storm of blood and death and insanity, until the Psy race becomes nothing but a terrible memory.*

In 1979, Silence was a beacon of hope . . . but 1979 was more than a hundred years ago.

Those first children are long dead and the PsyNet has been rocked by the initial volley of a civil war that might yet tear it apart, taking the changelings and humans with it. A civil war that has awakened a whispering understanding in the populace about the ugly irony of Silence: in creating a society that rewards lack of emotion, the Psy have created fertile ground for the rise of psychopathic personalities to the leadership of their race.

An individual who feels nothing is, after all, the perfect graduate of Silence.

Ruthless. Cold-blooded. Without mercy . . . without conscience.

I

"You mean to tell me every single exorcist in this city is gone?"

Perched on her crude stone chair like an ancient Greek actor shadowed in darkness and smoke, Alessandra rolled her luminous green eyes to the ceiling. "Why is it everyone who stands before me must repeat everything I say?"

Because you say the craziest things? I thought, keeping a straight face.

Under the bowl-shaped seat, a bundle of laurel leaves smoked in a copper basin wedged between thick tripod legs. The fine material she wore over her head and shoulders caught the sweet-smelling smoke rising from below, billowing the fabric and directing much of it toward her lungs. Her hand stroked the back of a python curled in her lap, its fat head resting over her forearm.

Stone, python, laurel leaves—all primitive, powerful things that enhanced the sight and gave Atlanta's resident oracle a spot at the very top.

There was a time long ago when oracles were killed for being wrong, but Alessandra—with her pale, ageless skin and softly glowing eyes that never focused on anything for long—hadn't stayed in business the last two thousand years by being wrong. Confusing, frustrating, pompous to a staggering degree? Absofucking-lutely. But *never* wrong.

The smoke hit the back of my throat, tasting of burnt leaves and bitter wood. I coughed, waving at the ghostly ribbons drifting my way and cursing the oracle's refusal to install ventilation in her temple.

She called it a temple. *I* called it a decrepit forties-style theater in Underground Atlanta. There was one stage, mezzanine seating, and staggered seating in the pit. You got a number, waited your turn, and then walked onto the stage to face the hooded oracle seated above her burning leaves.

Alessandra also owned the club next door. She'd had it connected to her temple via a wide, arched tunnel that allowed the beat, the strobe lights, the smoke, and the club patrons to trickle through. Sandra loved an audience, and milking the drunks for every penny they had was an added bonus to an already lucrative career.

The smoke, the saccharine sweetness hanging in the air like jungle humidity, the unbelievably hard time Alessandra felt compelled to give me—not to mention the constant throbbing beat from the club next door—were ingredients for The Perfect Migraine.

And The Perfect Reason why I kept my visits few and far between.

"You waste my time, Charlie Madigan. As usual. Track them down if you want. Search until you expire for all I care. You've found how many in the last week? None. Nada. Zip. Zeroooo." She sang the last word, making an *O* with her thumb and pointer finger. Her red nails flashed in the dim light. Such a small distraction, but one that made her musical note fade as she fanned out all five fingers in admiration. "Gods, I *adore* this shade. How can you not love a color called 'Spanked Bottom'? You tell me." She flashed her nails at me. "Pretty accurate, no?"

My brow lifted. "I wouldn't know, Sandra . . . can we cut the BS for once? I've spent the last few days tracking down every exorcist in this city. I have no one left to tell me. Is my sister possessed or not?"

"I see only what the leaves tell me. They tell me nothing about spirits lurking in her belfry."

"Of course not." Alessandra could try the patience of a saint, but I swear she only did this roundabout cryptic shit to me. "And the exorcists leaving the city? I suppose that's just a coincidence."

"Well, they're not stupid. They know when the danger is too great to stay. And who said they left willingly . . . or even alive?"

The fact that all the exorcists in the city had suddenly vanished didn't bode well for Bryn. And there was no doubt in my mind the danger Alessandra spoke of was most likely attributed to one person: jinn tribal chief, organized crime boss, and Sons of Dawn cult member Grigori Tennin. He was the only one with a direct link to the off-world drug *ash*, the cult, and my sister's possible possession.

"Why do you even question her possession?" Alessandra asked me. "Wishful thinking, no? And here I thought you were a lifelong pessimist."

"I have to question it. Not a single mage in the League, not even the Elders, can sense another presence in her."

"Yet, only a week ago she killed the warlock mage, the one she loves."

"*Llyran* killed Aaron. Bryn just . . ."

"Helped him."

My heart sank. It was true. And even though we'd brought Aaron—my friend, my teacher, the man my sister loved—back from the dead, Bryn didn't remember the part she played. And the only thing I knew for sure was that Bryn was there with Aaron, his blood on her hands, when he died.

The Sons of Dawn cult had developed *ash* to suppress human will. *Ash* made humans pawns. The cult needed pawns to further their agenda, needed vessels in which to place the spirits of their dead priests. Just waiting for a new body, a new life to fuck up . . . And now all the exorcists were gone.

"Well, I think we both agree she wasn't in her right

mind," Alessandra said. "If she is under their control, she's in an excellent position to help the cult recover what they lost during your fight atop Helios Tower. Surely you have considered this."

"Of course I have—that's why I'm here. I need solid proof before I go pulling a spirit from her without being certain there's one to pull."

"Otherwise you'd take hers, and that would leave her quite dead, wouldn't it?"

I rubbed a hand down my face, letting out a tired breath. White tendrils of smoke drifted my way again, and my head was starting to pound. "C'mon, Sandra, you've got to give me something. Anything. *Please.*"

She regarded me for a long, thoughtful moment. "There is another in the city," she said slowly. "Drawn by the darkness, can see inside and do many things . . ."

Relief swept through me. "Great. Who?"

"The sylph."

I blinked, questioning with a look.

"Creatures of mist, smoke, earth . . ." She leaned precariously to one side and then swayed to the other, eyelids fluttering. "Left Elysia . . . branched off . . . evolved into shifters of a *different* kind." Her voice went deeper, breathier. "Been here, part of Earth, *tied* to Earth so long. Yes, yes. A different kind altogether."

I was only familiar with one kind of being that could alter its shape at will without the use of crafting—

nymphs. The nature-loving beings from Elysia, and the inspiration for much of Celtic mythology (along with the darkling and sidhé fae), were born with the ability to shift into an animal form. But a creature that shifted into mist? "Never heard of them."

"And why would you? They prefer to stay hidden, unknown. Why should they reveal themselves when Elysia and Charbydon were discovered? The sylphs were already here, long before the nymphs and fae even. They did not see the need to enlighten mankind." Her voice dropped to a mutter. "And they're not the only ones . . ."

That was comforting. "Where do I find the sylph?"

She waved an impatient hand, glancing at the entrance to the club. "Here and there. Above. Below. I'm an oracle, Charlie Madigan. *The* oracle. Not a map. I do not keep track." She paused, eyeing me with open calculation. "I can, however, get you an introduction. You want one?"

Alessandra being helpful was a recipe for some kind of disaster. Nothing was cut and dry when it came to her information or her idea of help, but . . . "An introduction would be great, thanks."

"Mmm," she said, nodding and closing her eyes for a few seconds. "No need to thank me. You'll be charged extra."

Figures. My bank account was about to take a major hit.

"And where's your partner tonight?" she asked. "As

I recall, last time he was here with you, Tuni broke his nose." She cast an admiring glance at the rogue jinn warrior standing off to the side of the stage.

Tuni stood with both feet apart, large arms crossed over his chest, his gray skin a near match for the darkness behind him. Only the light reflecting off his violet irises, smooth bald head, and ear piercings saved Alessandra's Goliath of a guard from blending completely into the shadows. I knew for a fact that the guy had a fist the size of a grapefruit. A grapefruit made of steel as Hank told it.

The last time we were here, inquiring about the new off-world drug, *ash*, Tuni had indeed broken my partner's nose. A minor scuffle. My fault, really. Hank's face just happened to be in the way when I opened my big mouth and insulted the oracle.

I sighed, wondering where the hell she was going with this, but knowing it was part of her game, her ritual. Her boredom. "I don't keep tabs on my partner, Sandra."

"Mmm. Maybe you should. Now that he has full use of his siren abilities once more, I wonder how many potential mates will be crawling out of the woodwork. New Year's Eve is coming. Time for kisses. I'll be kissed. Will you?"

"You're the oracle. You tell me."

A genuine laugh breezed through her painted lips. "I think I'll keep that one to myself, Charlie." She leaned forward with a conspiring gleam in her eyes. "You want me to tell you what your siren will be doing tonight?"

My teeth ground together. *He's not my siren.* "I'll pass." Because I knew exactly what my partner was doing tonight. Sleeping. Just like he'd done yesterday and the day before and the day before that.

When Hank had used his siren voice to issue a massive power word atop Helios Tower, it ended the battle between us and the war-obsessed cult Sons of Dawn. But there was a consequence for that kind of energy drain.

He'd held it together after the battle—long enough for us to find a hiding place for the cult's most prized possession and to check on Aaron—but as soon as Hank had walked away from me at the station, he'd gone straight home, crawled into bed, and sunk into a near comatose state.

That was a week ago. He'd missed Christmas. And he might even miss New Year's if he didn't wake up soon.

"So certain you know, eh?" A smug grin crawled across the oracle's face. "You of all people should know you can never *truly* know another. Trust. Faith. They are only hopes, not absolutes. *Never* absolutes. Thin hopes, at best, to ease the mind and heart."

Me of all people. Nice. *Hit me where it hurts, Sandra.*

I gave her the most annoyed expression in my arsenal even though she spoke the truth. My ex-husband Will and I had been together for eleven years. I would've sat across from the devil himself and bet my life on Will's faithfulness and honesty. And the devil would've collected my soul, leaving me completely blindsided. Alessandra was right. You can never *truly* know another or what they're capable of. Will and his secret life of black crafting had taught me that. It was a lesson I'd never forget.

"There are limits on love and loyalty, Charlie. Everyone has a line, a truth, a sacrifice they are unwilling to make for another no matter how much devotion and love they have. Your siren has secrets just like you and everyone else. The only one who can truly know all is"—her white teeth flashed from within the darkness of her hood—"*me.*"

My expression went flat. She might *know* the future as it was tonight, but I firmly believed the future was fluid, changeable, affected by constantly varying factors.

Whatever.

No matter what Alessandra saw or knew about Hank and me, she wouldn't get to me. Not this time. I gave myself enough hell as it was. Every time I thought about losing control and blatantly falling under the siren spell like your average groupie, and then getting that damn truth mark, I could barely breathe let alone think about Hank's last words to me. *You don't stand a chance.*

And what the hell did that mean anyway?

Dating? A fling? Something more? The answer hinged on what happened next. Except the "next" had been put on hold while Hank recuperated.

"How long?" I asked tightly as her eerie green eyes laughed at me. "How long will it take to contact the sylph?"

Alessandra waved the smoke away as though just realizing it bothered her. "As long as it takes. Now leave your token at the altar." Which was code for: *We're done; get the hell out of my temple.* "And for Dione's sake, get your Revenant out of my club."

I turned, immediately finding the seat Rex had promised to stay in. "Shit," I whispered through clenched teeth. Damned if he hadn't gone into the club. I looked at my watch. Thirty minutes to gather Rex and get to the Mordecai House to pick up my kid from visiting with Bryn.

My token consisted of a credit card swiped through a conveniently placed machine (aka the altar) by the steps. Tuni and the twelve other bodyguards lurking around the theater made sure everyone paid and everyone treated Alessandra with the utmost respect.

I glanced down at the receipt and cringed. Three hundred bucks. *Great.* I shoved my card back into my wallet and then made for the steps.

"Oh, and Charlie?" Alessandra called. I turned on the steps and waited to be wowed by her next vital and coherent piece of information. "Do me a favor and don't summon your power tonight, 'kay?"

I paused on the steps.

"Number one hundred and twenty." A booming voice called the next patron over the loudspeaker as I started back up the steps to ask her what the hell she meant.

Tuni blocked my path. "Move along."

I leaned to the side. Alessandra wasn't even looking my way anymore and I knew from past experience she wouldn't elaborate once she was "done." With a sigh, I left, making for the giant archway that led into the club.

The music grew louder as I approached. The blood vessels in my head pounded in time to the deep bass. Strobe lights flashed through the tunnel, making the smoky air light up in bursts that did nothing for my developing headache.

"Let me come with you. Don't worry I'll be good as gold," Rex had said earlier.

Yeah. Good as gold, my ass.

As I approached the two guards at the archway, one reached for the snap to the velvet rope as the other one went to step in front of me. I swore if he asked for a cover charge after I'd just spent three hundred bucks, I was going to blow. He pulled out a stamp, pressed it to the back of my hand, and allowed me to pass. Smart man.

Inside the tunnel, the music was louder, the smoke suffocating, the strobes brighter. The faintest hint of nausea spread from my gut to my throat. With every step farther down the tunnel, my desire to kill Rex mounted. Now I just had to hurry up and find the—

A record scratched. The music stopped. And a voice rang out loud and clear.

"Come and get it, muthafuckahhhs!!!"

Rex.

2

Club patrons raced past me, down the corridor, and toward the temple. I eased back the side of my jacket. As soon as my fingers curled around the cool polymer grip of my 9mm sidearm, a sense of calm and familiarity came over me. I didn't pull the gun from the holster, but I was ready if the need arose.

Rex stood at the end of the tunnel where it opened into the club, his back to me, wielding two legs of a metal chair; the rest of the mutilated chair lay nearby. He swung the legs around and around while exchanging insults with a group in front of him. And he was enjoying every minute of it.

Spread out over the recently vacated dance floor were eight black mages, otherwise known as Pig-Pens for the thin, dirty aura surrounding them. The aura was a result of an Elysian giving up their inborn power for the dark power of Charbydon, which lent itself better to black crafting. A lot of Elysians looked upon Pig-Pens as though they were abominations of nature. But I knew better than most the lure that black crafting held. Enough to destroy lives . . .

Pig-Pens could be any Elysian race, but the ones facing off with Rex were a collection of sirens and nymphs. Males and females. All dressed in dark clothing. All black-eyed, pale, and wearing grave expressions.

I'd never seen more than four together at one time, and even that number was noteworthy because Pig-Pens usually worked in pairs.

"Mind explaining this?" I said to Rex, stopping at the head of the archway, out of his swinging range.

"They were asking around, looking for you, about to head into the temple. Call it saving your ass. You can thank me later."

"So, what, you decided to play Super Ninja all by yourself?"

Rex might have remembered his jinn past and his training as an elite warrior, but he was still in a human body, my ex-husband's body to be exact. Rex would survive a mortal blow—his Revenant spirit would simply be set free. Will Garrity, on the other hand, would die. And I wasn't about to let that happen.

One of the Pig-Pens stepped closer, his dark eyes zeroing in on me. "Where is it?"

"Where's what?" I asked innocently, even though I knew exactly what he referred to.

"The sarcophagus. Where is it?"

"We destroyed it," I answered.

"You lie!"

"Why would I? Do you really think we'd risk keeping it? Gee, let's see . . . destroying an object for the greater good of mankind or keeping it around. I don't know . . . seems like a no-brainer to me." The lie flowed easily from my lips, but my heart raced. Destroying the sarcophagus hadn't been an option, so we hid it the best we could. The fact that these guys were here now meant that Tennin and his crazy-ass cult hadn't bought into the rumor of its destruction. "What did he promise you? Money? Power?" I asked, knowing these guys were just hired hands; they had no clue what was inside of the sarcophagus.

Footsteps shuffled to my right. Alessandra's jinn bodyguard Tuni appeared next to me as another one of her enforcers took up position on the other side of Rex.

"Madigan," Tuni's deep voice echoed in the lofty space. "Should've known."

I leaned toward him. "For the record, I did not start it. If they back off, I'll walk out of here without another word in their direction."

"Enough of this talk! Where is it?" the Pig-Pen shouted at me. The others behind him shifted, eager to pounce. Their energy intensified, building, getting ready . . .

Three sidhé fae appeared behind them. Straight

out of thin air and practically glowing in their silvery chain mail tunics and pearly skin. Each one had a crisscross of sword hilts peeking from behind his shoulders. Two blades that I knew were curved, thin, and razor sharp. What I didn't know was what the hell they were doing here. And where they'd come from, because these guys looked old-school; I'd only ever seen armor like that in books.

The tallest one in the middle took a step forward, assessing the situation with a quick, perceptive eye. The guy was at least six and a half feet, long, lean, and agile-looking. He had a noble face, ruthless and hard as granite. Light hair had been pulled back into a ponytail, accentuating his widow's peak and giving him a sharp visage. He wore black leather pants and boots and a leather belt over the silver chain mail, arm guards, and thigh guards.

The familiar, light pink irises typical of the sidhé fae fixed on me. "You are the one they call Charlie Madigan, aye?"

Half of the Pig-Pens turned in surprise at his voice. The air went thick with hostility and an underlying confusion. This new development threw everyone off balance, including me.

I glanced around, wishing there was another Charlie Madigan in the club, and wondering what the hell I'd done this time. I returned my attention to the sidhé. "That depends on why you're asking, and if you're here for the same reasons as these guys." I gestured to the Pig-Pens.

A haughty eyebrow lifted as if to say breathing the same air as them was appalling.

"Stay out of this," one of the Pig-Pens growled at the fae. "She's ours."

As they exchanged heated words, I glanced over at Tuni even as goose bumps spread over my arms. "I'm apologizing in advance. Make sure you tell Alessandra I was only defending myself." He crossed his thick arms over his chest and grunted. "So . . . you just gonna watch or help me clear the dance floor?"

The jinn were a warrior culture. I wasn't surprised to see the corner of Tuni's mouth twitch into a grin. His big fists clenched, his rings flashing in the light. He nodded. "Just this once. Since they *are* disturbing the peace."

A welcome spike of adrenaline surged through me.

Rex let out a huff and his arms dropped limply to his sides as he glared at Tuni and me. "You guys are like two little old ladies over there talking. Shut up already and let's kick some oinker ass."

"Rex," I warned, as the argument between the Pig-Pen and the fae continued, "stay behind me. I don't want anything happening to Will."

An incredulous snort came out of his mouth, just as one of the Pig-Pens shoved a fae.

And that was it.

I ignored the thrumming vibration of power stirring inside of me and whipped my Nitro-gun from the holster under my arm, flicked the setting to stun, and fired as Rex engaged with his chair legs.

"Damn it, Rex!" I yelled at him.

He didn't have to fight, since the odds were in our favor to begin with. Sure, there were eight of them, but the sidhé fae were preternaturally efficient and could dispatch ten times their number with ease.

"Charlie, duck!" Rex shouted. I dropped to the floor and rolled, barely evading the bolt of power that surged over my shoulder. "Damn it, Rex! What the hell are you doing?!" I pushed to my feet, angry that he put Will's body in danger, no matter how good he was.

"Again, with the saving your ass!" he shouted back.

One more attacked him, and the black mage went down swiftly. "Come on! Who's next?! Here piggy, piggy, piggy! Soooo-eeeeey!" Rex's voice rang with laughter as he faced another.

I never knew a human body could move that fast and beautifully. Rex had tapped into his former self— the jinn warrior he used to be before his spirit had been forced from his body during the Great War in Charbydon. He'd said he was the best . . . and watching him now, I believed him.

A boot connected with my kidney.

I flew forward, gun tumbling from my hand as hot pain burst through my torso. I fell to my knees, gasping. Fuck. I'd allowed Rex to distract me. Stupid mistake.

I rolled onto my back as the electric hum of power began to flow through my limbs.

The Pig-Pen attacker stood over me with a leer, his hands cupping a bright red ball of energy.

My chest swelled and my arms and hands went numb—a searing, painful numb like the pricking of a thousand red-hot needles. A scream built in my throat and all I knew was that I had to get rid of it. I sat up, overwhelmed and blinded, and threw out my hands, releasing my chaotic energy.

It all happened so fast. Once second I was flat on my back and the next, a bolt of blue energy slammed the Pig-Pen square in the chest, sending him flying across the room and through the drywall.

Jesus. I sat there panting as the faint hum of power receded. The room had gone quiet.

The sidhé fae calmly sheathed their weapons. They hadn't even broken a sweat. I put my palms on the dance floor, about to push to my feet and approach the leader of the fae, when a deafening report tore through the club.

I bent over, hands pressed over my ears. An enormous vibration rang through the club, as though some kind of sonic boom ripped the air apart. The shock wave shook the ground and my surroundings, every bit of glass in the club shattering.

What the hell?

As the roar diminished, I let my hands fall from my ringing ears. Glass pinged the floor, the lighter bits rebounding and hovering in the air for a split second before being whisked sideways as if caught in a freak current. Another shock wave?

Other things were picked up in the strange current—paper, napkins, credit card slips . . .

Warnings darted under my skin like tiny fireballs. I crawled a few feet to retrieve my gun and shoved it back into the holster under my arm.

"Rex!"

More debris began to tornado around the club.

"Charlie!"

There. He was hunkered down behind an overturned table. "Run!" I shouted. "Get out of here, now!"

Rex stood to yell back at me, but a flying bar stool hit him in the back of the head. He landed motionless at the feet of the sidhé fae leader. The fae's gaze went from Rex to me, and in that grim, knowing expression, I understood. He knew *exactly* what was happening.

The fae shouted a stern order to the others in his old language.

And then it dawned on me—nothing close to me was moving. While debris spun around the perimeter of the club, I sat in the center of an eerie quiet.

The eye of the storm.

Fear threaded into my psyche. I swallowed hard, slowly standing, wary of the circle of spinning debris. *Stay calm. Balance. Be ready.* I bent my knees, centered my weight, and crossed my right hand over my chest, poised to grab the gun under my left arm.

Something darkened in the spinning debris, catching my eye. A shadow. Then it simply glided out of the chaos.

A tall mass of gray. A suggestion of a tall, cloaked

being. Yet it swirled and moved, becoming so thin at points that I could see straight through it.

It was in front of me in less than a second.

I stayed rooted to the spot. A shot, a kick, a punch, would go right through this creature. Still my fingers flexed over the grip of my weapon. A comforting gesture, because the more I looked into this . . . *thing*, the more darkness I saw—a terrifying, empty void.

It leaned closer. My pulse thrummed like a freight train.

A deep voice spoke, and there was so much power in it that I swayed on my feet. Primal. Ancient. Frightening as hell.

And then it enveloped me.

One gasp was all I had before it flew at me, passing completely through my body and coming out the other side.

Invaded. Turned inside out. Violated.

I dropped like a stone.

I awoke to Rex's tiny, repetitive taps on my cheek. For a moment, all I could do was stare in shock as my brain scrambled to make sense of my last coherent memory—the terrifying shadow passing through my body. All five senses came flooding back with the memory, leaving me feeling exposed, raw. Weak.

I honed in on the worried face above mine.

But in my disoriented state, all I saw for a moment was Will. Will's face. Will's body. Handsome. Tall.

Athletic. The concern shining in those stormy blues and the gentle smile was so much like him . . . But it wasn't him. It was Rex in control now. I let my head fall to the side, irritated that my mind had gone there for even a second.

The club was in utter ruins. Employees and body-guards picked over the rubble, righting chairs and tables . . .

"Come on, sunshine," Rex said. "Time to go."

I grabbed his outstretched hand and let him pull me to my feet. My vision swam and my stomach gave a sickening wave. The groan was out of my mouth before I could stop it.

"You okay?"

"Yeah," I said through gritted teeth. "Let's get out of here." Before Alessandra got there and started assessing damages.

I started moving toward the exit until her last words struck me still.

Do me a favor and don't summon your power tonight, 'kay?

"Charlie?" Rex was a few feet in front of me, his brow wrinkling.

I'd summoned my power. The loud crack. Then . . . that thing had come. And she'd *known*. I turned and marched toward the tunnel, my strength and fortitude returning.

"Oh man, here we go again . . ." Rex muttered from behind me, shoving debris out of his way to catch up.

Alessandra was already striding through the tunnel toward me, her angry steps matching my own.

The light from the temple behind her lit the veil over her head and shoulders like a halo. Her eyes glowed in what could only be called Pissed-off Green.

We met in the middle of the archway. I'd never seen the oracle so angry before, but the implications of her wrath—and their consequences—were lost on me at the moment because I was just as steamed.

"What the hell was that thing, Sandra?"

"I *told* you not to summon your power."

"*What. Was. It?*"

Emotions cycled through her expression and finally settled on something akin to spite. "Fine." She leaned in close. "*Sachâth*. Destroyer. Death. Call it what you will. But *you* brought it here." She poked me hard in the chest. "Now *you* have to deal with it."

She shoved her way around me, shouting Tuni's name and leaving me standing there in the smoky tunnel with my mouth open.

The air on Mercy Street was blessedly cleaner than the acrid haze contaminating Alessandra's temple and club. After several purifying breaths, I threaded my fingers through my hair and gave a hard ruffle to remove the burning smell and bits of glass and debris. My jacket came off next, and I gave it a good shake.

After I was finished rearranging myself, I tucked my jacket between my legs and brushed off Rex's shoulders.

"Ow! Take it easy there, Nurse Ratched." He stepped away from me. "I can do it myself."

I shot him an eye roll as he brushed off his clothes and then bent over to ruffle his hair. Small fragments of the club hit the sidewalk. He straightened. I smiled despite being so rattled. His brown hair stuck up, making him look like a kid just out of bed.

"What?"

I shook my head. "Nothing. Come on."

I chose a path down the center of the carless street to avoid the after-Christmas-sale shoppers populating the sidewalks. January was just a few days away, but you wouldn't know it from the temperature. The darkness hovering over Atlanta seemed to insulate everything beneath it from the winter weather. Or maybe, like some theorized, the darkness was generating its own energy, its own heat . . .

Whatever the case, I didn't need the light jacket I slipped back on as I walked. But it covered my weapons, and I'd rather not be gawked at for parading around with three different firearms strapped to my body.

Without warning, the hair on the back of my neck stood. I glanced over my shoulder with the distinct feeling of being watched, but there was nothing unusual. Just your typical day in Underground Atlanta.

"You ever see anything like that before?" I asked Rex as we walked.

"Those old fairy dudes? Nuh-uh. And now that I think about it, I've never seen a Pig-Pen do that much damage."

"I meant the creature."

"What creature?"

"What do you mean, what creature? The one that came out of the wind. The one that went *through* me. The reason I was out cold on the dance floor."

"I thought you just couldn't handle the Donna Summer remix." He reached over and patted my head.

I swatted at him. "What are you doing?"

"Checking for a bump."

"There is no bump. It was there, right in front of me." I used my hands to explain. "Yea big. Tall. All gray and floaty-like . . ."

He frowned. "That must've been *after* you made me get hit with a flying bar stool."

Oh. Yeah. I'd forgotten about that. Might explain why he hadn't seen the creature.

I pulled out my phone, hitting Sian's cell number. "Hey. It's me." I proceeded to tell my new office assistant every detail I could remember about the creature and asked her to put her research skills to work. "Oh, and while you're at it, access the gate logs and see if any new sidhé fae visitors have come through from Elysia within the last two months. And I want whatever you can find on their warrior classes, groups, sects, cults, whatever . . ."

My steps slowed as I came upon Hodgepodge, my sister's variety shop, which catered to crafting, odd off-world items, and rare plants from all three worlds. "That's it. Thanks," I mumbled, hanging up. The doors were open for business and shoppers browsed the aisles.

What a relief.

I'd finally convinced Bryn to take advantage of her part-time employee's offer to run the store while she dealt with the *ash* addiction. Gemma was a retired schoolteacher and had been working for Bryn for almost two years now—just weekends and some evenings, but she'd been around long enough to know exactly how Bryn liked things done. And Bryn desperately needed the sales after having been closed during the holidays.

Seeing the female figure behind the counter made my chest tighten. It should be my sister standing there, stealing M&M's from her stash, and talking to her array of herbs and plants. My gaze traveled up to the second story. The blinds in the windows were down. No light from within. Barren.

And it was all wrong. So damn wrong.

Bryn was currently staying at the Mordecai House, the League of Mages headquarters in Atlanta. Her choice, not mine. Bryn was afraid. Afraid to be alone, afraid of what she was capable of, and more determined than ever to uncover her lost memories. Her guilt in possibly aiding or even directly causing Aaron's death was eating away at her faster than her addiction to *ash*.

"Okay," Rex said after we'd passed the store. "You can say it."

"What? That you promised to stay in the temple?"

"No, not that part. The part where you tell me how awe-inspiring I was back there. You know"—he slid a look my way—"you might make a pretty good sidekick one day."

Oh my God.

"Rex . . ." I paused, forgoing the lecture because it wouldn't make a damned bit of difference anyway. "What am I going to do with you?"

A slow grin spread across his face. "Now *that's* one hell of a question." He threw an arm around my shoulder and picked up our pace. "So glad you asked. I have plenty of ideas. First . . ."

3

A slow, familiar zing snaked through me as I entered the crowded plaza where Mercy Street, Helios Alley, and Solomon Street converged, and made for the wide concrete steps that would take us Topside. Like the first jolt of a drug-induced high, the Charbydon genes inside of me responded to the forty-mile swath of darkness that hovered above Atlanta and its outskirts.

I hated that I was getting used to it . . . that, little by little, I was coming to terms with the incvitable. The Charbydon and Elysian DNA that had been given to me as I lay dying ten months ago was altering me from the inside out, changing me into something new, or something old if I believed Aaron's "divine being" theory.

But it wasn't the darkness that made me stop in the middle of the plaza.

It was Alessandra's comments about Hank that had quietly tunneled beneath my confidence, making fine cracks in my trust.

Just like she'd intended.

People passed by, conversations came and went along with the sounds of traffic from the city above. And I just stood there, knowing I should keep walking, that I should have some measure of belief.

I bit down hard, grinding my teeth together with indecision. But when you've been burned before . . .

I cursed under my breath and turned away from Topside, heading toward my new path: Helios Alley. Damn her.

"Uh, Charlie?" Rex said from behind me. "We told Bryn we'd pick Em up at ten."

Was Hank really in bed recuperating? And, worse, how totally pathetic was I for having to check? "I know. This won't take long. I just want to check on Hank." I cleared my throat. Since when did saying his name become so uncomfortable?

"Oh, *really*?"

I didn't need to look at Rex to know he was smirking. I sidestepped a baby stroller. "Yes, really. Someone should go check on him."

"No one needs to check on him. You were there when the chief told us the deal. He's in a self-induced coma. Doesn't need to eat, drink, or take a piss . . . When he wakes, he wakes. What are you going to do, stand there and moon over him?"

My stride increased. "What the hell's that supposed to mean?"

"What the hell are you getting so defensive about?"

"I'm not getting defensive."

"You sound defensive."

"No I don't."

"Yes you—"

"Rex!" I stopped, letting him see just how tired I was of being provoked. "Knock it off."

He held up his hands in surrender. "Just trying to figure out which way the wind blows these days."

I growled and kept walking. Rex could think whatever the hell he wanted. Hank was my partner and I had every right to check on him.

I knew Hank had his secrets. He was close-lipped about his Elysian history and why he'd come here. He evaded personal questions as easily as picking lint from his sleeve. Sure, he was entitled to his privacy, his secrets, like everyone else. But at the same time, we'd been partners for three years. I'd welcomed him into my world, shared my home, my life, my trust. We'd become friends. And recently, something more than that. Hadn't I earned some small degree of sharing in return, some trust from him as well?

Sounded reasonable.

I chewed softly on the inside of my cheek, not liking the questions the oracle put into my mind. But how much could I lay the blame on Alessandra? My trust and faith in people—or, more correctly, men—had been shaken considerably since Will.

I wasn't ready for a serious relationship, I knew that. But it didn't stop my feet from carrying me deep into Helios Alley until I was staring at the polished brass numbers attached to the black door leading to

Hank's apartment above Skin Scripts and Off-world Exotic Pets.

Heat formed in my belly and made the journey into my limbs and my face. Last time I was up there, the windows got blown out, and I'd almost killed my partner with the twig of a Charbydon Throne Tree. Among other things.

I rolled my shoulder, thinking of the mark Hank had given to me during our fight. It was healed now, but not even my new healing abilities could erase the light indigo scar. Odd that it wasn't giving off the strange, feel-good sensation that signified when we were close. But maybe the brick walls and the fact that he was a story above me and out cold had something to do with it.

What the hell did I know about marks?

"We going in or what?"

I ignored Rex and let my gaze fall to the big front window of Skin Scripts. All I had to do was open the door. The artists there could tell me everything I needed to know about the mark permanently pressed into my skin. It would be even better if they could tell me how to get around the truth issue.

In the heat of our fight, Hank had given me a truth mark, which meant I couldn't lie to him if he asked me a direct question. I could evade it, choose to not answer, but if I lied outright, the ink embedded in my skin would release a toxin into my bloodstream. It wouldn't kill me, but it would have serious consequences. There was a time when a broken mark could cause death, but legislation and regulations had long since prohibited actual death marks.

I headed over to Skin Scripts's entrance, but before I opened the door I turned to Rex with a stern warning. "Not a word. Not a single word. Got it?"

An exasperated look crossed his face, but he nodded in agreement, and we stepped inside to the tiny jingle of the bell above the door.

Behind the counter, the darkling fae artist looked up from a sketch. His long fingers were splayed over a piece of heavy paper, holding it down while he drew with a charcoal pencil.

Like the sidhé fae, the darkling fae possessed a fascinating, otherworldly skin tone—a sheen, a luminescent quality that put one in mind of pearls. And it was easy to tell them apart. The darkling fae's skin tones were indicative of Charbydon—shades of gray, some with hints of blue and violets—while the sidhé possessed lighter skin tones that reminded me of a very pale human, except for the soft, pearly glow.

Darklings were thin, too, with long, graceful limbs and large, slanted eyes with irises that ranged from the lightest sea green to the darkest shades of violet. This one gazed up at us with pale blue eyes painted with heavy black eyeliner. His black hair was short and spiky, and he had a wealth of tattoos and markings on both arms and around his neck.

"Can I help you?" he asked.

I cleared my throat. "I was wondering if you could tell me about ceremonial markings? The ones having to do with truth between two people, a vow not to lie . . . that sort of thing."

The guy didn't blink an eye, but then, why would he? The things people came here asking him to do were a hell of a lot crazier than what I'd just asked.

He turned in his swivel chair to the shelf of books lining the wall and pulled one out. He set it on the counter in front of us, flipping it open and skimming. It was an encyclopedia, a collection of ceremonial markings complete with sketches, incantations, and definitions. "Any of these interest you?" He turned the book so I could read right side up.

Rex leaned over my shoulder as I scanned the six sketches, finding one that was very similar to the mark on my shoulder—a curved, incomplete arrow-shaped symbol with two slashes and a dot, though it lacked the correct combination of slashes and dots.

"We can do them in traditional tattoo ink or we can do them in Throne Tree ink. Tats will run you about eighty, and the tree ink will cost you a couple hundred to a couple thousand, depending on what you want."

Rex pointed. "Ooh, I like this one."

"I'm not buying," I said to the artist. "I already have one. I just want to know what the hell it means because it's not on this page."

That caught his and Rex's undivided attention. "Let me see," they said at the same time.

I drew in a deep breath, turned, and tugged my shirt down over my shoulder, exposing the mark on my shoulder blade. Since we shared a home together,

Rex would see the mark eventually. The bigger deal I made about it, the more hell he'd give me.

The artist came around the counter and studied the mark, letting out a low whistle. "You got this and you don't know what it means?"

Rex's laugh and the smart-ass comment that was about to come out of his mouth died a premature death thanks to the murderous glare I gave him.

"No," I answered the artist, truthfully. "I know it's a truth mark, but that's about it."

"Well, it's an old version of a truth mark, one that signifies truth between lovers or a mated couple. These are illegal for humans, you know that, right?"

"The only illegal ones are the death marks," Rex said, working it out for himself.

I didn't respond. I *hadn't* known. And I seriously doubted Hank had known that either when he marked me. As angry as we both were at the time, he'd never intentionally give me a death mark. Although, since I was no longer one hundred percent human, I was pretty sure the ink wouldn't work in the same way on me as it would on your average person.

"That's hard-core, man." Impressed, the darkling went back behind his counter. "Your work's not bad," he told Rex, mistakenly attributing the mark to him.

Oh boy.

A blinding grin split Rex's face. "Why, thank you. It keeps my old lady"—his hand dropped possessively onto my shoulder—"in line."

I gave the artist a tight smile and ground the heel

of my boot into the top of Rex's foot. He hissed, but I kept my attention firmly on the artist. "Is it normal for the mark to get warm when I'm near the person with the corresponding mark?"

He nodded. "Yep."

"How close do we have to be to feel it? Could I feel it if the guy was upstairs or in the building next door?"

"You should, yeah."

My gut tightened into a wary ball. "What if he was that close and it didn't respond at all?"

"Then he isn't where you think he is . . . or he's dead."

Shit. "Thanks," I said and then hurried out without another word.

Rex caught up with me at Hank's door. "So. He's not up there or he's dead. Not a whole hell of a lot you can do about either one, I'm thinking."

"Rex?"

"Yeah?"

"Stop thinking." I faced him, finally at my Rex limit for the day. "In fact, stop talking. Stop egging me on."

"Fine," he said without a hint of remorse. "Just admit you're crushing on the siren and I will."

Count. Just count until you don't want to wring his neck.

I ignored Rex yet again and instead pressed Hank's buzzer before stepping back, biting on the inside of my cheek and staring up at the dark windows. *Come on, Hank. A light. A light coming on is all I want to see.*

Nothing.

Growing more concerned by the second, I pulled

out the spare key Hank had given to me for emergency purposes only, unlocked the door, and ran up the stairs.

I hesitated at the landing, my heart pounding. The tat artist's "dead" comment had my hand shaking as I shoved the key quietly into the lock. Hank couldn't be . . . gone. I would know, would have felt it somehow. My mouth went dry.

"Don't say a word," I whispered to Rex as I drew my weapon and then entered the spacious loft, concentrating on my senses, trying to feel any auras I didn't recognize.

I eased forward, noticing the place had been cleaned somewhat since our fight. The Throne Tree was upright and back in the corner of the dining room. The floor had been swept, though not totally free of debris, telling me that Hank had attempted the cleanup himself.

I kept my weapon trained as I made my way slowly over the hardwood floor. I cleared every room and then went into the bedroom, all the while knowing he wasn't there.

I used the nozzle of the gun to push open the un-latched bedroom door and entered. The blinds were drawn, the room dark. I flicked the light switch on the wall near the door.

Empty room. Empty bed. Sheets pulled back. A depression in the white pillow where Hank's head had been. The initial wave of relief washed through me with such intensity that I slumped against the wall. I lowered my weapon and let it rest lamely against my thigh.

His scent clung to the room: the subtle aroma of dryer sheets, the faint mix of fresh citrusy herbs used at the Bath House, the barest hint of cologne—the good kind, the kind that probably cost me a week's worth of wages—and lurking below all of them was a very basic, very potent, very masculine note.

"There. See? Happy now? He's obviously awake and has gone out." I didn't move. Rex let out a loud sigh. "No signs of forced entry or a struggle. He woke up and he went out. Elementary, my dear Watson."

As I holstered my gun, Rex let out a soft *"Oh."* And then, "Oh shit. He didn't call and tell you he was awake."

"So? Hank doesn't have to tell me every move he makes, Rex."

If Hank was feeling better and had gone out . . . more power to him. He didn't have to call me, didn't have to tell me he was up and okay. I wasn't his mother, his wife, or his girlfriend. We were friends and partners, and beyond that I wasn't quite sure what we were.

But I couldn't lie—it would've been nice to hear from him.

Alessandra was no doubt laughing her head off. I holstered my weapon and left the bedroom.

"Come on, let's go get Em. We can stop for ice cream on the way home." Rex reached over my head to hold open the door.

"You think this is an ice cream moment?"

He paused, careful, as though treading on very shaky ground. "Umm . . . yes?" I didn't respond.

"No?" He searched his mind. "This is a Charlie needs to kick someone's ass moment?"

The hint of a smile tugged my lips. "No. You were right the first time. This is definitely an ice cream moment."

Because, damn it, I was crushing on the siren.

He was awake, whereabouts unknown, and he hadn't bothered to let me know.

My cell rang at a quarter to midnight. Em was asleep. Rex was downstairs watching TV, and I was sitting on my bed in a tank top and underwear, reaching for the bedside lamp. My first thought was of Hank.

I picked up the cell from the bedside table. As soon as I saw that it was the chief's name flashed on the screen, I got up and went for my discarded clothes. "Hey, Chief." I began tugging my jeans on, the phone trapped between my ear and shoulder.

He wasn't the chief of the Integration Task Force anymore. He was boss only to me and Hank and our small division on the fifth floor of Station One. But his old moniker wasn't in any danger of dying out. He'd always be the chief to us.

"Charlie." His tone was deep and quiet. Not good. I sat on the bed to get my other foot into my jeans. "We have a situation."

"Go ahead."

"Two jumpers. At the bottom of the Healey Building, Forsyth Street side."

I frowned. "Since that's normally the ITF's problem, I'll take it there's something special about the jumpers?"

"They were *ash* victims. Casey Lewis and Mike Everton."

I froze, jeans halfway up my thighs, hands still, and staring at nothing. It took me a second to process his words. "Anyone see them?"

"Only the entire metropolitan area. It's all over the news, online . . ." The chief's heavy sigh crackled the speakers. "No one was up there with them, Charlie. They just held hands and . . . jumped. I don't think I have to tell you what we might be up against."

I settled in because whenever the chief said that, it meant he was going to do the opposite.

"Fact is we got ten people hooked on *ash*. Ten people who are perfect hosts for possession because of that damn drug and the Sons of Dawn. After last week on Helios Tower, the cult's been exposed; they know we're coming after them. If Casey and Mike were possessed by the spirits of deceased Sons of Dawn members, the cult could've ordered the suicides, Charlie. It means they're scared, scared one of them will talk. They don't want us knowing the names of their high-ranking members. Anyone who might be possessed is now a liability."

I struggled to keep the shake from my voice. "We need to contact everyone, the other ten *ash* vics." Not twelve anymore.

"Already done. They know. We've got a man on the

inside for those who agreed to it and guys on the outside for those who didn't, whether they like it or not. If any of our *ash* vics go climbing rooftops or standing on bridges, our guys will stop them."

I continued getting dressed. "That won't stop them from opening a vein over their bathroom sink or swallowing a handful of pills if they're told to."

"I know. And as much as I hate to admit, there's not a goddamned thing we can do about it. I can't force a man into their homes."

"We have to find a damn exorcist and fast. Call outside the city, fly one here, whatever it takes."

"Sian's here right now," he said. "She's been on the phone for the last hour. The exorcists' union has issued a warning to all registered members not to come to Atlanta. They know that several exorcists have already fled the area and some have gone missing. It'd take a miracle to get one to come here right now."

Or a whole lot of cash. "Tell her to keep trying. Offer them whatever they want. I'm heading to the scene now."

"Look." His voice dropped. "I know you're worried about Bryn, but she's fine. She's been called, and the League knows what's going on. There's a guard in her room. You just get to the Healey and find out what you can."

After I agreed and hung up the phone, I sat back on the bed and pulled on my boots, debating on whether or not to call Bryn anyway. I knew she was sleeping.

With a whispered curse, I picked up the cell and hit her speed dial number.

She picked up on the sixth ring. "Charlie." Her voice was groggy.

I went to my mirror, dragged my fingers through my chin-length hair, tucked one side behind my ear, and then left the room. "Hey. You okay?"

"Yeah." She yawned. "I'm fine. Are you?"

No. I feel like putting my fist through a wall or, better yet, murdering Grigori Tennin. "I'm okay. Just checking in. Someone there with you?"

"Uh-huh."

"Good. I don't want you doing anything alone, even going to the bathroom. I mean it. Leave the door open. Just don't be alone. Please. Promise me." I left my room and walked down the hallway.

"I promise."

A relieved breath escaped me. "Okay, thanks. I'll come by first thing tomorrow."

"Okay."

"Now let me talk to your guard." As expected, she sighed into the phone. But I wasn't taking any chances. If I couldn't be there myself, I had to know she was being protected, even if it was from herself.

After talking to her guard, saying my piece, and being assured Bryn would not make a move without his knowing, I hung up, clipped my cell on my hip, and inched open Emma's bedroom door. Our adopted hellhound lifted his gray head.

"Just me, Brim," I whispered under my breath.

His eyes caught the light from the hallway and flashed red. He blinked in that quiet way of his and then resumed his position on the rug by my daughter's bed. Those two shared an incredible bond. Brim and I would never so close that we could communicate without words, but ever since he'd given his life to protect me on Helios Tower and I brought him back from the brink of death . . . well, I loved that ugly beast and I got the feeling he might just love me too.

I crept to Emma's bed, brushed the hair from her temple, and kissed her softly, not worried about waking her; the kid slept like the dead.

After closing her door, I went downstairs and headed toward the living room, where the blue glow of the TV told me Rex was either still watching or had fallen asleep.

I went for the hall closet, pulled out my shoulder harness, and then walked into the living room. Rex was stretched out on the sofa, hands folded over his chest and out cold. I nudged his leg. Nothing. "Rex."

"Hmm?" His eyes didn't open.

"I have to go to work." I picked up the remote and turned off the TV. "Not sure when I'll be back."

"Hmm. Fine. I'll take Em to school . . ."

"Rex. There *is* no school. It's Christmas break. *Rex.*"

"Huh. Yeah. Break. Sure. Hey, turn off the TV, will ya."

I rolled my eyes, grabbed the afghan off the back of the sofa, and spread it over him.

Me leaving in the middle of the night for a case was

nothing new to Emma and was no surprise to Rex. I knew they had shopping plans tomorrow and Rex would look after her. That was our deal—he had a place to stay, and in return he helped with the house and played stand-in parent to Em. As much as Rex bitched and complained, it was clear that the Revenant inside my ex's body was trustworthy and he liked living here, being a part of our family.

I went into the kitchen and left my daughter a note, pretty sure she'd be up in the morning before Rex, and then I left the house.

It was only after I pulled out of the driveway and headed downtown that I allowed myself a moment to freak out about the suicides and what this all meant.

Murder. I was sure of it.

No one needed to be on the roof with them, not if they weren't in control of their minds and bodies. The Sons of Dawn could've given the suicide order to the spirits controlling Casey and Mike. Death would set their spirits free, and would keep law enforcement from containing them and using an exorcist to find out what they knew. Like the names of the high-ranking cult members.

My fingers tapped impatiently on the steering wheel. Shit, shit, shit.

This was not like Grigori Tennin. He'd never get rid of a useable commodity. So, what the hell was going on?

Could it be that he wasn't the big man in charge

after all? A faint tremor ran up my spine. Not a comforting thought.

The Healey was one of my favorite old downtown buildings. Sixteen stories. Took up an entire city block, and had a grand Gothic presence I loved. Will and I used come here with Emma to see the massive Christmas tree they'd place in the rotunda for the holidays, eat at one of the restaurants, and do a little shopping in the ground-floor stores. Much of the building, however, was luxury condos. It was right near Five Points and Woodruff Park, and convenient to Station One.

An ambulance and a few police cars blocked Forsyth Street. A cop directed traffic at the intersection. I drove up and flashed my badge. He waved me through. A TV crew was hurrying down the sidewalk. Pedestrian onlookers had gathered on both sides of the street beyond the tape.

I parked behind a cruiser, ducked under the tape, and approached the uniformed officer already walking toward me. "ID?"

I flashed my ITF badge. *Federal Division, Detective Madigan*, it said. What it *didn't* say was: *covert division, license to use deadly force, no disclosure necessary, deal with it*. Hank and I did what the ITF did not and could not. We cleaned up messes. We hunted down monsters. We killed that which fought to the death, that which could not be integrated into the prison system or stand trial, that which was a danger to society on a level far beyond the average criminal.

But the only thing I cared about now was that my badge opened doors. The officer stepped aside as I clipped the badge back onto my belt and proceeded to the sidewalk, just a few feet down from the grand entrance of the Healey.

I glanced up, the windows above me ablaze with light, with onlookers from above. Finding the broken one wasn't hard. Twelve stories up. Guess they hadn't bothered to go for the roof. No doubt the falling glass had alerted someone to start recording. Don't call police. Don't try to talk them down. Just turn on your camera and start filming. I'd never understand that mentality. Everything was reality porn these days— even a tragedy like this.

A thirty-something guy stood in the street talking to investigators. Eyewitness, maybe. Or could be the person who caught the footage. Might even be the owner of the car where one of the victims had landed. I'd find out later.

I turned my attention to the second "crash site" on the sidewalk, bracing myself and taking a hard analytical line to process the scene of blood, fluids, and brain matter with a detached approach. The body had already been bagged and was being hoisted onto a gurney.

"Great way to end the year, eh?" Liz came up beside me. "Looks like your average double suicide," she said. "So how was your Christmas?"

"Fine. Rex and I took Emma to Jekyll Island. We spent most of our trip on the beach in the sun. Nice getting away from the darkness for a while."

"Tell me about it. I need to drive out for lunch on my next day off. Could use some real sunlight instead of this fake crap from a bulb . . ."

"What'd you do for Christmas?"

"Slept. All damn night. No one woke me until dinner. Best Christmas ever."

"I thought you loved the night shift."

She rolled her eyes. "Yeah, about as much as paying full price for Beausoleils."

"Never heard of them, but I'm guessing those are eyeglasses."

She turned to look at me, giving a model-like wave at her face. "Yeah. You like?"

I studied the glasses she wore. The fifties-style secretary look she had going was cute on her small frame and Asian features. "I do. They're very nice."

"I know, right? So, two fatalities," she said, switching gears. "Broke the window up there, twelfth story. Female landed on the Ford Fusion. The other on the sidewalk. Computer geek over there"—she indicated the guy I'd put on my radar earlier—"saw the glass fall and recorded it with his phone. Guys are up in the condo now, but so far no signs of a struggle, nothing to suggest this was anything but a suicide."

"Who owned the condo?"

"The female. Lewis." She scribbled on a piece of paper and then tore off the edge. "Here's the male vic's address. Heard Ashton talking about it. Said he was heading over to notify next of kin and see if the guy left any kind of warning. You know he won't be too happy to see you."

"Ashton's never happy to see me. Didn't you hear? I'm not only a Tri-racial Bitch, now he thinks I'm the Antichrist."

Liz glanced up, her eyes narrowing. "Well, you can get scary." I opened my mouth to argue that summation, but she cut me off. "But I find it cute, endearing, more like a rabid puppy than the Antichrist." Her lips twitched.

"Ha ha." I rolled my eyes.

"I would say one of these days Ashton will get over it, but I think we both know it's a lost cause."

Couldn't argue with that one. Ashton Perry was one of ITF's lead detectives. He'd never had a problem with me in all the years we worked together in the department, until I stopped being "one of them," as he called it . . . until it was known that I had the genes of all three worlds in me, that I was the one who'd brought darkness to the city of Atlanta to save my kid from Mynogan, the now deceased Charbydon noble and Sons of Dawn cult member.

But more than anything else, Ashton hated that I'd taken a federal job, one where I didn't answer to the department or the reigning chief. Ashton and everyone else in the ITF were on a need-to-know basis when it came to my job. And Ashton *hated* that. He hated even more the fact that I now had the freedom to work on the really big cases, and that my new division had the power to take cases away from him, if necessary. Such was the power of Washington.

And Liz was right. He'd never let it go. He took every opportunity to insult me, call me out, push me to the edge, which usually involved insulting my daughter somehow. Asshole. "Well, he won't see me at all," I said. "I'd rather not deal with him making my life miserable. All he'll know is that I was here nosing around."

Liz chuckled. "You'll be wanting autopsy details, yes?"

"As soon as you have them."

"Will do. How's Bryn holding up?"

Boy, that was a loaded question. "She's been okay. Under watch at the League. But now . . ." I dragged my hand down my face, gazing up at the building. "We need to get every *ash* victim under lock and key. This can't happen again. Not until we know more."

"Hey!" Liz shouted suddenly. "Hands off my body!" She mumbled a quick good-bye and then marched over to the detective who'd been about to lift Casey Lewis's hand from the hood of the car with the tip of a pen or pencil.

Damn, I'd meant to ask her if she'd heard of any new sidhé fae in the city.

I walked away from the scene, shoving my hands in my pockets. It could wait.

4

"What do you mean, Aaron moved out?" I leaned against a dresser in Bryn's room at the Mordecai House—the League of Mages headquarters in Atlanta—cradling a venti Starbucks coffee like it was a lifeline. I'd had very little sleep last night and had gotten up early to check on Bryn.

Bryn stood near one of her upstairs bedroom windows, one shoulder against the wall, her arms wrapped around her middle as she stared out at some mysterious point beyond the glass. She was so quiet, so enigmatic, and with her blank aura, I couldn't even begin to guess her mood.

"Why would he leave?" I went on. "The League is his home."

My sister turned her head—the first time she'd visually acknowledged me since I'd arrived just moments ago. "He didn't leave the property, Charlie. He's staying in one of the guest houses on the grounds. Says he wants his *solitude*." Her attention returned to the window.

I expected the pale skin, the somberness, the muted-out version of her former, vibrant self, but it was her eyes that thickened my throat and squeezed my chest. Round. Tired. Hollow.

"I think he just wanted to get away from me. I did"—she tossed an uncaring glance at the guard sitting quietly in the corner—"kill him, after all."

I took a step toward her, denial and sadness filling me. But she was so distant. For the first time, I wasn't sure my sister would welcome my embrace. "You don't know that," I said instead. "Aaron knows whatever part you played, whatever happened that night, it wasn't you in control. He knows you'd never do something like that willingly."

"I'm sick of this room. I'm sick of being tired all the time."

Her depression dominated the space, heavy and stifling, covering everything like a dreary, sepia-toned picture. It scared me to death. Two *ash* vics had just committed suicide. Could depression, intensified by *ash*, be the cause, and not murder?

I kept my voice neutral. "You want to get out of here? Take a walk. Go get some breakfast. We can raid the kitchen, make some nachos . . ."

A faint smile tugged on her full lips, but didn't reach her eyes. "Haven't had nachos for breakfast in a while . . . What did Alessandra have to say?"

Emma had stayed with Bryn last night so Rex and I could go to Underground and see the oracle. My visit wasn't exactly a secret. And, though it was unspoken between us, we both knew I couldn't share details with someone who might still be possessed. I hated that part . . . Hated to think there was something else inside of my little sister pulling the strings, wanting to know what Alessandra said, wanting to get to the hidden sarcophagus . . .

It was clear from Bryn's look that she understood the direction of my thoughts. "Don't worry about it." She pushed away from the wall. "Come on, I'll take you to see Aaron."

Bryn turned to the guard. I'd tagged him the minute I walked into her temporary living space. Human. Midthirties. Typical mage aura—a wash of intelligent greens. Warlock tattoo—a black dragon swallowing its tail, and always placed around the right wrist. It all equated to a bodyguard more than capable for the job. "Charlie and I are going outside," she told him in a robotic tone.

"She'll be fine with me." His dark eyes met mine. "Why don't you go take a break? We'll be back in a little while."

He stood, clipping his phone on his hip. "I'll follow behind."

Ah. Yes. It would be just like Aaron to give the orders where Bryn was concerned. Orders that'd be followed to the letter. I nodded in reply.

No doubt, every single one of her guards was a warlock.

Since warlocks were the warrior sect of the mage class, Aaron's decision made perfect sense. Not only were they skilled mages dedicated to study, craft, and knowledge, but they trained regularly in the art of warfare. And since Aaron was a warlock himself, it made even more sense. He'd trust them more than any other. Even if they knew Bryn had a hand in his death, they'd *still* put their lives on the line for her, because Aaron had asked them to. Simple as that. Warlocks were a *very* tight band of brothers.

Bryn took the lead, going down the wide second-floor hallway toward the service stairs at the back of the house, instead of the main, sweeping staircase that commanded the front. Her blue tri-colored skirt swished around her legs and her ankle bracelets tinkled like wind chimes in a slow breeze as we went; the sound so normal and comforting. So . . . Bryn-like that it gave me renewed hope.

The warlock stayed true to his word and trailed us at a leisurely pace.

Once we were through the massive kitchen and out the side door into large herb and vegetable garden, Bryn slowed enough for me to walk on the stone path beside her. "I've never been in the back before," I said in a low voice. "It's huge."

"It's hard to see everything with the darkness, but there's a swimming pool, veranda, gazebo, patio . . . The grounds and gardens make up about seven acres.

The woods, or the park as the League calls it, make up another three. And then the school"—she flung a gentle hand to her right—"makes up another five."

If she hadn't sounded like an emotionless robot, the tour guide bit would've been interesting. As it was, it only cemented the fact that she was changing.

"Wasn't always like this," she said.

After buying the old Mordecai House a few years ago, the League set about buying up property around the mansion. They cleared the land, put their earth mages to work, and created a park-like setting within downtown city limits.

Even though it was morning, the sky was dark, the kind of deep ominous color that heralded thunderstorms and tornadoes. Every once in a while a green flash would snake like otherworldly lightning through the churning mass of gray and bathe the ground in a fleeting, eerie glow.

There was enough outdoor lighting to see over the lawn dotted with old oak trees to the school where street lamps illuminated the massive, gray stone church and monastery, which had been converted into the League's private school. One of the most exclusive in the country. One that Emma begged to attend, now that her secret was out and her abilities known.

"So how's the school coping with the darkness?" I asked, wondering if attendance had been affected.

Bryn shrugged. "The kids are on break now. Maybe some won't come back. I don't know. We just installed sunlamps in the classrooms. Our teachers are scholars and crafters, so to them the darkness is fascinating, an opportunity to study and learn. Before break, they were teaching Abuse of Power. Rituals. Properties of Raw Energy. History of Charbydon, et cetera . . . They take full advantage of this new development. It's a good school. Emma would do well here."

She probably would. But to say I was torn was an understatement. On one hand, I wanted Emma to have a simple, normal, *human* life; to have friends, do well in school, play sports. It was hard enough to deal with all the usual growing pains of preteen and teen years. How much harder would it be if crafting and arcane knowledge were added to the mix?

I had to weigh the benefits. Had to figure out what would provide the best environment and life experience for my child. What would give her safety, security, confidence, and yet allow her the independence she craved. From the time Emma was born, I envisioned this happy, ideal life she'd have—that I was determined she'd have—but lately, it wasn't working out the way I'd thought it would.

We stepped off the path and into the yard. The scent of tangy grass filled the air. While there'd been no sun for the last two months, it was winter and the grass should've gone dormant and slightly brown. Yet the park at the Mordecai House flourished.

"Is this your work?" I asked.

Bryn looked up from the ground and out over the green field. "Mine and the other earth mages here. We do what we can, maintaining the grounds until the sun comes back." More hope swept through me. Bryn loved communing with nature. It was easy to imagine her working her magic on the earth, using her gifts to cultivate plants, to give back to nature, even as she drew energy from it.

Placed sporadically through the grounds in isolated spots were small guest houses that looked more like quaint country cabins or cottages. We skirted a large pond ringed with weeping willows and finally entered the woods, following a small dirt path. I never would've found Aaron's hideaway amid the maze of gardens, orchards, greenhouses, ponds, and outbuildings.

Bryn was right. Aaron did want his solitude.

The air was cooler and fresher in the dark woods. The leaves smelled earthy and old, crunching under our feet as we walked. "So, besides him wanting his solitude, how are you guys doing, okay?" I finally asked.

A bitter snort came from her. "If not talking and walking on eggshells is okay, then, yeah, we're freaking brilliant. He probably has no idea about the suicides," she said at length. "This should be interesting."

"Maybe you should let me break it to him."

"Maybe," she echoed. "We're here."

In front of us, nestled in a thicket of pines, was a small cabin. Light glowed softly from the two small windows framing a narrow door. If not for the curtains in the windows and the smoke coming from the chimney, I'd think the place was a simple gardener's shed.

Bryn stopped. She didn't make a sound, just stared silently at the building.

Unlike most nymphs who lived at the Grove downtown under protection of Pendaran, the Druid King, Aaron was a loner. A scholar. A warrior. One who went his own way and didn't live by the customs and laws of the Kinfolk.

And it was no wonder he needed time to recuperate. Physically and mentally. The Sons of Dawn had done a number on him. They'd targeted him for his power, had ripped his life force from his body and stuffed it inside the famous ring of their founder, Solomon.

And they'd used Bryn to help them do it.

Their sole purpose was to insight a war between the nobles of Charbydon and the Adonai of Elysia. To do that, they had to go deep into ancient off-world mythology to a forgotten history and find proof that the nobles had once ruled the beautiful and heavenly world of Elysia.

They'd found their proof all right.

The being lying inside of the sarcophagus was the link, the ancestor to the Charbydon nobles, Elysian Adonai, and humans. A First One. One whose existence alone would prove that the other myths were true and that the nobles had indeed once lived and ruled in Elysia.

Once the nobles had physical proof, they'd leave the dark world of Charbydon and lay siege to Elysia. Heaven and hell at war again. And we'd be stuck in the middle.

With the nobles gone from Charbydon, the path would be clear for the jinn to take back control of their home world or worse, use the chaos of war to gain new territory and control here.

Bryn knocked on the slatted wooden door, pulling me out of my thoughts of war and chaos.

We waited a few seconds. She knocked again. A soft thud sounded behind us and we both turned in time to see a black wolf jump down from the tree in front of the house.

Aaron had been in the tree. Odd. *Since when do wolves climb trees?* But then, this was no ordinary wolf, was it?

Emerald eyes regarded us in a quiet, predatory way before the wolf padded past us and shifted en route, clothes following in a blur as wolf became a masculine, black-haired nymph male. Without a word, he opened the door and went inside.

"Joy," Bryn muttered, following him.

The interior of the cottage was cozy, with two timber beams running the length of a low ceiling. Aaron went to the fireplace and poked at the red coals before placing a stick of wood on the fire. His bare feet peeked out from the ends of frayed jeans. Reflected flames danced on an untucked black silk shirt. A couple days' worth of beard covered his jaw, and the emerald green aura that was usually so vivid appeared dull.

As he set the poker down and turned to us, I noticed shadows curving beneath his solemn eyes. Black eyebrows were drawn together in a thoughtful frown and his hair was in need of a cut.

Aaron put me in mind of a rugged, ancient Celt,

and now he looked the part more than ever. Battle weary, too, with his gaunt expression and noticeable weight loss.

I met his gaze. The intelligent light usually there was muted. A sigh of regret went through me.

"Have a seat." He gestured to the old floral-print sofa against the wall.

Aaron took the chair by the fire as I sat down. Bryn perched next to me on the arm of the couch. An uncomfortable silence descended, which brought the tension between them into stark relief.

"So what is this place?" I asked, trying to lighten the mood. "Looks like you're renting it from the seven dwarves."

A brief smile crossed his face. "It's sanctuary. I find the house too loud, too busy this time of year with all the decorating and planning."

"Oh, right. The New Year's Eve shindig." The League threw one of the biggest New Year's Eve parties in the city, going on four years now. Emma, Rex, and I had been invited and it would be our first League party. "Emma can't wait. She's already got her dress, shoes, and jewelry . . ." Unlike her mother. I had no clue what I was going to wear.

"Oh, that reminds me," Bryn said suddenly. "She wants to help decorate the ballroom. I told her it was okay with me if it was with you. She can come early the night of and help with last-minute details, too."

"Should be okay," I said. "Rex will want to come, too, and make a nuisance of himself in the kitchen."

And no one could argue with that—one of Rex's undying passions was cooking.

"While we're on the subject of your daughter," Aaron said, "have you given any more thought to her request to attend the League's school?"

My eyebrow lifted. "She's gotten to you, too, huh?"

"She did speak to me last night during her visit with Bryn."

I went right to the biggest obstacle when it came to Emma attending the League's school. "Honestly? I can't afford it." Not on my salary. Not since *Will* was no longer working and the child support had gone out the window. I was barely able to pay Emma's tuition at Hope Ridge; there was no way in hell I could make the League's astronomical tuition.

"We do take on a small number of scholarship students every year," Aaron said. "Students who show promise academically as well as in crafting. I've taken the liberty of submitting my recommendation to have her considered. All you have to do is fill out the application and sign the release form so we can get a copy of her current school records. Then we can set the ball rolling."

I blinked, totally caught off guard. Part of me was glad I couldn't afford it because the decision was made for me.

"I can see you hadn't expected this. I hope I didn't overstep. My thinking was that if you knew attendance was possible . . . well, at least then you have options."

"It's fine." Unexpected, but fine.

"She has a special gift, Charlie. Allowing her to explore it will only benefit her, challenge her, and serve as a measure of protection for her."

I ran my fingers through my hair and sat back, staring up at the low ceiling for a moment. "I know. I just never thought my own child would be gifted like she is. I mean, my mother isn't; I wasn't really, not like Bryn. Will certainly wasn't."

"Ah, but you were. Both of you. You were able to communicate without words with Connor, your twin brother. And let's not forget the very reason your body accepted the introduction of Charbydon and Elysian DNA was because your female line contains long-ago ancestors from both worlds. And Will demonstrated his aptitude for learning crafting, even though it was black crafting and behind your back. Gifts can skip generations, but, Charlie, I would've been surprised if your daughter wasn't affected in some way."

I sat forward again, bracing my elbows on my thighs and rubbing both hands down my face, letting out another loud breath. "She would be safer here."

"Safer than anywhere else."

"And learning crafting will help her protect herself and strengthen her abilities," Bryn joined in.

"Defense and offense," Aaron said. "She'll study them both."

"You do have a good academic program."

"The best in the country. Our academic program goes back eight years. And when we moved our headquarters here to Atlanta, the school moved locations with us. The last four years have elevated the school to one of the best in the country. Think on it . . . She can start spring semester, after the first of the year."

I nodded, still a bit dazed by the turn of the conversation and the scholarship.

"So," Bryn began after a long moment of silence. "As you know, Charlie saw the oracle last night . . ."

"The exorcists have all fled, left on their own or forced out," I told him. "I think we have Grigori Tennin to thank for that."

"*If* he's the one in charge," Aaron mused.

"Well, there's no doubt Tennin is a key player. If the nobles were to leave Charbydon, Tennin would become High Chief of all the jinn tribes."

"True. But we mustn't forget that there are nobles out there who believe in the old myths and who want war with Elysia. The Sons of Dawn might have started out as a jinn cult, with a jinn goal, but others, like Mynogan, believed."

To most nobles it was near heresy to imply that they were related to the Adonai, that they once lived in the heaven-like world of Elysia, and were cast out into Charbydon by the Creator. That myth was so old and obscure, most people didn't even know about it and the ones who did simply believed it was fiction. Only a small few knew it for what it was. The truth.

"Elysia is light. Charbydon is dark. Unpleasant," Aaron said. "All it would take is exposing the First One as truth, not fiction, and the nobles will wage war for a better home, a more abundant home."

Aaron was right. It was possible that Tennin might not be the leader of the cult. It could be a noble. Hell, Mynogan had been a noble from the royal House of Abaddon. You didn't get much higher in status than that. He was dead, but that didn't mean there weren't more like him.

"Did the oracle say anything about the *ash* victims?" Bryn asked. "If she believed they're possessed?"

"No," I answered truthfully. "But we should assume they are." And I hated to say it but added, "Even you, Bryn. It's the only way to keep everyone safe."

"And to that effect," Aaron said, "the cult certainly won't want an exorcist around to reveal the truth. They'll want to maneuver the victims, use them . . ."

"Use me," Bryn added, gaze fixed on Aaron, her words ringing with a touch of steel.

The strain between them increased with frightening speed.

Just when I thought things might escalate into something more, Bryn shrugged. "Unless they decide I've outlived my usefulness and have me jump off a building instead."

Oh boy.

Hot rage mushroomed like an atom bomb, then spread out to swamp the room. An eerie, dead silence seemed to stretch for eons. Aaron went completely still, so poised it made me a little uneasy. The light was back in his eyes, making the green color brilliant. I'd never seen him like this before, this . . . inflamed.

But then, I'd never witnessed my sister purposefully provoke a Magnus Level warlock. I wanted to grab her hand and get her out of there before things escalated any further. And then give her a good lecture.

"What do you mean by that?" Aaron asked in a steely tone.

A smug smile twitched at the corner of Bryn's lip. I glanced up, shot her a scolding look, and elbowed her in the thigh, jumping in before she could make things worse and start the fight she obviously wanted. "Two *ash* victims jumped from the Healey Building last night. We don't know why they did it. I'll be doing the rounds after this, talking to family, checking their homes . . . See if they left anything behind, a note, a reason . . ."

Aaron placed his elbows on his knees, putting his hands together to make a teepee with his fingers and resting his chin on top. "Murder?" His head cocked, eyes glittering, the word slipping from his lips like a threat.

"Well, like I said. We won't know until—"

"It is either murder," he interrupted in a dangerous tone, "the cult having possessed those two people and then deciding to get rid of them. Or it is the effects of the drug, creating depression deep enough to make suicide an option."

Obviously, he didn't appreciate my attempt at downplaying the situation. He wanted to hear it like it was, and I couldn't blame him; I was the same way. "All right," I said. "Here's what I don't get. If they were possessed, why would the spirits inside of them listen to that kind of order? I mean, without bodies and without being strong enough to take an unaddicted person, they're releasing themselves to the afterlife, giving up a life, a body. So . . . why would the spirits allow that to happen?"

Aaron scratched his stubbly jaw. "Depends on how devout a cult member they were in life. You have to remember, they've been kept in those spirit jars perhaps for thousands of years. They likely chose to await a new life, to serve the cult in this way. This is a cult that has lasted over two thousand years, Charlie. Even in spirit form, those members would follow orders. True that maybe some wouldn't, but these two obviously did."

"I don't know . . . It's not like Tennin to throw away a mole, you know? It's not his style."

"Then perhaps it's not him issuing this particular order."

Aaron turned to Bryn, his expression analytical and cold and totally not the approach she needed right now. Removed. Unfeeling. "Have you been having suicidal thoughts? Bad dreams, visions? Are you more depressed than usual?"

An inward sigh went through me. If only he'd injected some feeling behind his hard eyes, a little concern into those questions . . .

I didn't need to be in her line of sight to know her eyes were spitting copper fire. "Only when I'm around you."

Ouch.

The tension came roaring back to life.

"Careful, Bryn," Aaron responded with a hint of arrogance. "Your youth is showing."

Oh shit. That was the one thing Bryn hated about her relationship with Aaron—the fact that she was twenty-seven and he was a couple hundred years old.

"And for all your years and supposed knowledge," she said, standing, "you know very little about females." Her back was rigid, shoulders back, chin up. But below this show of anger, there existed a wealth of hurt. "I'll take this as my cue to leave. Wouldn't want me listening in on whatever the oracle said. Might use it against somebody . . ."

I watched her go, hoping that Aaron would call her back, to show her he cared, but he remained silent until the door was closed. "I'll double up her guards," he said. "I want someone by her even while she sleeps, while she's in the bathroom, while she's working in the garden. Every moment of every day and night, she'll be protected . . ."

Now why in the hell didn't he say that when she was here?

"Did the oracle say anything else to help us?" he asked.

"She's arranging an introduction with a creature she believes can see inside of a person and tell whether they're possessed or not. Called it a sylph. You ever hear of it?"

Aaron blinked, his surprise slowly replaced by

scholarly interest. "A sylph. They are little more than legend, even to us."

"Well, apparently it's real, so says the all-knowing Sandra."

"It's not an *it*, Charlie. It's a she. Sylphs are said to be female."

"Oh. What else do you know about them?"

"I only know what the legends say."

"And what do those say?"

"Some say that sylphs are a distant relation to the nymphs, that somewhere in our prehistory, they left Elysia for this world, first making their homes in the lakes, glens, mountains, and deep woods of what you now know as the British Isles. It's said that during this time they evolved, diverged, and developed into shifters of the earth, of this world and its elements.

"Supposedly they eventually mated with male Picts and Celts of the area, sent the male children back to their fathers or killed them, and kept the females. It's the females who have the ability to shift. Earth, air, fire, water. I'd guess they draw energy from their surroundings; develop a kind of symbiotic relationship with earth. I have long believed that this is where legends of your nature spirits come from. The Lady of the Lake, I assume you have heard of her?"

"The one from the King Arthur stories, sure."

"Perhaps not fiction, perhaps a water sylph tied to a particular lake. Perhaps, even, still there today."

"Any idea how they see inside?"

"None, I'm afraid. I wasn't even aware this was a talent they possessed. I'll research more. If I find anything, I'll let you know. How's your arm?" I followed his glance to my right arm. It was covered by my sleeve, but underneath, the scars from the battle atop Helios Tower remained. More precisely the scar or the imprint left from reaching inside of the agate sarcophagus and taking the divine sword from the grip of the First One lying inside, and using it to kill Llyran, the Adonai serial killer who'd been working with the Sons of Dawn for his own psychotic agenda.

That weapon was meant for a divine being to wield. It meant death to anyone who touched it. But because I had the genes of all three worlds coursing through my body—much like the First Ones—I had lived. And now I had what appeared to be some kind of ancient script/molecular-looking symbols running from my fingers to my shoulder.

"I'd very much like to copy the symbols, to study them. When you're up for it, of course."

Aaron felt strongly that the markings on my arm were from the language of the First Ones. Divine script. The first writings. The root language of the three worlds. And to him it was further evidence that I was morphing into—or evolving back into—a First One, a divine being, the first beings formed by the Creator and the genetic forefathers of the three noble races: humans, Charbydon nobles, and the Elysian Adonai.

"Maybe when *you're* up to it," I said, standing.

He actually smiled at that. Aaron was a long way from being healed and he knew it.

After I left the tiny hut in the woods, I took the meandering path that led to the school.

Bigger and grander than the Mordecai House, the League's school, all done in gray stone and Gothic architecture, seemed like the perfect atmosphere to study the arcane. The grounds were beautiful and just as immaculate as the grounds of the Mordecai House.

I really didn't think about what I did next, just let my feet carry me to the front of the main building and then followed the signs that pointed to the office, where I spoke with the administrative assistant. After looking over the scholarship application that Aaron had partially filled out, I signed my name to it, also signing the form giving permission to release my daughter's academic records from Hope Ridge.

There. Done. I swallowed tightly, handed the pen back, and left.

It was just one small step, I told myself. Just to see if she'd even qualify. It didn't mean I'd made a decision.

It was only a baby step.

5

I spent the rest of the day checking out the residences and workplaces of the suicide victims and talking to friends and family before heading into the office. There'd been no notes, no hints from family or friends that either *ash* addict had been contemplating suicide. Nothing to suggest they were about to take a leap from a twelfth-story window.

Walking across the back lot of Station One, a sense of defeat settled over me. I was tired. Anxious for a call from Alessandra. Worried about my sister and the other potential victims.

How did you fight something you couldn't see or weren't sure existed in the first place? How did you protect someone you love from an unknown like that? I shuffled up the steps and into the building, heading robotically toward the elevator that would take me to the fifth floor—home to my tiny office set amid a sea of overflow office equipment.

Hank and I no longer worked for the Integration Task Force of Atlanta. I'd gone rogue to save my kid and Hank had joined me. I'd known at the time it would cost me my job and end up in jail time.

Ask me to do it again and I would in a heartbeat.

What else could I have done? Tell my kid I couldn't break the law to save her life? That I just had to sit back and let her die? Please. I'd give my *life* for my kid. Saving her had been the *only* choice.

The decision had been a no-brainer, but it was that decision which gained us the attention of the covert bigwigs in Washington. It was either take the job or go to jail. We took the job.

There were teams like us in every major city. Anywhere there was a gateway into the other worlds, anywhere there was a large population of off-worlders you'd find two detectives like Hank and me willing to go above and beyond.

The elevator doors slid open with a whisper. My stomach growled as I walked down the hallway, reminding me that I never should've skipped lunch. I slid my key card into the lock and then made my way through the maze of discarded office equipment and furniture before coming to our nifty space in the back corner. With a heavy exhale, I dropped into my chair, laid my arms on the desk, and rested my forehead on my arms.

So tired—my stomach growled again—and hungry.

If only I could feel normal. Stop feeling so drugged out all the time and like I had to eat like a sumo wrestler, stop hearing random voices whenever I finally relaxed and stop seeing visions . . . My insides were being pulled in random directions all the time. I wanted to be normal again. Human again. At this point, I'd even settle for my evolution—as Aaron called it—coming to a close and leaving me in whatever state I ended up in.

The door to our office clicked open. I didn't raise my head. The air of calmness trickling through the room and the scent of mint and lavender told me all I needed to know.

I didn't know what it was about the jinn hybrid that brought about this sense of tranquility. When I first saw Sian in Grigori Tennin's strip club, she'd had the same effect on me and everyone in the place. I wondered if all jinn hybrids possessed that ability or if it was just something unique to her.

"Oh, good, you're back," she said, entering our nook and bringing with her the scent of food. My stomach twisted. A stack of files dropped beside me. "Here's everything on the *ash* support group, all the members, personal info, vital records, et cetera. Oh, and Hank called. He'll be in the office later."

I finally lifted my head and looked at her tall, cloaked form. "Hank called?"

"Uh-huh."

I waited for more, some message for me, but she continued on, going to her desk by the window, dropping her canvas bag and an armful of files before removing her cloak and draping it over the hook on the wall.

I grabbed my cell and checked it. No missed messages from my partner. What the hell was going on with him?

"You okay?" Sian straightened her black pencil skirt as she came back to my desk carrying a large brown bag.

The scent of dough, freshly baked and wonderful, wrapped around me like a warm blanket. Sian's white eyebrow rose, and she lifted the bag. "I think I should get a raise for supporting your eating habits."

Hunger pains radiated through my gut. I motioned with my fingers. "Hand it over." My hand shook as I sat back and dove into the bag, pulling out an everything bagel. The first bite was pure, one hundred percent, Grade-A pleasure. "Bless you," I muttered, cheeks full.

She parked her hip on the edge of Hank's desk, which was pushed up against mine. She wore a thin cashmere turtleneck in dark gray, much darker than her light gray skin. Her snow-white hair was pulled back into a braided bun and her indigo and violet eyes held a note of apprehension.

Sian was gorgeous—high cheekbones, full lips, almond-shaped eyes . . . Yet she didn't go outside of her home or the office without covering herself with her cloak.

Bias and racism was alive and well even in the off-world community. And while the jinn prized the extremely rare product of jinn and human offspring, the rest of the Charbydons and Elysians did not, nor did some humans.

I wanted Sian to hold her head high, to ignore the criticism and step out into society as the beautiful, alluring, and harmless being that she was, but after a life spent growing up in the confines of the jinn underground, she had miles yet to go. There was one good thing about being forced Topside and taking this job—she was slowly gaining confidence.

After I'd wolfed down the first bagel, I went in for another. "Thank you," I told her. "So you gonna keep staring at me or tell me what's on your mind?"

Sian's father had used a blood debt against me to secure his daughter a job within the ITF so she could feed him information. He gained a lot of useless fluff instead. Sian didn't have the cunning chops of dear old dad. He knew this, refused to accept it, and had placed her here anyway. Grigori Tennin used everyone and everything, even his own daughter.

"I have no loyalty to my father now. And I don't want Daya's death to be for nothing. I want the Sons of Dawn stopped. I don't want war. For anyone. She'd want me to do this."

"Do what exactly?"

Sian was still mourning the death of Daya Machanna. And Tennin had no idea his involvement with the Sons of Dawn and Llyran had resulted in the death of someone Sian had loved. Their relationship had been a secret: totally forbidden, since Sian was a jinn and Daya was an Elysian whose life force had been sucked dry and stored in Solomon's Ring along with Aaron's and those of the others Llyran had murdered. All to raise the Star, the First One . . .

"I'm in the perfect position to keep an eye on my father."

I stopped chewing and considered her words.

In the end, I didn't think it was my place to deny her the opportunity to get some closure for Daya's death, and if this was how she wanted to do it . . . "I wouldn't want you to play spy. No riffling through his things or anything. But if you want to take a mental note of who comes and goes, keep your ears open, learn his routines . . . I think that would be okay. You'll have to clear it with the chief."

"I'll talk to him as soon as he comes in. I can tell you already that he's the one who hired the Pig-Pens to go after you at the club last night. One came early this morning to report to him, and she mentioned the sidhé fae you asked me to research, but neither she nor my father seemed to know why they were in the club. They think the fae are also after the sarcophagus.

"My father doesn't believe it was destroyed. He's convinced you know where it is. Is he right, Charlie? Was it destroyed? Did you see inside?"

"Yes." Because of the absolute necessity, this particular lie was easy to tell and I was exceptionally convincing. "There was a sword and a bunch of bones. But I didn't destroy them. I'm not strong enough to do something like that. The Druid King is, and he did. It's done. Your father needs to accept it and move on."

"He'll never do that. He asks me to find out, to listen to what you say, to follow you sometimes. He is angry over the loss."

Again, not surprising. But I doubted even Tennin himself knew exactly what rested inside. It had taken Llyran calling down the darkness and uttering the language of the First Ones to open the sarcophagus lid, and Tennin had never made it across the rooftop during the battle to see inside before Pendaran went dragon on his ass and took him down. Literally. Six feet into the pavement below.

Only Pen, Hank, and I knew what really rested within the thick agate. No bones. No remains. But a perfect, black-winged being at rest, in some kind of eternal stasis, but able to plead, to somehow fill my head with her sorrow and make me feel a connection with her. We couldn't destroy her. So we hid her at the bottom of Clara Meer Lake under the protection of the Druid King.

"Charlie."

I jerked. "Huh?"

"I said he is thinking, always thinking of ways to find out, to make you tell him."

I resumed chewing my bite of bagel. "What ways? Has he said?"

"Not anything that makes sense. It's mostly grumblings, bits and pieces of his thoughts. My father is very careful, he will think of every angle, every outcome, every way his actions might affect him and his goals. He is only rash when there is no time to be anything else." The corners of her lips turned down. "He is more of a beast to live with than usual. Maybe we can give him some kind of proof that the tomb was destroyed. Maybe that would put an end to his obsession."

I mulled the idea over. "Maybe," I said quietly, dragging another bagel out of the bag. "What's the latest on the *ash* victims?"

"All the bodyguards reported in at noon. So far everyone is accounted for and safe."

"Good. Any luck on the exorcists?"

"None. No one will come after the warning went out from the union."

I polished off the third bagel and pushed away from the desk, heading to the small corner kitchen for a bottled water. After a long drink, I leaned against the small countertop. "What about the sidhé and that creature? Did you find out anything based on my description and that name, Sachâth?"

She shook her head. "Not yet. I tried every variation and spelling of the word. I'll keep trying, though. As for the fae, I found a few warrior sects that might match. I'm going to work on getting that together for you now," she said, sliding off the desk and making for her own.

"You want a bagel?"

She gave a careless wave, her back to me. "Nope. They're all yours."

Smiling, I returned to my chair, stuck a fourth bagel in my mouth, and grabbed a sheet of paper to write the chief a Request for Salary Increase for our researcher/secretary/spy/bagel-bringing angel.

The boost did me good for the next hour as I worked on transferring my notes from earlier into my computer and then compiling my report on the suicides, which would then be encrypted via our new protocol, sent to the chief, and then passed on to Washington.

My cell rang, making me jump. Alessandra's number flashed on my caller ID. "Madigan," I said.

"You should try those Starbucks energy drinks or a SoBe Adrenaline Rush with an Aeva bun and that should kick your ass into high gear."

"Thanks," I said dryly. "You get the intro?"

"I did. Your first meeting will take place now at the covered bridge in Stone Mountain."

"Wait, what do you mean, first meeting?"

"You'll meet four sylphs. Ryssa, Nivian, Melki, and Emain. Each element is needed to see inside. That's how it works. Have fun. Oh, and don't bother holding your breath."

She hung up, but still I said, "Ha, ha," into the speaker.

I used the restroom, washed my hands and face, tucked my hair behind each ear, and then went back into the office, where I rechecked all three of my firearms. My 9mm firearm, my Hefty, and my Nitro-gun. Since sylphs were originally from Elysia, I was hoping the Hefty would perform as it should and the high frequency sound wave tag would do to them what it did to most Elysian races: drop them like a stone.

Not that I was going to battle. I was going to ask a big favor, to beg for help if necessary. If I succeeded, we could know in a few hours if Bryn was in the clear. That thought gave me all the energy I needed.

6

Stone Mountain was less than twenty miles from the city. Unfortunately, it fell within the forty-mile-wide mass of Charbydon darkness roiling overhead. But despite the drop in tourism, Stone Mountain wasn't the ghost town you'd think it'd be. Fireworks were planned for New Year's Eve. The granite rock would be lit up like always, and a concert on the lawn would go on as scheduled.

As I drove through the main gate and down Jefferson, lights blinked through the trees and across the water. Still some die-hard campers around and a ton of employees to maintain all of the features in the park—the animals, the country club, the marina, all the stores, inns, and attractions . . .

I navigated around Robert E. Lee Boulevard, passing one car before turning onto the road that would lead me to the covered bridge and across the water to Indian Island.

The headlights illuminated the long structure as I slowed my Tahoe to a crawl. There was no one waiting on this side of the bridge, so I drove inside. The lights from the vehicle beamed off the lattice sides, creating odd shadows as I went. The effect only heightened the apprehension already pricking my skin.

After parking, I took a moment to steady myself, turned off the engine, and got out. A mild breeze rustled the leaves and branches. My boots crunched the gravel. Spooky bridge, wooded island, darkness overhead . . . Christ. It felt like I'd just stepped into a damn horror film.

Ripples in the water caught my attention. I found the source standing at the edge of the lake near the embankment only a couple yards from the bridge.

Sylph at eleven o'clock.

She looked human, so that was promising. But I didn't see the other three.

Okay. Here we go.

Carefully, I made my way down to the grassy edge, where I had to completely readjust my initial thought on the sylph: human-looking, yes, but in a highly disturbing, heart-pounding way.

The sylph stood at arm's length from me, her feet in the water. She was reed-thin and willowy like the fae, but a tiny thing in stature, no bigger than my eleven-year-old. Her skin was the color of moonstone and oyster. Tiny blue spider veins threaded through portions of her neck, cheeks, and arms. Her face was technically pretty, petite nose, small mouth, but it was difficult to see beyond the fact that she looked like a drowning victim come back to life.

A slash of shimmering blue-gray cloth covered her small breasts and wrapped around her hips. Her dark hair fell in long, tangled strands, trapping bits of mud, sand, and what looked like algae.

Her eyes, though . . .

Unease curled up my spine. Her irises were a rich blue ringed in white, and a clear wash of water passed over them in a continuous stream, going from one corner to the other.

I glanced around, swallowing. "I thought there were four of you."

The creature looked in my direction with an unfocused stare. Water bled like tears from her eyes, running down her cheeks, and taking gravity-defying paths to her mouth, ears, and nostrils.

Her lips parted. A high voice came out, ringing in an unearthly tone and thick with a distinctive Irish-like lilt. "You'll meet each of us in turn," she said very slowly, as though talking was a rare occurrence for her. "I am Nivian. This is my water."

And territorial, I added to the list of strange attributes.

What didn't make sense, though, was the fact that these elusive beings had been in hiding for thousands of years, keeping themselves from the eyes of the world so well that they remained a question of uncertainty. And they chose *now* to reveal themselves, and to me? "So you're here in Atlanta because . . . ?"

A sniff and a few droplets of water trickled out of her delicate nose. Her pointed chin rose a fraction. "The portend. The darkness"—she lifted her hand to the sky and I noticed rivulets of water running down her arm; the water at her feet was trailing up, encircling her like vines, moving in thin streams around her limbs—"is a prophecy of the *Ceallachan*. Our wise ones. You will be granted our aid, Charlie Madigan. You must accept each gift we give."

My muscles had gone so tight, they ached. My heart pounded hard. Gifts. No problem. Who didn't like gifts, right? "Uh, thank you," I said, unsure of what to do next.

"You may remove your clothing if you wish."

I did a mental double take, floundering for a second. I might be about to get anointed and wet somehow, but I'd do it with my clothes on, thank you very much.

I removed my jacket, weapons, and cell phone, setting them in a pile on an even spot of ground away from the water's edge. Boots came off, then socks, before I walked back over the cool grass toward the sylph.

I rubbed my hands down my arms and drew in a deep breath. "I'm ready."

"Accept the gift," she told me in earnest. "You must accept it."

"Right. Accept the gift. Got it. Now what?"

The water around Nivian's ankles rose. Her pale arms lifted straight out. Her head tipped back slightly and a very small smile turned up one corner of her bluish lips. Higher the water rose, yet it didn't spill onto the embankment as it should've done. The way she commanded it, it was like she was a tiny, creepy version of Moses parting the Red Sea.

And then she stared straight at me with those watery eyes. "Accept the gift."

I had time to gasp once as she swirled, completely dissolving into water as it reared up and engulfed me. A great wave grabbed me off the ground and pulled me far out into the lake.

There was no time to prepare, no time to catch another breath. No time for anything as I was dragged under by the ankles.

Panic, stark and black, filled me. Water shot up my nose. My hands went to my face, but it was too late. Water slid down my throat. The urge to cough, to gasp for breath, burned a straining, searing path to my lungs.

A raw scream exploded in my head and I flailed for the surface somewhere high above me, struggling for air. For life.

Dear God!

Pressure built in my chest, my throat, my face. *Can't . . . hold it . . . in.*

"Breathe, Charlie Madigan, breathe," Nivian's strange voice came from all directions.

I can't! I screamed in my mind.

"Accept the gift."

I held on until it felt as though my face would explode from the pressure, my eyes squeezed tightly together in an effort to keep out the water. White dots appeared behind my eyelids. My fingernails finally punctured the rough skin of my palms.

Burning. God. Help. Me.

I gulped.

The pain that hit me was unlike anything I'd experienced before. Nothing happened. No air. *Oh God. Choking*. Another gulp and another. Like a fish on dry land. That primal, involuntary need to breathe, and yet I was suffocating. Water filled my lungs, the pressure so acute that every muscle in my body tensed into steel. Frozen, molded, in certain death.

I'd stopped moving. Black fuzz ringed my consciousness as I floated like a frozen statue in deep, cold, silent water.

"Accept the gift."

One more gulp. Pathetic. That final gasp.

The pain in my chest began to subside, and it was in that irrevocable moment that I thought about using my power. Hank and I had practiced manipulating water. And yet everything had happened so suddenly, taking me completely by surprise, that all my faculties were still left standing on dry ground.

Then I was jerked as though a small kid had reached down and grabbed a sinking plastic doll by the calf.

I had no sense of time.

One minute I was a floating Barbie doll and the next I was on the embankment, curled on my side as water ran out of my mouth and nose and ears as though it left me of its own free will.

It crowded my desperate airway, shoving its way out and making me feel bloated and suffocated all over again.

Once the water ebbed and air had room to make its way, I gulped and gasped, loud and noisy, as my fingers dug into the soft soil for purchase. I vomited, an action so violent that my bladder released. Warm liquid spread between my thighs as bile filled my mouth and soaked the ground, mixing with the scent of lake water and urine.

The shaking started then, fierce and uncontrollable, as my head fell onto the ground, turning slightly to avoid a face-plant.

Nivian stood in the water, at the very edge, watching me. Anger flared, stinging my eyes with wet tears. "Your next gifts will come within three days' time." She tossed my cell phone onto the ground in front of me in clear distaste. "It . . . shrilled. Someone spoke. He is coming to pick you up." A surprised look must have crossed my face because she said, "We are not oblivious, Charlie Madigan. We have watched the rise and fall of civilizations, watched as the population encroaches farther and farther into our territory, taking from it, killing it, killing the earth." An unnerving grin crawled over her strange elfin face. "You will all destroy yourselves and then we shall begin to heal this place and it will be ours once again." And with that, her ankles went watery and she dropped into the lake, disappearing and leaving me on the side of the embankment alone, cold, shaking, and nearly dead.

God, let it be the chief who called. Please, not Rex. Because Rex would have Emma with him and the last thing I wanted was for my kid to see me like this.

I curled into a tight ball, shivering and too exhausted to heal myself. Just a moment of rest . . .

The shutting of a car door woke me.

Through the cottony fog in my brain, I heard footsteps on gravel and the gentle lap of the water nearby. My own heat or spent tears, I wasn't sure, had made my eyes dry. I blinked several times, and tried to swallow, but stopped cold and moaned in pain. My sense of smell kicked in and my sore stomach rolled. My weight had made a nice little impression in the grass, where a wet stinking puddle formed beneath me.

Nice.

The faint vibrations of footsteps reached me. And fuck if my mark wasn't tingling. I groaned inwardly in utter disbelief.

The grass dipped behind me. I stayed curled on my side. A finger removed a wet strand of hair plastered across my face. A deep sigh wafted through the air, whispering, *What kind of trouble have you gotten yourself into this time?*

"Are you going to look at me, Charlie?"

Warmth burst in my belly at the sound of his deep, potent voice. The gentle zing of pleasure it brought me told me just how much I'd missed that sound in the last week. A siren's voice was their power. Their lure.

And Hank's voice washed through me like a shot of the smoothest whiskey.

I didn't want to look at him. I knew what I'd see—an insanely beautiful male, a being brimming with strength, masculinity, and carnal innuendo all wrapped in a package that grinned like the devil and spoke like an angel. While I was the total opposite, a dark, wet mess lying in a stinking puddle.

Was I going to look at him? Hell no.

I moved my arm over my head to hide my profile, curling tighter and shrinking away. Weakness stole over me. Tears stung my eyes and thickened my throat. Just that small bit of action hurt.

"Would you like to rinse off in the—"

"No!" The word shot out my mouth on wings of pure horror. It hurt, but there was no way in hell I was getting back in there, reeking or not. No. Way. Just the idea had my heart leaping wildly. I removed my arm just a little and turned onto my back to face him.

Gently assessing, intelligent eyes stared out from a rugged face blessed by the gods, designed to strike devotion, lust, obsession in the hearts and minds of most living things. Sure, darkness rolled above us, but right then I felt like the sun had finally come out.

Emotions flipped through me, one after another, like the turning pages of a book. I finally managed a swallow and a lame "Hey."

A slow, crooked grin made a little crescent in his left cheek. "Hi, Charlie."

7

Hank glanced beyond me to the lake, his smile fading. One hand slipped beneath my knees and the other went around my back. Without a word, he lifted me off the ground.

My hands came around his neck, the skin hot to my cold fingers. His clean scent filled the air as my head fell against his shoulder. The image of Hank's ex-girlfriend Zara came to mind, all tall and gorgeous and perfect in her siren beauty. As comparisons went, she was probably looking pretty good to Hank right about then. My humiliation increased with every stride he made up the embankment.

My hands slid off his wide shoulders as he set me on my feet, one hand around my waist while opening the car door with the other. Sleek black Mercedes coupe stared back at me. Oh, great. Humiliation complete. "Don't put me in your car," I begged in a whisper. "You'll ruin your seats. Just put me in the back of my Tahoe. I'll drive when I feel better."

"They're just seats, Charlie. It's not a big deal. I'll call the chief and see if he can get someone out here to get your truck."

I slid wet and stiff onto the expensive leather seats, totally grossed out by myself. Hank got in, opened our windows, and then started the car.

I faced away from him, curling toward the door and shaking uncontrollably. My thoughts turned to Nivian. That watery little bitch had tried to drown me. I wanted to choke her with her own damn lake water or, better yet, stake her to the hot sand beneath the blazing sun of the Sahara Desert. Let her dry up until she resembled a tiny piece of sylph jerky.

Imagining revenge, however, didn't make me feel better.

I watched the miles go by, letting my mind drift to one vague thought after another. The mark on my shoulder stayed warm, the heat seeping into my cold limbs. By the time we pulled into my driveway in Candler Park, my tremors had become minor.

Hank turned off the engine and got out. I reached for the door handle, but it slipped rather violently from my weak fingers. Frustration flared; I was so tapped out that I couldn't even pull a fucking door handle.

My door opened on its own. Hank stood back, one

hand on the top of the car as he bent down to extend me his other hand.

"Thanks," I mumbled, sliding my hand into his. He hauled me from the car. As soon as my full weight settled into my legs, my knees gave way.

"Whoa," Hank said, picking me up and shutting the car door with his foot.

"Anyone home?" he asked.

"No, Rex and Emma went shopping and Brim is in the kennel."

Hank used his own key, the one I'd exchanged with him a long time ago, opened the door, and took me straight up the stairs and into my bathroom, where he set me on the counter and then turned on the water in the tub.

"Shower or bath?" He glanced over his shoulder.

I stared at him. I hadn't seen him in a week and suddenly he was here, his six-foot-four frame filling my bathroom, and taking care of me like it was the most natural thing in the world and I didn't reek like a sewer.

"Earth to Charlie."

"Oh, um, shower." I needed to stand, to get the strength back into my legs.

Hank adjusted the water temperature, turned on the shower, and closed the curtain. As he straightened, I was thrown back to a similar situation when I'd stabbed him with the Throne Tree branch and he'd been unable to get into his bathroom on his own or undress himself. He'd relied on me. He hadn't told me to go, to leave and not see him so weak. He let me in, and I suppose that was a form of trust after all. For all he didn't tell me about his past, I knew he did trust me with his present.

"Could you . . . ?"

He didn't blink, didn't register any kind of emotion, just stepped closer, grabbed the hem of my shirt, and pulled it over my head. He tossed the nasty thing into the corner and then stood me up to help with my pants. I was so shaky and weak; I grabbed both of his shoulders for support as he knelt down and took on the difficult job of trying to peel off my wet pants.

"For the record," he said, looking up at me with a crooked smile, "this is *not* how I pictured removing your pants for the first time."

"That confident, are we?"

His smile filled out, deep and brimming with humor. "When something is this inevitable. Yes."

I rolled my eyes, but couldn't help but smile. I pulled one leg free and then the other.

He tossed my wet pants into the pile with the rest of my soiled clothes, then turned back and froze. "You're wearing SpongeBob underwear."

Shit.

My gaze flew downward and my mortification was finally complete. "Emma got them for me . . . for my birthday." What the hell. Might as well get it over with. I turned around. "Patrick is on my ass."

God, it was so ridiculous. I glanced over my shoulder to see him grinning like a damn fool. Our laughter came at the same time, his rich and easy and mine scratchy and hoarse. When it died, we stood there in an odd moment when comfort and tension seemed to exist in tandem.

"I can take off the voice-mod, Charlie." His voice dropped. "I can make you feel better with a word."

A hot flush burst low in my belly. The steam from the shower was taking all the oxygen out of the room. Or maybe that was Hank. I couldn't help but wonder what he'd say. How it would feel. *Silly girl. You know exactly how it would feel.* And without a doubt I'd like it way too much.

"No." The word came out high and broken. I cleared my throat. "I'll heal. I'll be fine. I can handle it from here." I wrapped my arms around my bare midriff, starting to shiver again. "If you want to clean up, you can use the bathroom downstairs. There are clean shirts of Will's in my closet . . ."

"Thanks." He lingered at the door. "You need help getting into the shower?"

I shook my head. "Nice try, siren." He flashed me a grin and then left the room.

"You're not seriously thinking about going through with this. There are three more of those crazy bitches out there," Rex said in disbelief.

I spooned another bite of hot tomato and orzo

soup with shredded chicken into my mouth, savoring the rich, creamy flavor.

Thank God for Rex and his cooking skills; by the time I got out of the shower and came downstairs I was ravenous, my stomach leading me right to the Crock-Pot. He must've made the soup this morning before going shopping with Emma. They returned while I was the shower. Em had already scarfed down a bowl and was in the backyard with Brim. Hank was just finishing up his second bowl, and Rex was looking pretty pleased with himself—well, except for the sylph bomb I'd just dropped on him.

I swallowed another bite. "I don't really see another way, do you? We might've been able to wait before, to convince an exorcist outside of the union to come here, but now with the suicides, there isn't any time."

"So we just have to sit around and let them nearly kill you? Three more times?"

I shrugged, "Well, that's just it. They're not going to kill me, Rex. Look, in a couple days, we'll know. We'll have our answers."

The sylphs were our only option. I'd accept their "gifts" and then somehow they'd work their magic. We'd know if Bryn was in danger and which *ash* victims to protect. And if Titus Mott hurried his genius ass up and found a cure for *ash*, the danger for all of them would be over. Then I could concentrate on tearing down Grigori Tennin and the Sons of Dawn for good.

Hank pushed his bowl away and leaned back in the chair. "Good soup, Rex."

I snagged a chunk of chicken with my spoon, about to agree, when Rex turned abruptly in his chair and faced Hank. "So," he began in a stilted tone, "Charlie and I stopped by your place last night. You weren't there. Where were you?"

I froze, feeling like every ounce of blood had drained from my face as I stared wide-eyed at Rex. *Just shoot me now.* I sank deeper into the chair, wishing I could just keep going. I forced down my bite.

Emma burst through the back door. "Mom, where did you put the tea tree oil?"

I blinked, unable to wrap my mind around her question. Rex threw a casual glance over his shoulder. "It's in the junk drawer." And then his eyes were back on Hank, brow lifted high and waiting.

Em rooted around the last drawer beneath the kitchen counter. "I want to try it on Brim's elbow . . ." She found the oil and shut the drawer and went back to the door, waving behind her. "Carry on, old people."

Silence greeted us after she left.

Hank was still leaning back in the chair, looking completely at ease. "I was out." He cocked his head at Rex and then folded his arms over his chest.

"It's no big deal. I just wanted to check on you," I said, glaring at Rex as I gathered the empty bowls. "It's *none* of our business."

I was hoping Hank would elaborate anyway, but

he remained quiet as I set the bowls on the kitchen counter and then opened the dishwasher.

"I was out," Hank finally answered. "Shopping."

I turned. "Shopping?"

Em came in at that moment to put the oil back. "There, maybe that'll grow some hair on that elbow."

Hank rocked back in the chair, looking particularly amused. One corner of his mouth turned up. "Christmas presents."

I frowned, not expecting that answer, while Emma went instantly on alert, her expression like that of a prairie dog that had just popped up out of its hole.

"If you hadn't noticed," he continued, "I missed Christmas." Hank dug in his pocket and tossed Emma the car keys. "They're in the trunk."

"Figures." Rex rolled his eyes and got up. "I'm hitting the john," he muttered.

Em squealed and darted out of the kitchen with the keys. I winced as the screen door banged against the frame.

I just stood there, back against the counter, hands still wet. Ever since we began working together, Hank had gotten Emma a Christmas present. Usually something way too expensive. I gave myself a mental shake and rubbed my hands on my cotton drawstring pants. Right. The usual. For a second there, I'd thought he'd meant me and that would just be . . . weird. I mean, we'd never exchanged gifts before . . .

I turned to wash out the bowls. My mark flared. I stiffened, not needing the mark to feel Hank's presence behind me, swamping me. His hands fell on other side of the counter, trapping me. Immediately, my pulse skipped and my senses went into hyperdrive.

He leaned down, taking advantage of my momentary lapse. My mouth went dry. I tried to swallow. Warm breath breezed faintly against my neck, the short ends of my hair doing a soft wave toward my chin.

His lips were too close to my ear, his voice husky and low with an edge of humor. "I got you something, too."

And then he was gone, back to the table and leaving me more disoriented than I'd been before. The ceramic bowl in my hand shattered. I jumped. "Damn it!" Great. Perfect. Thoroughly embarrassed now, I went to work cleaning up the shards from the sink with a paper towel while trying to calm myself with slow, regulated breaths, wishing like hell the heat would drain from my face.

I ran the water to clear the sink of the tinier fragments, wiped my hands on a dish towel this time, and then turned to throw the paper towel in the trash. Hank was back in his chair, leaning back so that the two front legs were off the floor and looking pretty pleased with himself.

"Since when do we get each other gifts?" I asked, sounding more composed than I felt. "I didn't get you anything."

He sat forward. "It's just a gift, Charlie. Every year I shop for Em, I see something that makes me think of you. This year things are different . . ."

There'd been no gifts before because we were friends. Because I was married and happy. Because there were never any romantic feelings between us. Not like that. At least on my part there hadn't been. While I had no choice but to acknowledge and grow accustomed to my partner's extraordinary allure, I'd never crossed the bridge of developing *those* kinds of feelings for him.

Had he?

My thoughts must've been pretty transparent. "I wasn't longing after you while you were married, Charlie. It wasn't something I even allowed myself to think. I was too new to this world, too new to my freedom and all the things I wanted to experience . . ."

Wait . . . freedom? "What—"

Emma stormed back into the house with a giant bag smelling like the bakery in Underground. Sweet, warm dough. God, I loved that smell. She set the bag on the table and pulled out a large wrapped box, rolling it around in her hands. "This one is for me." She set it aside and then dug out a plain brown box, the size of a boot box. "There's no name on this one. Is this mine, too?"

"That one's for your mom," Hank answered.

Em turned to me, her smile goofy and her expression silly. She sang the words, "You got a present."

I took it with an eye roll at her teasing. My pulse thrummed; I hadn't gotten a gift from a guy in a long time.

I set the box on the table and opened the lid.

Gasped and then shut it again, my gaze flying to Hank's. He was grinning broadly now, his eyes a brilliant topaz blue. I was a hard person to buy for, I didn't collect anything, didn't talk about things I wanted to buy . . .

"Mom! What is it?"

"It's a dozen Aeva buns," I said in awe and then laughed. "Oh my God."

"There's a subscription notice in there, too. Every month, you'll get a dozen delivered to your doorstep for a year."

I clutched the box to my chest, though not too tightly—didn't want to damage those heavenly concoctions. "You got me a Buns for a Year subscription? Are you kidding me?"

I was smiling like an idiot, smiling because this was just like Hank. And he hadn't gone and done something like get me jewelry or a scarf or perfume or a useless trinket I'd never use. He bought me something I raved about on pretty much a daily basis, something no one had ever gotten before even though every year I casually threw out the mention to those around me.

Maybe I'd never gotten it because everyone else thought it was a goofy idea. But I always thought if you were gonna give a gift, it should be something the person wanted, really, really wanted. And boy, did Hank hit this one out of the park.

"Mother," Em said in a serious tone, "I hope you know you *will* be sharing those."

My eyes narrowed. "I might give you one . . . if your room is clean, you do the dishes, empty the trash . . ."

"Mom!" She reached for the box.

I held it aloft, laughing. "Okay, okay. You can have *one*." I set the box on the table and opened the lid, selecting a fluffy white creation with reverence.

Made by the Elysian imps who were known in all three worlds for their skills in the baked goods department, the Aeva buns were their highest achievement. I handed Emma one and took one for myself, biting into the soft, cloud-like creation, so sweet and light that it melted in your mouth.

Rex came down the hall. "I smell Aeva buns."

My gaze stayed on Hank. I managed a thank-you through my stuffed cheeks. He gave me a small nod and a half-smile, yet so much swam in his expression—satisfaction, relief—something that spoke of vulnerability. If I wasn't mistaken, he'd been just as nervous as me about the gift. Christ. That realization disarmed me completely and my heart gave a hard knock.

8

After Hank left, I sat on the porch swing and stared into space. Despite the last hour of fun, I couldn't shake the ominous feeling that descended after all the distractions had gone.

I pulled one knee up and chewed on my pinky nail.

Em's head poked out of the front door. "Hey. What's wrong?"

"Nothing."

"You're chewing on your nails and you only do that when you're worried about something."

Smart aleck. "Just thinking about Aunt Bryn. And I'm tired. As usual."

"Go to bed, then. I'll send Brim up with you. Trust me, having him in the room makes you feel better."

Before I could turn down the offer, she whistled for the enormous beast, opening the door wider and telling him to stay with me. That was all she had to say and that damn beast would stay with me until she told him otherwise. It was uncanny, their bond; the way they communicated with each other. She didn't just order him around; she loved that ugly beast. And he loved her right back, enough to run all the way downtown, up fifty flights of stairs, and onto the roof of Helios Tower to save my life.

Brim stuck his big, goofy face in mine, sniffing my breath. I ruffled his ears affectionately.

"Thanks, kid."

"Don't mention it."

The door closed and I smiled to myself. Sometimes she sounded just like me. Other times like Bryn. Always trying out new sayings, trying to grow and figure out who she wanted to be, and how she wanted to present herself to others. It was fascinating to watch. But I worried, too; I worried about this special talent she had for communicating with Brim. Hell, she'd even sent *me* flying through the air with only the force of her will.

Emma had raw, and apparently very strong, abilities. And more than anything I prayed they wouldn't hurt her.

I stayed on the swing for another ten minutes or so. "Well, beasty boy, you ready for bed?" He turned away from the screen with a whine. Poor Brim, he looked so lost when Emma left him. "Come on, let's go in."

Dutifully, he climbed the stairs and then circled

repeatedly in the corner of my bedroom before lying down and settling into relaxed yet watchful guard dog mode. It was like having a gray, bald tiger in the corner, only this one had the jaws of an oversized pit bull and eyes that reflected red in the light.

And for some odd reason, I was starting to think the thing was cute.

I chuckled at that thought, lifted the down comforter, and slid into my cool bed.

I am on the rooftop of Helios Tower watching a sporadic replay of last week's events. Dawn of the winter solstice. Llyran parts the darkness churning above and then uses its power to slide the lid off the agate sarcophagus.

The agate no longer masks the power inside. An enormous surge radiates over the tower, a pulse of energy so heavy and thick that it steals my breath, a surge that flows through every fiber of my being, so deep and powerful and stunning.

There is fighting all around me. It comes in broken flashes.

Brimstone attacks Llyran.

My chest tightens painfully. I know what comes next. Tears sting my eyes as Llyran kills my daughter's beloved hellhound.

Then I am crawling toward the sarcophagus, pulling myself up, and grabbing the only weapon I can find. I hold the sword aloft, over Llyran's head. The hilt sears my hand, but I don't care. It doesn't matter. Tears slip hot and fat from my eyes as I bring down the weapon with every bit of strength I have left.

And then suddenly, they are gone and I am standing alone beside the agate tomb, gazing down in wonder at what it contains. Llyran is dead. My hand is useless, but I am transfixed as I stare at one of the most beautiful creatures I've ever seen. A divine being. A First One. Ahkneri. The Creator's Chosen One. His Star, and then, later, His instrument of Vengeance, Retribution, and Punishment. The sword is back in her grip as though I never touched it, held between her breasts. It is a named weapon, a divine weapon called Urzenamelech, "Anguish by fire."

And now I understand why because my hand and even my arm burn from the inside out.

The scene shifts in a blur.

Gray landscape. Valleys. Mountains. Cloud-laden sky. Mist-covered ground. All moving by at great speed. Down over foothills covered in grass to flatlands that eventually turn to sand. To a desert and a sparkling river under a blazing white sun. To the walls of a massive temple rearing up on the other side.

Straight up the face of the wall and over the balcony. Between massive columns, so high their tops are lost in shadows. To a courtyard.

"No!" A voice pleads. Feminine. Familiar. And I know immediately who this is. Ahkneri. She speaks in an ancient language that somehow I understand.

Then another voice. "Our purpose is at an end. Our lives here, in this state, are over. It was always meant to be like this. You know this."

Another denial. Anger. Shouting.

And then the scene is speeding away again back through

the columns and out over the land to a dark place, a place of mist and jagged mountains that scrape the sky.

Then inside a tunnel of light so blinding.

Darkness. Inside of the mountains. Into blackness. Earth.

An eye blinks open.

My eyes flew open. A cold, heart-pounding sweat covered me. Foreboding tensed every muscle and dried out my mouth. That dream, or whatever the hell I'd just experienced, struck me with bleak fear.

Brim's sudden whine made goose bumps spread over my skin.

My sight quickly adjusted to the dark room, and I stayed beneath the covers, moving only my head so I could see the shadow of the hellhound—still lying down, but his head was up, short ears pointed.

His soft panting was the only sound in the room. But still I hesitated to move. I could detect auras, sense presences, and those senses were telling me there was nothing else here. Nothing. Yet it didn't feel right; something wasn't right.

Slowly, I turned my head to the other side. The street lamp from outside faintly illuminated my dark curtains. There was nothing in the bedroom. I drew in a deep breath and let it out. It had to have been the odd dream. And Brim's response could be due in part to the vibes I was giving off.

Just as I decided to turn over and go back to sleep, a small hand slapped down on my right arm in a bruising grip. A second hand landed flat between my breasts, shoving me back into the mattress.

A body materialized into a pert-nosed waif with clear blue eyes, white hair in two long braids, dressed in some type of silvery, body-hugging tube around her flat chest and a matching miniskirt. Her midriff was bare and sported a belly button ring. Oh, and she was floating—I squeezed my eyes closed and opened them again—yep, still hovering over me.

"Do you accept my gift?" she asked vehemently, producing a giant syringe and pressing it against my skin.

"What the— Stop!"

Her eyes went narrow. "So you deny my gift, then?"

"What? Yes. No . . ." Jesus. *Okay. Calm down.* Gift, *she'd said* gift. "What are you doing?"

"What I'm doing is not fooling around with some stupid test of worthiness like my backwoods sisters. You want it or not?"

My eyes fixed on the syringe. "Want what exactly?"

"Air. A hundred mils of it, pulled from yours truly, clean, blessed, and ready for the joining. Snagged this big boy"—she nodded toward the syringe—"from a horse farm in Conyers."

"I thought that was just a myth, that air couldn't—"

"Kill you? Sure it can. In big enough doses. Look, you don't have to accept death to accept a gift. That's my sisters' deal." She shrugged. "If you're big enough to take the risk, then it's fine by me. So, are you?"

"And the risk would be?"

"Brain damage. You in?"

"Brain damage," I repeated numbly.

"Yeah. See," she snorted, "you're already halfway there." When I didn't laugh, she rolled her large, slanted eyes.

It was like I'd just woken up in some alternate never-never land, where Peter Pan was a smart-ass little female floating above me.

"My gift will move slowly because I told it to. Once you accept all the gifts, and use them for your purpose, you'll be fine, and what I just gave you will be used up. Should you fail to accept the other gifts or don't use them within four days of receipt of the first one, then mine is free to make its merry way into your brain. So, what'll it be?"

These *tests* were all about worth and sacrifice. If you were willing to show you meant it, you were given the gift: the element.

I knew my heart, and because of that I wasn't afraid.

I met her eyes and nodded, tensing as her grip on my arm tightened. She still hadn't removed her other hand from my chest.

"Once I have all of the elements inside of me, how do I use them to see inside of my sister?"

"I'm not sure how it works. It just does." A lethal grin spread across her face. "Don't worry. I'll try not to hit an artery."

And then she shoved the needle into my skin.

I gasped at the sting and the instant bloom of hot pressure as air forced its way into my tissue. The sylph drew back and finally lifted her other hand off my chest. "It should only hurt for a little while."

I sat up, rubbing at the burning skin. My arm was beginning to numb.

She glanced around the room, saw my small trash can, and tossed the syringe inside. "Later."

"Wait!"

But she was already spinning into . . . nothing but air. And as air, she had no problem going wherever the hell she wanted—through cracks, under doors, through window screens . . . Nice power to have.

I fell back onto my mattress, heart pounding, and pressed my palms to my eyes and cursed. Great. I was a walking air embolism, and I had no idea how to use the elements inside of me to see inside of Bryn and the other *ash* victims.

Brim stood, stretched his long body, and then began circling again several times before lying back down.

I'd received the water gift first, so I had roughly three and a half days left before I needed to use what was inside of me or die. Funny, Alessandra never mentioned that part.

Two more tests to go. And the next time I saw a sylph, she wasn't going anywhere until she told me exactly what to do with my *gifts*. Not if I could help it.

*   *   *

"Mom." I was shaken so hard, my teeth clattered. "Momma, *wake up!*"

I groaned in protest, trying to turn over and pull the comforter over my head. "Stop, Em. Not time to get up yet . . ." The alarm hadn't even gone off.

"Momma, get your butt out of bed. Miss Marti is on the phone. Something's wrong with Amanda."

I rolled over to see my daughter leaning over me in her pajama tank, hair in a cloud of wavy tangles, with the phone in her hand. I took the phone, my stomach already knotting. "Hello?"

"Charlie," Marti's unsteady voice came through the speakers. *Please, don't let this be bad. Please . . .* "We're at the hospital. Mandy"—she broke off with a sob—"tried to kill herself this morning."

Amanda was one of the *ash* victims. She was also supposed to be under guard like the others.

"Where?"

"We're back at Grady." The same place Amanda had been taken a couple months earlier when *ash* had begun making its way into the population, when she'd ingested it out of teenage curiosity, and was later found lying on the bathroom floor of Hope Ridge School for Girls. My daughter's school. My daughter's good friend—older, yes, but those two had developed a sisterly relationship in the years since Marti and I became friends and carpoolers.

"I'll be there as soon as I can." I ended the call and

got out of bed. Em stepped back and watched me jerk my shirt over my head. "Get dressed," I said. "I know you'll want to see her."

The breath she'd been holding released in a long whoosh. "Come, Brim." And then they were gone.

I stepped to the bedroom window, praying my SUV had been dropped off like Hank promised. Thank God, it was there. I dressed quickly. I could hear Em's racing footsteps on the stairs, the sound of the back door as she took Brim outside to the kennel, and then her heading back to her room to dress.

Twenty minutes later, we hurried into the hospital and up to Amanda's floor, passing a nurses' station and heading a few doors down to where a plainclothes officer stood against the wall. He straightened as we approached.

"You were the one guarding her?" I asked.

"Who are you?"

Badge out. "Madigan. What happened?"

Red tinged his eyes. Unshaven. Dress shirt wrinkled. The guy could use a coffee or two. He stared over my shoulder for a moment, gathering his thoughts, and then opened his mouth, but the door to Amanda's room clicked and Marti poked her head out.

"You're here. Come on in. Titus is here, too." She stepped back, opening the door wider. Emma went first. Marti gave her a gentle smile and a hug.

"Give me a sec," I said to the officer and went inside of the room.

Atlanta's resident genius, the man who'd discovered the alternate dimensions of Elysia and Charbydon, stood as we entered. I could tell he'd come from the lab, most likely working all night as usual. Titus also happened to be Amanda's uncle, and with his brother, Cassius, having fled the country after his involvement in the production of *ash* came to light, Titus was the only one left to help pick up the pieces and lend support to his abandoned niece and sister-in-law.

He was a better man, by far, than Cassius had ever been. The incredibly wealthy scientific empire Titus had built on the foundation of his discovery over a decade ago hadn't gone to his head. He was constantly working, constantly trying to invent better things and help our world deal with the influx of off-world immigrants and the crime factor that came along with it. Titus had invented every single one of our weapons, and he'd streamlined a better portal device to compensate for growing inter-world travel. The terminal here in Atlanta was the biggest and busiest, but there were terminals now in all the major U.S. cities.

Marti returned to the chair by Amanda's bed. She still wore her pajamas, a matching set of soft pink silk pants and top. I didn't know how she managed to look put together even here in this situation, but she did, as always. Only the tight line of her lips and the haggard look in her eyes gave her away.

It was easier to focus my attention on them first and not the girl who lay in the bed—Amanda.

But it wasn't so for Emma. She went right to her friend and placed her hand over Amanda's. "Is she going to be okay?" she said, looking at the array of monitors, the thick neck bandage, and the oxygen mask covering Amanda's nose and mouth.

"She'll be fine," Titus spoke up, sliding down his glasses to rub the bridge of his nose. "The restraints are for her protection."

I turned to Marti. "I'm going to talk to the officer. I'll be right back."

I could've asked them what happened, but I didn't want to put Marti through telling the tale. I closed the door behind me and walked a few steps away, motioning for the officer to follow. Then I turned and waited for an explanation.

"It all happened so fast," he said, guilt eating through his voice. "We did everything we could think of . . . got rid of every razor and knife, took all the doorknobs off the doors. She was never alone. Marti even sat in the bathroom while Amanda showered. And then this morning . . ." He rubbed a hand down his face. "She shoved a plastic protractor from her book bag into her jugular."

"Christ," I said on a faint breath of shock.

He rubbed a shaky hand down his tired face.

"There's no way you could've known," I told him. There was only one way to stop something like this from happening again. I walked away from the officer and hit the chief's number.

"Hello?"

"Hey, Chief, it's Charlie."

"You at the hospital?"

"Yeah. Are you thinking what I'm thinking?"

"That an eight-by-ten holding cell looks pretty good right about now."

"So let's round them up, get them all into the station. Whatever strings you have to pull, whatever lies you have to tell them, just get them into a goddamn cell, like now."

"Already working on it. We've alerted the guards we have out there as to what's happened, and have personally made contact with the *ash* victims. Most of them are coming in on their own after this latest . . . attempt. I'll handcuff and drag the others if I have to. They can sue us later."

"And Bryn? Have you talked to Bryn?"

"She's on her way in."

Oh, thank God. "Thanks, Chief. And will you send a fresh officer to the hospital? Amanda's guard is here now and the guy could use a break."

"Will do. Is Titus there yet? If we had a cure for *ash*, our problems would be solved . . ."

"I know." Without *ash* in their systems, they'd be strong enough to force out an unwelcome spirit. "He's here, I'll talk to him."

And then I proceeded to fill the chief in on the sylphs. He was just as thrilled with the idea as Rex, but he also knew the stakes. And he believed in me. "Christ Almighty," he breathed through the phone.

"If Titus doesn't come up with a cure soon and we can't get an exorcist here . . . this is the only option we have to identify the ones in danger." Not to mention an option that I had to see to the very end. The process had already been started. Neither Alessandra nor Nivian had stated the facts and then let me decide beforehand. I was underwater, drowning, before I accepted the first gift, not even knowing what that really entailed, not knowing the elements would kill me if I didn't complete the process. Even if I wanted to, I couldn't back out now. Even if a cure was found, I still had to complete the sylphs' ritual.

"For God's sake, just be careful. The warlocks are bringing Bryn in now. So just focus on the job at hand, all right?"

"I will."

After I hung up, I headed back to the officer. "Thanks," he said, and I knew he meant the request for relief. I hadn't exactly been whispering on the phone.

"Sure. Why don't you go get a coffee or something? I'll stay until you get back."

He gave me a nod and walked off. The guilt pouring off that guy was pretty heavy. I had no doubt he'd done the best he could . . . I just wished we'd corralled everyone sooner.

Titus stepped quietly from Amanda's room, his shoulders slumped, his look weary. He removed his wire-framed glasses, rubbed the bridge of his nose again, and then slipped them back on. His brown hair was a mess as usual and he needed a shave and a cut.

Titus's rise to fame and fortune as the genius who'd discovered "heaven" and "hell" had come in his late twenties. The guy was in his early forties now and was still going strong, still making new discoveries, modifying his inventions, and growing his scientific and research empire.

"How close are you close to finding a cure?" I asked him, my voice as tired as he looked.

"Close. We've been testing a type of Elysian seaweed. It looks promising. So far it's breaking down the Bleeding Soul extract found in *ash*. That extract is the active ingredient in the drug. It's quite remarkable. Once it's introduced into the system, it bonds to the neural pathways in the brain. Once there, it begins to fade, to break down all on its own, but it starts breaking down the brain, too. Which, as you know, is why we have to keep giving the victims *ash* in small, regulated doses. But if the Bleeding Soul is neutralized or made to turn on itself, destroy itself without destroying anything else, then . . . then maybe they'll be free."

"And this seaweed does that? Breaks down the Bleeding Soul without harming anything else?"

"In a petri dish, sure. I have yet to move my tests to live subjects."

"We're running out of time, Doc. If you can cure them of the *ash* addiction, they'll be strong enough to fight off what's inside of them."

"I know, Charlie." He let out a weary sigh. "I know."

As we stepped back in the room, I saw that Em had taken up Titus's earlier position on the other side of Amanda's bed.

"Can I stay here for a while?" she asked as soon as she saw me. "I don't have school."

"I can drive her home later," Marti offered. "I'll have to go home and change at some point anyway."

I met my daughter's eyes. They were hopeful, soft, worried . . . "Sure. You can stay." I turned to Marti. "Rex should be home, but have Emma call him when you're on the way. I don't want her home alone."

Marti nodded, and my chest ached for her. I knew what it was like, to fear for your child's life, for your hands to be tied, and there was nothing you could do but wait. Mentally and emotionally, it was the toughest thing I'd ever had to deal with.

Emma crossed the room and gave me a tight hug, which I returned wholeheartedly. She gave me strength and she didn't even know it. "You're wearing all your amulets, right?" She nodded. "Good. I'll see you after work, then. Call me if you need to."

I paused in front of Marti, unsure. Wanting to give her some words of comfort, some support; but I froze up. I didn't know what to say to make her feel better. First Amanda had almost died from ingesting *ash*, then her husband had been involved with the drug— using one of Titus's labs to manufacture it into an easily ingestible form—then he'd fled the country, leaving his wife and daughter. Now this . . .

"She's a strong kid. She'll be okay," I said, feeling my words were so inadequate, but needing to say them anyway. She gave me a grateful nod.

On my way out, I stopped at the nurses' station, flashed my badge, and told them to keep Amanda in the restraints. She wasn't to get out of that bed, not even to use the bathroom. It was catheters and bed-pans until we figured this thing out.

Amanda might be the one in restraints, I thought as I walked out of the hospital, but it sure as hell felt like it was *my* hands that were tied. I paused just outside of the main doors, glancing up at the rolling darkness above me. My mood was gray like the sky.

How do I fix this?

Ash had only been on the market for a few weeks before we'd gotten it taken off the streets, but in that short time it had long-lasting, devastating effects. All because of some stupid flower—the Bleeding Soul, *Sangurne N'ashu*, an extremely rare, bioluminescent flower from Charbydon.

Cassius Mott was gone, Mynogan was dead, and the only other person of the three responsible for putting *ash* on the market was Grigori Tennin.

And he was right here. In my city.

And he was about to get another visit from a very pissed-off, potentially divine ITF officer.

9

Hank was waiting for me at the plaza in Underground. I'd called him from my car, but I didn't need to see him to know he was there; I felt him, my mark going annoyingly warm and happy.

He was rising from his seat on the fountain before I cleared the steps—the siren felt it, too.

As Hank straightened to his full height, he drew the gaze of at least a dozen eyes. Men, women, kids, all drawn to him by something they couldn't control, all willing to jump off a cliff for him and thank him going down. All he had to do was ask.

One of Titus's many inventions, the torque-like device worn by Hank and every other siren by law subdued the majority of their potent voice, but not all of it. And it didn't do a damn thing for the natural lure that seemed to emanate from every pore.

Also annoying.

Hank shoved his hands into his leather jacket and strode forward as I came down the last step, the zing from being so exposed to the darkness above lessening, now replaced by a different kind of zing. I bit down hard, clenching my teeth and stealing myself against the sudden one-two punch—first butterflies, followed by a sharp stab of heat, which I refused to define as lust.

He wore khaki cargo pants, black combat boots, and a white T-shirt beneath a blue button-down shirt that set off his tanned skin. His wavy blond hair curled past his ears, brushing his collar. He hadn't bothered to shave, which I liked. *A lot*. It gave him a rugged appearance. Unkempt. Wild. Slightly bohemian.

I rolled my eyes.

Yes, I liked Hank. I knew it. He knew it. But it would've been nice to feel unaffected in the midst of work. Once I saw him as someone *other* than my partner, I'd fallen down the rabbit hole, on a fast track to wanting it all. It was confusing and quick and so unlike me . . .

His blue eyes glittered as he approached. One corner of his mouth was drawn into a knowing smile. I frowned harder, clamping down on my emotions and aura.

Hank stopped in front of me. "How are the Motts holding up?" The words were deep and rich, and lowered to an unnecessarily intimate tone. *No, a concerned tone, so maybe you should stop imagining things and get on with it*.

I stepped around him, focusing on crossing the plaza as he fell in step beside me. "As well as can be expected," I answered, looking straight ahead. "Amanda should pull through as long as she stays under watch and in the restraints."

"Em doing okay?"

Some of my ire deflated. "She's worried . . . I wish—"

"Wish what, Charlie?" When I didn't answer, he said, "It doesn't make you weak to say how you feel."

I shot him a flat look. "I *do* know that."

Usually, I wasn't one for lamenting things beyond my control. But I'd taken all I could take. The Sons of Dawn had been behind everything, from creating me to be the only being in all three worlds capable of bringing darkness to the city, to letting *ash* loose upon the population, to making puppets out of its victims . . .

I went a few more steps before I finally answered. "It's just that . . . all this crap they've put into play from the very beginning . . . I just wish it was over. Wish they had picked someone else."

Everything that had happened since I died and was brought back ten months ago had been, in one way or another, the cult's doing. Their plan. Their interference in my fucking life. And I was sick of it.

"You don't mean that," Hank said quietly. *You'd be dead if they had picked someone else to revive,* was his unspoken thought; I could hear it in his voice. I knew it, but I needed to rant, to get it out.

"It's not like there aren't other people out there with off-world blood in their family tree. Any one of them could've survived the gene manipulation and been able to complete the darkness ritual just as well as me . . ."

I shoved my hands deep into my pockets and let out a loud sigh. "But . . . no," I admitted, belligerently. "I wouldn't wish that on anyone and I know I wouldn't be here if they hadn't interfered."

If I'd been conscious before my heart stopped, if Titus and Mynogan had stood above me and offered me life or death, knowing exactly what I'd be getting into, I would've agreed. I'd do anything to keep my kid from suffering that kind of loss.

"That was their first mistake—choosing you," Hank said softly, his shoulder knocking mine for a moment as we walked around a jewelry cart. "No one else would've been able to do what you did, Charlie. Defeat Mynogan. Stop the ritual before it spilled darkness over *more* than just Atlanta. I bet the cult is kicking itself for involving you." His voice went firm. "The bastards created the very thing that will destroy them."

I did a mental blink, nearly bumping into a shopper who'd stopped to window-shop. The absolute surety of Hank's tone and the fact that he thought this way about me . . . It was nice hearing it out loud. It took me several seconds to respond. And then when I opened my mouth I didn't have any words.

We fell into an easy silence, both lost in our own

thoughts and emotions as the light grew dim and the air thickened. If Underground was the heart of the off-world population in Atlanta, then Solomon Street was Charbydon central. Home to a few nobles, some ghouls, and a large population of jinn, darkling fae, and goblins.

The street grew darker as we went. Years ago, the Charbydons had petitioned the city for the right to burn open fires on Solomon Street. They used the fires for light, for cooking, for warmth, for getting rid of things . . . It was part of their lifestyle, something that they didn't want to give up. So in went ventilation shafts and city-approved fire barrels, and up went the soot and grime to cover the glass of every street lamp, giving the Charbydons a world that mimicked their own—sweltering, smoky, dark.

The jinn had gone one step further, and dug a subterranean village out of the bedrock beneath Underground, a maze of corridors, chambers, and dwellings that reflected the way they lived in Charbydon. Here, tribal customs and laws ruled.

The main entrance to the jinn's underground territory, which I'd dubbed The First Level of Hell, was located at the dead end of Solomon Street, Grigori Tennin's base of operations, the Lion's Den—a gambling house, bar, and strip club.

Sweat formed on the small of my back as I walked down the street. The smoke from the fires made it hard to breathe; the city needed to overhaul the ventilation system big-time. The scent of tar hung heavy here—a telltale sign of a large jinn population. Like on the other streets and alleys in Underground, doors were thrown open, sales carts rolled slowly over the brick pavers, music and voices blended into a chaotic hum.

It was too early in the morning for the Den to be open for business, but that didn't stop Hank from opening the heavy iron-and-wood door. No need to lock up—everyone knew who owned the place, and you'd have to be an idiot or looking to get yourself tortured and killed if you took from the boss himself.

Inside, the space was quiet and empty. Our footsteps thudded loudly on the planked floor as we made our way past tables, the bar, and to the door that led below.

"After you," Hank said.

I stepped through the open door and then went carefully down a flight of wooden stairs. A female jinn, part of Tennin's personal guard, turned and glanced over her shoulder. She wore traditional jinn war regalia and was just as deadly and strong as her male counterparts. When they said *warrior race*, they weren't kidding.

"We're here to see Tennin," I said.

Her violet eyes assessed us, unimpressed. And why should she be—she was six feet tall, armed, and had biceps that rivaled Hank's. "This way."

Deep, angry echoes filled the corridor, followed by the high-pitched crash of glass or pottery. Not unusual, as the jinn relished fighting and were quick to anger. The sounds grew louder as we approached the main chamber, where Tennin usually had meals and held court. The Charbydon language was being shouted so loudly that it vibrated off the bedrock walls—echoing and bouncing and filling the subterranean village.

As we entered the chamber, I immediately noticed Sian standing near Tennin's great wooden table. Her eyes flashed to mine in alarm, and she warned me with a slight shake of her head as Grigori Tennin threw another jar at the massive fireplace across the chamber, his booming Charbydon words jolting through me.

I understood none of it. But I did understand the tension and fright filling the massive space, emanating from the other jinn gathered in the room. I flinched as another vase crashed into the bedrock wall and rained pieces down over the floor.

The guard turned and went to usher us back out of the chamber, her face a shade paler than before. But before she could do so:

"YOU! CHARLIE MADIGAAAAAAN!"

Shit.

It got so quiet I could hear Tennin's ragged breathing from where I stood.

Slowly, I turned, swallowed, and leveled my voice. "Tennin."

His thick chest and shoulders rose and fell as he panted like a raging bull. His gigantic fists clenched and unclenched, his face a dark gray mask of seething jinn rage. His eyes glowed red violet and scary as hell. Veins swelled and ran over his temples and over his smooth bald skull. His earrings flashed in the firelight.

In front of the fireplace, scattered over the floor, were remnants of alabaster jars. Tennin strode to the table and grabbed the last intact jar in his big hand.

And then it hit me. My eyes grew round. I knew what that was. A spirit jar.

Tennin grinned, feral and evil, his white teeth flashing. He tossed the jar and caught it again. Christ, Aaron was right. I glanced at the debris on the floor. How many had there been? Had they been empty when he threw them? Or full?

Better question, though: why was Tennin destroying the jars?

"Another *ash* victim tried to kill herself this morning," I said slowly, observing his reaction. "But then, you already know that, don't you?"

Hank chuckled, completely devoid of humor and full of hostility. Sian's indigo eyes went wide and more frightened than before. I glanced over as realization settled warily in my gut. Tennin had planted an axe in Hank's back during the battle on Helios Tower. And Hank, obviously, hadn't forgotten.

"What's wrong, Tennin?" he asked in a menacing tone. "Your moles not listening to you anymore? Or maybe," he ventured, "you're not the one in control after all? Is that it?"

Tennin's eyes brightened even more. I'd only ever seen them this bright once before, when he'd killed one of his own tribe members here in this very room with a thought. Something, I hoped, he could do only to other jinn.

He pointed the jar at Hank. "The last time, I was aiming for your skull." He stuck out his other arm and the battle-axe hanging on the wall flew into his outstretched hand. "Let me try again." As soon as it met flesh, Tennin threw it. It sailed end over end, whooshing like a countdown clock. One. Two. Three.

Hank ducked as I leapt to the side. The axe slammed into the wall behind us, cleaving the rock and sending pulverized bits flying in all directions.

I swallowed, heart pounding as I straightened and rested my hand on the hilt of my firearm. This was not good.

Hank rose to his full height, casually wiping the bits of rock from his jacket. He gave Tennin a challenging look. "Missed again."

"Who's giving the suicide order?" I interrupted before they went at it.

A slow grin split Tennin's face. "You're like a blind nithyn in a nest full of moon snakes." He waved his hand around. "Going around and around. Lost. Stumbling." He shook his head, turned, and then flung the last spirit jar at the fireplace. It hit the mantel and smashed into a spray of tiny fragments.

After the last piece hit the ground, Tennin moved to his table and sat down, propping his booted feet on the corner of the table. "Tell me, Charlie—how is your Revenant companion? He remembers his jinn past now, yes?"

"You know he does. But if you think he plans to join with you, you're wrong. Rex is one of the good guys."

"And I am not? Come, Detective. Be nice. Your Rex will turn in time. He is a jinn after all. He knows what he is. Matter of time. That is all. You will see."

Rex had come to Tennin to find a way to repay the twenty-one-thousand-dollar collection debt I'd been hit with, thanks to Rex's oversight. Tennin had waived the fee in return for Rex agreeing to drink a potion that made him remember his past life, his original, physical life as—surprise, surprise—a jinn. It had worked. Rex remembered. And Tennin got what he wanted, though what his ultimate goal was regarding Rex remained a mystery.

"Run along, blind nithyn, run along," Tennin said, shooing us away and chuckling to himself as a pair of jinn brought out his meal.

I had to actually tug on Hank's arm to get his feet moving. I'd gotten the information I'd come for, and I sent a silent prayer of thanks to the Powers That Be that we'd arrived when we did.

Once we were in the club upstairs and headed for the door, I said, "He's not the one giving the suicide order. And he's pissed about it." So pissed that he was destroying the spirit jars. "Could you tell how many jars there were?"

"No. But there had to be at least four, judging from the debris."

If there had once been Sons of Dawn spirits contained in those jars, Casey and Mike could've accounted for two of them. Amanda, and possibly Bryn, for another two.

As we left the Lion's Den, a flash of movement to my right caught my attention. I followed it, peering into the darkness as my eyes adjusted to see a dark figure—female and small in stature. The shadow darted into the alley that ran between the Den and the apartment block. Soft, feminine laughter echoed in her wake, a daring kind of laughter, the kind that said *Are you brave enough to follow me?*

"You heard that, right?"

"The laughter? Yeah." Hank was looking in the same direction.

"I bet that's a sylph. Come on." I took off at a run toward the dark alley. And she was not only going to give me her gift, she was damn sure going to tell me how to use it.

The alley was pitch-black, reeking of urine and tar mixed with smoke. Obstructions rose up in front of me so fast I only had a second to adjust and then jump or dodge as I hurried after her. A dim light illuminated the end of the alley and the narrow delivery street that ran behind the backs of the buildings.

Laughter again. Echoing. Taunting. Calling my name. Oh, yeah. Definitely a sylph.

A shadow passed through the light. Metal banged. I raced around the corner and slid to a stop, scanning the area. *There.* A small metal service door hung open. I scrambled over a discarded couch to get to the door.

This was one of the entrances that led to the old sewer tunnels and supposedly intersected with the MARTA rails. The sewage system was long gone, leaving behind some impressive Gothic architecture and brick-domed tunnels.

My boots on the metal steps rang softly through the dark space below me.

"You sure about this?" Hank whispered above me, following me down.

"Yeah. Once you've seen a sylph . . ." I dropped to the ground and stepped away from the ladder. "Shadows or not, there's no mistaking it. I know it's her and I need that gift."

I pulled my ITF-issued flashlight from my belt and aimed it down both sides of the long tunnel. Hank dropped down beside me and clicked on his light. We followed the soft echo of laughter.

The scents of earth, bricks, and musty water hung heavy in the air as we went through the tunnel. The ground vibrated. A loud rumble filled the space as a MARTA train passed somewhere close by.

As the rumble slowly disappeared, a shadow appeared far down in the center of the tunnel.

The hairs on my forearms stiffened. My fingers flexed on the barrel of the flashlight. Anticipation heightened my blood pressure and added to the adrenaline already pumping through my system.

Hank turned to me suddenly and grabbed my arm.

A deep frown marred his shadowed features. "Christ, Charlie, what the hell am I supposed to do, watch it kill you?" He glanced down the tunnel. "Don't ask me to do that. Don't ask me to step aside and just stand here."

I hadn't thought about that. I knew what was coming for me, but the idea that Hank would have to stand by and watch . . . He just wasn't made like that and it showed in his aura and the chaotic anger emanating from him. He was tense, jaw tight, holding the flashlight so tightly, his knuckles were white.

He released me, his frown deepening in exasperation. "Why are you smiling?"

Before I could think better of it I grabbed his face. His stubble scratched my palms as I rose on my tiptoes and kissed him full on the mouth and then stepped back.

He stared at me, dumbfounded.

"Thank you," I said, removing my jacket and weapons and then handing them to him. "Stay here. I'll be right back."

I jogged down the tunnel toward the sylph.

She was petite, pretty, stockier than the other two. A tough little thing by the expression she wore. Her brown hair was braided in several small cornrows and pulled back into a high ponytail. It made her large eyes look more slanted and her cheekbones more prominent. A brown tattoo fanned out from the corner of her eye in a swirling design, like some intricate leaf, and her irises burned a mean green flecked with brown.

She wore a gold torque and two gold armbands, and a bare minimum of clothing like her sisters, though hers looked like some kind of suede material.

"Earth, I presume," I said, coming to a stop before her.

"Emain," she introduced herself. "And you're Charlie."

"I am."

No sooner than the words were out of my mouth, the ground trembled at my feet and opened up. Hank's shout behind me filled the tunnel and mingled with my gasp.

One minute I was standing and the next I was waist-deep in the earth, completely trapped. The faint beginnings of panic flirted with my mind. Dirt hugged me from my chest down. But my arms were free, thank God.

My flashlight was kicked out of my hand. It hit the wall and landed on the ground. It remained on, however, and while it wasn't pointed directly at me and the sylph, it was enough to illuminate the space and allow me to see the legs in front of me.

The bare knees bent and Emain's face appeared in front of me, one side illuminated and the other shadowed. The skin closest to the ground shifted color, blending into the shades of the dirt like a chameleon's. "Neat trick," I said, trying to control my breathing.

Her face moved closer, eyes narrowing. "Tell your siren to back off or he's going under."

Hank's shadow fell over us. I angled the best I could to see him standing there, chest heaving from the run, one hand holding the flashlight, the other holding his Hefty. His gaze was pinpointed on the sylph.

"Hank."

He wouldn't look at me, determined to keep the sylph at bay. Finally he flicked a glance my way and his eyes were hard as granite.

"No, Charlie, I—"

"Damn it, Hank." From the first moment I accepted Nivian's gift, I was on a path I had to complete. He knew it. I *had* to do this. And worse, he had to let me. "Just be here when it's over."

He swore. Turned, took two long strides to the wall, and punched a hole in the brick with an Elysian curse. I might've heard the crack of bone, but I tried not to think about it as Emain flicked the ends of my hair and smirked. "Do you accept my gift, Darkness Bringer?"

"Yes. Just get on with it." *Before Hank goes ape-shit.*

A slow, menacing grin grew on her face. The earth shuddered around me. I swallowed, commanding my heart to slow. *Don't panic. This is her price, whatever it is. She won't kill you. This is for Bryn. For Bryn. For Bryn . . .*

And then I was sinking, the ground eating up my sides, forcing my arms up above my head. My eyes went wide, fixing on the sylph in horror as she slowly sank into the earth in front of me, feetfirst as though in quicksand. A sigh of pleasure went out of her.

The dirt was to my chin now.

Hank slid down, digging the dirt around my chin before it claimed my mouth. It was too late for him to stop things, but despite that, he dug frantically. His tormented eyes met mine. Despair thickened his voice. "Damn it, Charlie . . ."

Cold ground touched my bottom lip. "It's okay," I hurried. *Oh God.* I started gasping, knowing I'd need air and trying like hell not to panic. Emain stopped her descent into the ground and winked at me at eye level. "See you below, Charlie Madigan."

Adrenaline shoved my heart into overdrive. I took one large draught of air and held my breath as my mouth and nose slid into the ground. Dirt filled in my ears, but not before I heard Hank curse with a catch in his voice and then threaten the sylph with every possible torture imaginable if I didn't come back up.

I said a quick prayer and closed my eyes.

The last thing I felt was Hank's hand. He grabbed mine and squeezed with encouragement before the earth swallowed me whole.

And then there was silence.

I was cocooned in pressure and weight. The sound of my own heartbeat drummed loudly and rapidly in my ears.

Oh God, oh God, oh God.

Going down. Down deep into the ground. My lungs burned. I couldn't move, couldn't struggle.

Claustrophobia took hold. It was worse than drowning because at least in the water I could move, I could struggle.

The pain, the pressure in my chest, burned a hot path through my blood vessels, stinging them, vibrating them. My mind went cloudy. *For Bryn.* My fingers curled, packing dirt beneath the short nails. It was the only movement I could make. My arms were trapped straight above me. The dirt pressed in on my body, my neck, face, eyelids, and mouth. God, my mouth . . .

I bit my tongue.

White erupted behind my eyelids.

I gasped.

For a split second I felt relief but that was immediately taken away by the dirt sucked into my mouth. No air. Just dirt. And then I was gagging, gagging without air to facilitate the action. Desperate, painful, familiar gulping for something that wasn't there.

Finally my mouth stopped moving as it filled with dirt. My chest kept lurching. In and out. Slower and slower. Still mimicking the need to breathe.

The hum is what first stirred my detached senses. It was a welcome sound, a sound that carried life. Energy. Connection. I felt wrapped in the Earth's womb. And she was alive. Pulsing. Powerful. And I was part of her, part of the cycle now. All of me, splitting apart, degrading, nurturing and feeding the soil.

Time disappeared. Ashes to ashes, dust to dust. Reclaimed. Dispersed. Just particles. Matter.

Eventually there came, at some point, a sense of body.

Floating, contained, wrapped in dirt, eyelids once again feeling the pressure, the weight. And it felt nice. This quiet. This cocoon.

So quiet, the city began to leak into this place. A thousand voices. A thousand random thoughts not my own. They came at me, at first just a slow trickle that became stronger and stronger until the pressure built inside of me, bloating me.

"Fighting, always fighting," came a soft voice.

Emain.

My mind withdrew from the edge of panic. She was all around me, forcing the hum into my skin, pressing the earth closer around me, filling me, opening me up, and breaking me apart at the same time.

"I see you, Charlie Madigan. I see you now. You are as they say. Never doubt the *Ceallachan*. They spoke of a day when darkness would come. And here you are." This pressure, this suffocating invasion, was too much, even for my unconscious self. "So much chaos inside of you. Fractured. She, Mother Earth, can repair this. Fix this. You'll need to be whole for what's to come."

No, no. No more, my mind cried.

"Fighting, always fighting . . ." The space went silent again and peace settled around me.

Then Emain's voice again. "The gift is yours. Your

last gift will come soon. Once each element is inside of you, they will join to make a new element. Nwyvre. You will be transformed, able to see the energy, the magic inside of everything because you will *become* magic. It will happen at once. And then, after a time, Nwyvre will fade and you will be as you once were . . ."

Her voice faded, and I relaxed back in the embrace of Mother Earth, letting my mind go.

The easing of pressure woke me.

The dirt was thinning fast around me as though drawing back. My mouth and eyes opened at the same time. Dirt scratched at my irises, and even though I closed my eyes immediately, dirt clung to my lashes and the rims of my eyelids, scratching, damaging.

My lungs contracted, wanting desperately to breathe, burning hot and painful. The burn of failure. Of denial. My throat thickened. Every time I clawed or moved, I lost the little bit of ground I had gained. *Goddammit!* I struggled, panicking.

My nails broke as I fought.

My hand suddenly hit flesh. Strong fingers wrapped around my wrist and pulled. The bones in my wrist cracked under the pressure, my shoulder nearly ripped from the socket. The dirt seemed to work against me, sucking me back in.

Then out. My head was free. I opened my mouth and sucked in air. Bits of dirt flew into the back of my throat, down my esophagus, and into my stomach. I hacked and coughed and choked, every draught of air into my body a welcome, dirty pain.

Strong, bruising hands re-gripped my weak, useless body lower and lower, climbing down my arms, pulling, until my shoulders came out. Arms went beneath mine, wrapping around me, dragging me out of my would-be grave.

My hips slipped free and I collapsed on top of Hank.

He held on to me as I heaved, lungs burning fire, and turning me when I started gagging and finally puking dirt onto the ground beside us.

When the worst of it was over, he sat up, skimming me for injuries. His dirt-caked hands finally settled on my face and I felt the faint tremble in them. He pushed back my hair and removed chunks of wet dirt from the corners of my eyes and ears.

I slumped against him, grabbing on to his bicep, the side of my face planted in the crook of his shoulder. Tears continually leaked, my body trying to shed the dirt from my eyes. Hank's heart beat hard and fast in his chest. He wasn't letting go of me, and I wasn't arguing.

"Asking me not to fight," he muttered in a shaky voice. "Never again. You understand? Never again."

Hot pain radiated through my wrist, and pretty much everywhere else on my body, but I heard his words and held them, stored them for a later time.

My muscles grew stiff as we sat there in the dim tunnel, both of our flashlights remaining on, lying on the ground nearby and giving me enough light to see. Another MARTA train rumbled by, shaking the earth.

After it passed and the tunnel grew quiet again, Hank leaned back to look down at me, gently laying a hand on my arm. "Your wrist is broken. I'm sorry."

"I'm not. If you hadn't pulled me up . . ."

He reached up with both hands and unclipped the voice-mod from his neck. I went still and slid back, off his lap and onto the ground beside him, our legs touching. "What are you doing?"

Determination settled over his features as his eyes held mine, shifting into a dark sapphire blue. "I broke it. I fix it. Don't argue." He spoke true and deep, and without the voice-mod adjusting his voice, it flowed over me and through me in a warm wave of contentment and pleasure.

"But I—"

"You're not human anymore, Charlie," he said softly, "you can handle my voice without . . ."

Without jumping his bones, declaring my undying love and devotion, offering him everything I had . . .

Not exactly the kind of one-sided relationship I was after. But then, he was right, I wasn't exactly human anymore.

His hand trailed down my arm. I went still; the only reaction was the light burst of awareness in my stomach. His fingers closed around my wrist. Pain shot up my arm, stealing my breath. His other hand cupped the back of my neck as he leaned forward, pulling me in, his scruffy cheek brushing against mine. My heart started to beat wildly. Pain? What pain?

I waited, knowing he was going to speak. He was so close, the act so intimate. His fingers clamped harder on my neck as his lips parted against my ear, so close I heard the faint intake of his breath.

And then he spoke.

Slow, rhythmic, deep words flowed from his lips. Words I didn't understand, but the exotic language and the accent that came with it seemed to give them power, persuading, demanding, an alluring kind of power. My wounds would obey him. Happy to re-knit and mend for him. Every muscle relaxed, every nerve ignited with vitality, pleasure, contentment, bliss . . .

My mouth dropped open and the stunned curse that formed languidly in mind never made it out. My broken nails dug into his arm, an initial burst of pain replaced by goodness as the cuts healed.

And the words kept coming, going deeper into my senses, and somehow more personal—far more intimate than those first healing words.

My mark burned—a good kind of burn that matched the heat building in the rest of me. My mouth still hung open and my breath was coming out swift and ragged. I wanted to reach up, to slide my hand around the back of his neck and pull him closer, but my body and mind were too overwhelmed to move.

His words ended in a low whisper. His lips smiled, brushed past my ear, and pressed into my temple.

I blinked a few times and finally was able to close my mouth and swallow the lump in my throat. My heart pounded like a damn drum and my entire body hummed with something pretty similar to an endorphin rush.

As he pulled back and released his hand at my neck, I felt the faint, feathery touch of his breath, and wondered if I was imagining it or was his breath as shaky as my own?

10

Hank stayed quiet as he reattached his voice-mod, head bent, expression unreadable.

Look up! I wanted to shout at him, but he didn't. I wanted to know he was affected, that this moment wasn't some usual siren event for him, that I wasn't the only one feeling something on the inside.

I drew in a deep breath and immediately started hacking, dislodging the dirt clinging to the back of my throat. I grabbed Hank's knee, bent over, and spit a glob of dirt onto the ground.

A wry chuckle echoed in the tunnel. "Well, I've never gotten that kind of response before."

I shot a dark look over my arm as I wiped my mouth. "Funny."

And the idea of him doing what he'd just done to me to someone else? Absolutely maddening.

"The aches and stiffness will return," he said. "Your wrist is healed, but it'll be sore for a while."

"Thanks." I sat straighter. "For healing me." My hands were covered with dirt, so I grabbed the end of my shirt and used the inside edge to wipe the dirt from my eyes, but it was just as grainy on the inside as it was on the outside.

"Here." Hank pulled off his button-down, and then yanked his T-shirt over his head, using the inside end of it to help get more dirt away from my eyes and off my tear-streaked face. He held it to my nose. "Blow. You've got dirt shoved up your nose. That's why you're breathing out of your mouth."

I hadn't even noticed, but he was right. Now I knew why I was still feeling a ton of pressure in my face. I grabbed the shirt and blew the corks of packed dirt from my nose, thinking maybe I should just accept the fact that Hank would always see me at my worst.

Hank pulled his button-down back on, and I finally got a good look at him. Streaks of sweat-soaked dirt on his face. Pants, hands, and forearms covered in dirt and grit. Mostly dried blood had made tracks on his fingers and hands from where he'd broken nails or sliced his skin and palms against sharp rocks, digging me out.

"Jesus," I managed, staring at him.

How long had he been digging for me?

"Nothing compared to what you look like," he said, pushing to his feet and extending a hand. "Well enough to stand?"

"Yeah." I rolled onto my hands and knees, and stayed there for a moment to regain my equilibrium. Then I brought my legs in one at a time and slowly stood. A little wobbly, but otherwise okay. I went to brush the dirt from my clothes, but what was the point? It wouldn't help. I could feel the small, gritty particles on my scalp, in my bra and underwear, in my shoes and socks . . .

Hank picked up our flashlights and handed me one, his light beaming over me in a quick downward slash. "You look like a deranged cavewoman."

"Gee, thanks." I sniffed and gave him a haughty look. "I have dirt everywhere," I said, walking past him. "I'm going to Bryn's to clean up."

Oh, the looks that were thrown our way as we made our way down Solomon Street, into the plaza, and then down Mercy Street. The walk was brutal. Dirt rubbed me raw in all my delicate places.

One foot in front of the other, that's all I could concentrate on until I made it to Hodgepodge and Bryn's apartment above the shop.

Shower. Rest. Food.

Or maybe shower, food, rest. I wasn't sure yet, but Abracas was smelling pretty damn fine as we hobbled by. And they delivered.

I used my key and let us inside, barely able to make it up the stairs and refusing Hank's offer of a "lift" at least three times. At the top of the stairs, I paused to catch my breath before inserting the key and entering my sister's dark apartment. Hank came in behind me, shutting and locking the door and then proceeding to find the light switches.

The couch beckoned me like never before, but I bypassed it and went into the kitchen, where the dirt could be swept from the floor. I grabbed the counter for support and then slowly removed my boots. Dirt fell in streams onto the tiles. And more fell as I held them over the trash can and shook.

Hank and I worked in silence, things coming off—our shoes, socks, weapons, harnesses, and belts, all of it piling onto the countertop in a dusty heap.

Once I was down to my pants and T-shirt, I glanced at Hank to see him still dressed, but shaking the dirt out of his socks and shoes. Even sweat-soaked and grimy, he looked obscenely good. I rolled my eyes, bent over, and shook out my hair. His lure never seemed to take a day off, but I guessed I couldn't really fault him for what was as natural to him as breathing.

Get used to it, Charlie, I told myself. Then frowned inwardly. I thought I had.

"I'm taking a shower," I said, straightening as he sat on the stool, pulling his socks back on. "What are you doing?"

He grabbed his boot off the floor and shoved his foot in, not bothering with the laces. "Going back to my place to shower and get clean clothes. There's nothing here for me to wear. I'm just one street over. I'll be back before you even get out."

The other boot followed and he stood as I pulled

Bryn's key off the counter and tossed it to him. "Bring some food back with you," I said.

"Planned to." He shoved the key in his pocket and grabbed his wallet, leaving his other things. Then he leaned down, kissed me on the cheek, and walked out. As normal as you please. As though he'd been doing that for years.

I blinked, staring at the closed door for a long moment, trying to wrap my mind around this new and sudden step—no, *leap*—in our relationship.

There was so much mud in the tub that I worried about clogging Bryn's drain. I had to keep mashing it with my feet to thin it out, but finally the water ran clear and nothing backed up from the drain. My wrist ached, but I could move it without too much trouble. Soap stung the scratches on my face and the tender skin around the corners of my eyes, mouth, and nose.

As I massaged my scalp with suds, my eyelids closed and I let my thoughts drift into the background. The natural energy inside of me took over, working and healing.

I went into a calm, meditation-like state, relaxing every muscle and letting go of the worry, anxiety, and pressure to make things right.

The vision started so slowly, sneaking up on my unprotected mind, overtaking me before I knew what hit me.

★   ★   ★

Gray landscape. Valleys. Mountains. Cloud-laden sky. Mist-covered ground. All moving below me at great speed. Down over foothills covered in grass to flatlands that eventually turned to sand. To a desert and a sparkling river under a blazing white sun. To the walls of a massive temple rearing up on the other side.

Straight up the wall face and over the balcony. Through the massive columns. To a courtyard.

"No!"

"Our purpose is at an end. Our lives here, in this state, are over. It was always meant to be like this. You know this."

Denial. Anger. Shouting.

And then the scene speeds away again, going back through the temple columns so massive I can't see the roof. Over the land, to a darker place of mist and gray jagged mountains.

The blinding light comes next.

I'm on the rooftop of Helios Tower. Dawn of the winter solstice. Llyran removing the sarcophagus lid.

The agate no longer masks the power inside. The pulse of energy steals my breath and flows through every fiber of my being, so deep and powerful, it feels as though it has taken part of my life force with it as it ebbs.

And with that pulse the scene shifts to the black Earth. An eye blinks open.

I came out of the vision with a heart-pounding gasp, losing my balance in the tub and flailing for the wall before I slipped. The water still ran warm, and the suds were still in my hair. I ducked my head under the spray.

Apparently, only a few moments had passed, yet it felt like I'd been gone for a lifetime. It was exactly the same as before, but this time I couldn't call it a dream. It was much more than that.

A tingle of fear crept over my wet skin as I turned the water off, stepped out of the tub, and grabbed a towel.

As my body morphed into something more than human, I had experienced some odd things. Seeing through and inside solid objects, hearing voices . . . All things I hoped would go away once my body decided on what it wanted to be. The vision could be just another one of those things.

But still it was hard to shake the ominous feeling that came along with it.

I went to my assigned drawer—Bryn had gotten so tired of me coming by and borrowing her clothes if mine were ripped, bloodied, or soiled that she gave me my own space for my things. I pulled on a pair of underwear and a tank, and then crawled under the covers, curling onto my side.

It was dim in the room, the blinds drawn, the light off, and I was so spent that even just a few minutes of sleep would do me a world of good.

I heard the voice before I saw it. Deep. Ancient. Powerful. Familiar. Vibrating with a natural echo, the language containing hints of Elysian, Charbydon, Aramaic . . .

I turned onto my back. My eyes widened. The shadowy creature was back.

It hovered above me. A dark mass of terror. So close. So black and empty, yet something had to exist within. Preferably something with a heart.

It spoke again, sounding almost . . . *curious*.

I didn't even have time to breathe before it flew at me and my vision bled to black.

I woke with a jerk, the shadow creature leaping into the forefront of my mind. But I was still in Bryn's bed, head on her pillow. The thing had appeared, did its "in and out of body" trick, and then disappeared, leaving me knocked out for a little while but otherwise unhurt.

I relaxed back into the mattress as other elements in the room began to filter through my senses, namely the extraordinary warmth at my back. The air was filled with the smell of masculine skin and hints of cologne, soap, and dryer sheets.

Hank was back. And his scent wasn't the only thing surrounding me; his arm was thrown over my hip and my back was tucked nicely against his front.

The creature's visitation must've really done a number; I hadn't heard the siren come in, hadn't smelled the food that wafted in now from the kitchen, and definitely hadn't noticed when he lay down on top of the covers behind me and pulled me close.

It was nice. Good. Right, even. And then another

feeling struck me in a novel way. Protected. I felt protected. A disbelieving laugh bubbled in my throat as I lay there, a small smile parked on my face.

I was always the one out there protecting people. And after Will and I had split, I'd had no one to go to for comfort, to let *all* my guards down, to take a rest from being the caregiver, provider, guard, and detective. To let someone else be tough for a while.

Had to admit, I liked it. And I never thought in a gazillion years I'd find this feeling with an off-worlder. I liked Hank's strength, his power, his quirky humor, even the badass attitude he caught sometimes.

I was in so much trouble.

My stomach growled loudly. Hank stirred, voice sleepy. "Was that the gargoyle?"

I turned onto my back, letting my head fall to the side, facing him. "Gizmo is at the League with Bryn. That was my stomach."

Hank's eyes opened and studied me for a long moment. "You look better."

"So do you."

Several seconds passed and it hit me that we were just lying there staring at each other. And even though I tried, I couldn't stop smiling like an idiot.

"What did you bring?" I asked.

"Food, woman."

He got up from the bed and swaggered into the kitchen, calling as he went, "I saved you, I healed you, I brought you food . . . I am a god."

I threw the covers over my head and laughed—not

giggled—letting the feeling wash through me, a rare moment of feminine happiness.

Then my stomach rumbled again.

Without delay, I scrambled from the bed, dressed quickly, and hurried into the kitchen, finger-combing my hair as I went.

Hank was pulling utensils from the drawer as I ze-roed in on the two big takeout boxes on the table. One was filled with bow-tie pasta with chicken drenched with a thick, creamy pink sauce—my absolute favorite dish from Abracas. The other contained a large cheeseburger and steak fries. Hank sat down, handed me a fork, and then lifted the burger.

I stabbed the pasta, impressed that he'd remembered what I liked.

We ate for several minutes in a food-frenzied silence before he asked, "How was your nap?"

I speared a piece of chicken. Now that I had food in me and had gotten over Hank's presence in the bed, my thoughts went back to the mysterious creature. "The nap was fine. The shadow thing that keeps showing up, not so much." I stuck the food in my mouth.

An eyebrow lifted high and he regarded me for a long second. He grabbed a fry. "Why am I not surprised." He shoved the fry in his mouth and made a rolling motion with his hand. "So what does it want?"

I told him everything, about the visions I'd been having, the altercations I'd had with the creature at the club and then here, earlier, in the bedroom.

Hank stated the obvious. "I think it's safe to assume, based on what Sandra had to say and its appearances so far, using your power triggers its arrival."

I nodded, stabbing a couple bow ties with the fork. "Yeah, but why? Alessandra said it was a destroyer, death, called it Sachâth. Ever heard of that?"

He shook his head. "No, but if that's true, it makes it even more strange that it's not attacking."

"I know. At first I think it's going to—that's the feeling I get—and then it hesitates . . . I'm not even sure if that's the right word. Sometimes it sounds confused or questioning. Frustrated, even. And then it just sweeps right through me, knocks me out cold, and vanishes.

"Well, we know how to keep it away from you."

"Yeah, if I don't screw up and use my power. That little bit in the shower was just healing . . ." And the creature was sensitive enough for that tiny slip to trigger its arrival.

Hank chewed another bite of his burger. "I think we should pay a visit to the Grove."

"You think Pendaran will know what this thing is?"

"If anyone does, it'll be him. He's been around for a while. Couldn't hurt to ask. Besides, we should check on the progress he's made with the Old Lore."

I nodded. The Old Lore, a collection of Elysian prehistory tales and accounts, resided with the Druid King. Llyran had stolen it from Elysia and brought it to Earth. In it was the only known record of the First Ones.

The Lore had been another priceless item, spoils from our battle with the Sons of Dawn. And within those ancient pages might be a ritual to disperse the darkness over Atlanta. And because of that, we were keeping it here in the city. For now.

Bellies full, we cleaned up the best we could, put Bryn's kitchen back to rights, and then left the apartment.

As we walked down Mercy Street, I checked my cell, listening to three messages. From Emma: she was home from the hospital, no change with Amanda. From the chief: all the *ash* victims were at the station and secure. And from Sian: Tennin had left the city to parts unknown, though she'd try to find out where.

I slipped my phone back on my hip. "Tennin's gone."

Hank let out a snort. "Probably hunting down the person who gave the suicide order."

While I suspected as much, I gave a turn at devil's advocate. I'd been wrong before. "We still don't know why they jumped, if they were possessed at the time . . . This might have zero to do with Tennin and everything to do with the drug's effects."

"True, but our instincts are hardly ever wrong. And if they are"—he threw an arrogant glance at me, eyes twinkling—"it's usually you, not me."

"Ha ha."

We emerged from Mercy Street, headed across the plaza, and up the steps to Topside.

Downtown Atlanta sparkled with a million multi-colored lights. Headlights, traffic lights, shops, and high-rises, all lit up beneath the ever-churning mass of gray hovering low in the sky above.

I rubbed the back of my neck, the hairs there standing to salute the dark power. I knew from experience what was in that mass—small particles of Charbydon energy, the stuff of magic, the raw material, the very thing that awakened the Char genes in my body and gave me this constant zing.

It was easier to handle when I was inside or down in Underground, but out here in the open it hit me hardest and made me jittery, energized; not altogether bad . . . just more . . . alive.

Hank paused on the sidewalk, shoved his hands into his jacket pockets, and lifted his face to the darkness. Quiet, thoughtful.

"Still there," I said.

Slowly, he withdrew his gaze and fixed me with a wry smile. I returned the look and led the way down the sidewalk to where I'd parked my Tahoe.

"Smart-ass," he muttered, falling in step beside me.

I took it as the compliment it was.

It was a short drive to the 10th Street entrance of the Grove, formerly known as Piedmont Park, where the

Kinfolk—the local nymph population—made their home. The nymphs had bought much of the park, put up a tall iron fence around their territory, and called it home. They'd built a Stonehenge on Oak Hill, and had somehow made the trees grow to incredible heights. Entering the Grove was like stepping back in time to the days when ancient forests blotted out the sun and tribes of Celtic gods and warriors ruled the land.

The iron fence loomed above us as we made our way to the massive gate. I couldn't shake the feeling of eyes on me and kept looking over my shoulder and across the street to the buildings and cars and shadows. Nervous unease mixed with the energized tingle from the darkness above, fueling my tension and anxiety. I swallowed the manic feeling, trying to quell its rise and regulate my thoughts.

"Charlie," Hank said. "Before we go in . . ." He paused at the gate, swiped a hand through his hair, and frowned, staring for a moment at the city skyline. "There's something I want to tell you. About that name Llyran called me. *Malakim*."

I blinked. Now? Now he was going to share, right before we went to see Pen, right when we were standing out in the open, being watched? Hank had insane timing, but at the same time, I really did want to know about him, his past, and the things he never talked about. Still . . . "Okay. You said it was a title, a form of greeting someone."

"In a way . . . yes."

A tingle of worry slipped down my spine as though he was about to drop a major bombshell that I couldn't live with.

Suddenly, I didn't want to know, didn't want anything to mess with whatever was happening between us. "You want to go have coffee after this? Sit and talk?"

"No," he began with a hint of frustration. "Look, it's not exactly easy to get this out and tell you what I've—"

"You two going to stand out there forever?" came a voice through the gate.

The hinges whined. Killian stepped out in his usual dark clothing, taking one last drag on his cigarette before grinding it into the palm of his hand, and then flicking it into the trash can nearby.

Sadist.

He saw my thought and grinned.

II

Killian led us a few yards down the straight path toward the lake. With no light filtering from above, the thick woods on either side of us appeared impenetrable. Of course, it didn't help that the nymphs' motto to anyone visiting the Grove was *Stay on the path. Don't stray from the path*. Could make anyone feel a bit anxious.

This time, however, our guide stepped off the stone path, between two burning torches, and led us into the dark woods. Our footsteps were muted by the soft ground. Sounds of the forest—rustling leaves, the snap of a twig, an owl call—were louder than I'd expected. Nymphs populated these woods, running free, letting their animal selves out to play, maybe even to hunt . . .

The land rose as we progressed and finally the trees

thinned to give way to Oak Hill, crowned by a ring of enormous stone monoliths at least eighteen feet high and capped with lintel stones. Inside of this massive ring were five trilithons arranged in a horseshoe pattern. The center trilithon was the highest stone in the ring, rising even above the height of the outer ring. From this, the next two on either side dropped in height, followed by the outer two, which dropped as well, but all were taller than the outer ring.

I'd only seen the site from the main path, but even from that distance, the power emitting from the stone ring had coursed through me like a pulsating subwoofer.

The closer we came to the top of the hill, the more the power intensified. The constant, deep *whoosh, whoosh, whoosh* had a slightly nauseating effect on me, and the drop in air pressure clouded my hearing.

Pendaran, the Druid King, stood in the center of the horseshoe, where a large gray stone slab rested on two fat stones. The altar stone. And even though the stone monoliths rose several feet above him, it didn't do a damn thing to diminish his stature or his presence. In fact, he fit right in.

He wore dark drawstring pants and a plain black T-shirt. His feet were bare. One hand was out, palm down on the stone. His head was bowed and eyes were closed, but even from this distance I saw that his profile was grim. His left side faced us, giving me a glimpse of the winding tattoo that ran up his neck, over his jaw, ear, and temple, disappearing into thick black hair.

I knew from seeing him—*all* of him—on an earlier occasion that his entire left side was inked with Celtic-style, interlacing symbols that ran from his toes all the way up to his temple. The guy was huge, solid, and brutal-looking. He'd earned his place as king and his title as druid, not by birth or vote, but by having indisputable strength, size, and power. He hadn't been given his role—he'd taken it.

There weren't many nymphs out there who could challenge a dragon and win. I'd seen the Druid King in action in his animal form. I'd watched his black wings stretch to the size of jet wings and I'd seen how deadly he was with his teeth and talons.

Good thing he was an ally; and that was something I wanted to preserve.

Killian cleared his throat, way too softly for Pen to hear, but the druid apparently had extraordinary hearing; he glanced over his shoulder. An abalone shimmer filtered over his irises and disappeared. His hand slid off the stone and with it went the intense power being conducted through the stones. The energy dropped to a low pulse.

Relief washed through me. Much easier to manage now, thank goodness.

Killian gestured us into the circle. As I walked over the cushy grass and closer to Pendaran in the center, the lines of worry on his face began to take shape.

"I'm afraid"—his head tipped back, mouth twisting into a brooding line as he scowled at the dark, moving sky; a troubled sigh parted his lips—"this is only the beginning . . ." With a quick glance flicked our way, he strode past us. "Walk with me."

Pendaran's manner wasn't at all what I expected. A sense of sadness and foreboding surrounded his big form as he passed me, his long strides eating up the ground. Whatever was bothering him seemed to have an instant effect on my frame of mind, as though his mood engulfed everything in its path.

I shoved my hands into my pockets, trailing the Druid King down the hill and through the dark woods. My mood and the quiet air of the place made it seem like the weight of the world had settled over the Grove.

The air was cool and clean here, the tall trees filtering out the scents of the city around the park. I breathed deeply in an attempt to release some of the heaviness I felt.

As soon as I started to relax, a familiar gentle whisper glided easily into my mind. I smiled. Soothing. Feminine. An instant calm. My tension dropped like a stone. I acknowledged the voice without words, but with a smile, a welcome.

Only occasionally did I understand Ahkneri's voice, sometimes through words, sometimes through emotion. And here, of course, it would be loudest.

Pendaran led us into the temple complex, which surrounded Lake Clara Meer. The temple seemed to grow from the ground itself; made of colossal carved timber, every precaution taken to honor nature, to incorporate it into the complex instead of destroying it. It felt sacred here. A church beneath the sky. Blessed and sanctioned by Mother Nature.

It wasn't until we were through the main temple and into the common courtyard area with a view of the lake that Pendaran stopped, ordering the three female nymphs sitting at one of the nearby tables to leave. Once they fled, he parked his rear end on a similar table and crossed his arms over his chest.

"I take it you're here about the Old Lore."

"Have you found anything yet?" I asked.

"It's a thick tome, written in the Old Tongue of Elysia. The translation progressing slower than usual. But if there's a ritual to rid the city of darkness, I will find it."

I inclined my head, my attention going to the lake and the faint whisper of the First One in my head. I could easily picture her in my mind, easily imagine her new resting place—in a cave at the bottom of the lake, warm and dry within her stone sarcophagus.

The reflection of downtown's skyline and its lights twinkled and glowed on the surface of the dark water. "And our guest?" I asked Pen quietly.

When he didn't answer right away, I withdrew my gaze from the lake and stared at him, but he wasn't looking at me; his attention had also been pulled toward the water.

"What's wrong?" I questioned.

"She speaks to you still?"

I gave a here-and-there shrug. "I wouldn't exactly

call it speaking. More like whispers or murmurs, most of which I can't understand. Some dreams lately . . ."

He nodded thoughtfully. "It is the same for me."

My eyes went wide. "You hear her, too?"

"I didn't at first, but when I go beneath the water and into the cave . . . she whispers."

Something about Pendaran's expression, the way he stared so quietly out at the water, made him seem so conflicted and grim.

"The visions Charlie's been having," Hank said to him after giving me a quick glance, "are you having them, too?"

Pen's black eyebrows dipped into a frown as he angled on the table and pulled up one knee. "What visions?"

"At first they seemed like dreams, recurring ones. Of landscapes, a temple, Ahkneri . . ." I bit the inside of my cheek, my gaze floating unfocused over the tops of the tall trees across the lake, and to the skyscrapers that ringed one side of the park like a steel mountain range. "On Helios Tower, when the lid of the sarcophagus was lifted, the power that went out . . . I don't know . . . it's like a warning. And I know that sounds stupid, but there's an eye. It opens . . ."

All the hard angles on Pen's face became starker. The hairs on my arms rose in response to the power that leapt in the air. A glimmer of abalone passed through his eyes, leaving behind a hard, calculating stare. "Agate masks power. Ahkneri and her weapon lie within the finest and thickest I've ever seen. It is not only a resting place; it is to protect them as well."

A thought occurred, one that gave me an instant chill. I hugged myself. "What killed the First Ones?"

"The myths suggest that they decided their time had come, their purpose was at an end, and they . . . slept."

"Anything in the Old Lore about that?"

"Not that I have read, but it is an ongoing examination. The Old Lore contains the only written account of the First Ones. Everything we have ever heard about them comes from this tome. But it is just a fraction of their lives. Stories. Written long after they roamed. The only one who could tell us all is Ahkneri herself."

"What about Sachâth?" Hank asked. "Ever hear of it before?"

"It is an old Elysian term for destruction, ruin, death . . . From the Old Tongue as well. Why do you ask?" He looked at me. "Is this word in your vision?"

"No. I heard the word from the oracle, Alessandra. Whenever I use my power, it seems to draw this shadow being. He has no face, no physical form. His voice holds a lot of power, though, and he speaks to me, but hell if I know what he's saying. Then he flies through me and I pass out."

"It doesn't attack?"

"No."

Pendaran scratched his jaw and pushed off the table. "Odd. I will look for this in the tome as well." He stretched his arms overhead. "You want a beer?"

A short laugh burst out. I shook my head. That was the thing with the off-worlders. Sometimes they came off as so ancient and knowledgeable, and the next they were ordering pizza and a beer. Just the way it was. "No, thanks," I said. "Let us know if you find anything, okay?"

We turned to go, but Pen stopped me, his voice low. "Charlie. Does she seem . . . sadder to you? When you hear her?"

I glanced from him to the lake, surprised by the question. I hadn't considered it before. I'd heard her cry, heard her plead, but those things I'd heard from her since the beginning. Sadder since then? "No more than usual, I think." I cocked my head, waiting for him to say more, but he just dipped his head and strolled into the darkness.

I left the courtyard feeling no better about things or any more knowledgeable than I had before I'd gone in. Pen had the same sense of foreboding that I did. *This is just the beginning.* Who the hell knew what was stalking me or why, but first things first—await the fire sylph and hope like hell she'd just be quick and get it over with. Three down, one more to go.

Tennin is right, the bastard. Like a blind nithyn . . .

Hank and I walked in silence back through the gate and down the sidewalk to my vehicle. "I think I'll head back to the station and check on Bryn, see how everyone is settling in."

"Sounds good. Liz's autopsy reports should be in. I'll drop by her office and see if she's learned anything."

It wasn't until after we were pulling into the back lot of Station One that I remembered asking Hank if he wanted to have coffee and talk.

Crap.

I slid a quick glance his way to find him staring out the window. His expression reminded me of a conversation I had with Emma when she was six years old and I found her sitting with her knees drawn up on the back of the couch, staring out the window.

"Hey, kiddo, what's wrong?"

"I'm looking out the window."

"Why?"

"Because that's what people do when they're sad. They stare out the window."

Emma's sadness had been because her kitten Spooky was at the vet getting spayed. Of course, I told her people stare out the window for all sorts of reasons, but her comment had been so thoughtful, so perceptive, that I hadn't forgotten it.

I couldn't tell from looking at Hank what was going through his mind or what his emotional state was. The last thing I wanted was to tap into my power to see his aura only to have Shadow Man come pay me another visit . . . But my instincts were telling me he wasn't in the mood for talking right now.

I parked the Tahoe and decided to leave the talk for another time.

*   *   *

After a quick pit stop in the ladies' room, I headed into the basement level, which contained our med units, cold cells, holding areas, and the morgue.

The holding area consisted of twenty cells, ten running down each side of the hallway. They were eight-by-ten, the back wall made of concrete blocks painted gray, and the sides and front made from a clear plastic as hard as steel. The only privacy consisted of a half wall that hid a small toilet. Everything else could easily be viewed by the cameras mounted in each corner, the other inmates, and the guards regularly walking the hall.

Granted, these cells were for criminals, not innocent people, but right now this was the best way possible to protect the *ash* victims.

After I showed my ID and headed down the hallway with one of the guards, nine happy faces greeted me. Most of those faces were familiar: known drug users who I'd seen on the streets in Underground or had arrested myself once or twice.

When *ash* hit the market, the jinn who'd been passing out the drug had targeted the users in Underground first. The only reason it had made it to Amanda was because of her father's involvement in the manufacturing process, and the only reason my sister was now an addict was because she'd been exposed to the drug during our fight to destroy the *ash* farm. Otherwise every *ash* victim, even Casey and Mike, had been users before.

"Hey, Madigan." A twenty-something former meth user named Kyle, if I remembered correctly, stood as I passed. "How long are we supposed to stay in here?" I really wanted to tell him that if he hadn't been a drug user looking for his next fix, he wouldn't even *be* here, but instead I said, "Until we know it's safe."

"Fucking cops," he mumbled, going back to flop down on the small cot pushed against the wall.

Bryn was in the last cell on the left, sitting on the cot, back against the plastic wall, one knee drawn up and her fingers toying with the ends of her long purple skirt. Her hair was down, hanging over one shoulder in a mass of auburn brown waves. Seeing my sister sitting in a holding cell was beyond strange.

I drew in a deep preparatory breath as the guard unlocked the door. Inside, I pulled the small stool from beneath the table along the opposite wall, and sat down in front of my sister. My posture slumped a bit. I rubbed my face and then gathered my hair back into a very tiny ponytail, using the band around my wrists to tie it.

"Sorry about all this."

"It is what it is," she said, eyeing me in an enigmatic way. "How's Amanda doing?"

"Got a text a little while ago. She's the same. Have you taken your *ash* dose today?"

She nodded. "A little while ago."

"Good. Has Aaron been by?"

Her gaze darted back to her skirt. "No."

I managed to keep the frustration from showing. Their relationship was none of my business, but damn, I wanted to give Aaron an earful. "I don't know why he's being like this," I finally said. Well, I did know *why*, but he didn't have to avoid her, or make her feel even worse about what had happened. By withdrawing right when she needed him most . . . it would make it that much harder to reconcile.

"I do have some good news," I told her. Since she was here in the cell and there was no way for her to do anything with the information, I wanted to cheer her up, to give her some hope. "There is a way to see inside of you, inside of everyone here, and hopefully fix things."

Her fidgeting fingers stilled. Her coppery eyes lifted, round and hesitant as though she was afraid to believe. "You found an exorcist?"

"No. The oracle told me that there's another way. Ever hear of a sylph?"

"A sylph? Alessandra must be inhaling more than just laurel leaves these days. Sylphs don't exist."

"Oh, trust me, they do." I leaned back, bracing myself with my elbows on the table behind me and linking my hands over my stomach. "Not very pleasant, either." I went on to explain my encounters with the vicious little females.

"So, one more," she finally said. "Fire."

"And then we'll know. We could know by tonight or tomorrow. Then at least we'll know how to protect everyone, who to keep here, who to let go . . ."

She was silent, digesting the information. The hope I'd wanted to give her seemed to have failed, but maybe it was too early yet to hope. Maybe better to be guarded.

"So how's Hank? Is he awake yet?"

"Yeah. He's over in the morgue talking to Liz."

"And?"

"And what?"

A rueful smile lifted the corners of her full mouth. "I am your sister. Sisters know things. For instance, I know every time his name has been mentioned in conversation, you get this weird look on your face. At Christmas when Em was talking about him, you even turned red. It's kind of obvious you're developing a thing for him."

I rolled my eyes. "Yeah, well, I don't exactly know what this 'thing' is, so . . ." I sat forward and draped my arms over my knees. "Temporary case of insanity, maybe? I don't know . . . something changed. We went from being friends to something more." I shook my head, baffled by it all.

"You think it's the whole siren thing? Why you're into him?"

"No." I stared down at the square block of tile at my feet. "If that were the case, I would've been into him the moment I met him. Before, I just would say, 'Yeah, really hot guy who's my partner, let's get back to work.' But now I get butterflies, actual physical responses."

She chuckled. "I never thought I'd hear the day my tough, kick-ass sister admitted to 'butterflies.'"

"Oh God. Did I really say that?" My head dropped into my hands. Laughter shook my shoulders. I straightened, trying to control the stupid grin that wanted to take over my entire face. "I swear, if you say a word of this . . ."

"I know, I know. You'll inflict some kind of horrible pain."

"Yeah. Bare knuckles and butterflies, that's me." Christ. When did this happen?

Bryn's laughter rang clear as a bell. It had been such a long time since I'd heard that. Open and free. Nothing shadowing it. Her smile widened to a blinding grin. "Well, good thing is, he's totally into you. Always has been."

"Please. What are you, the new oracle?"

"Say what you want. I bet you he fell for you the moment you *didn't* go all googly eyes for him and shot him in the belly. Remember that?"

How could I forget? I'd been so pissed about the new partner reassignments that no amount of male beauty could've affected me. And to make matters worse, prior to meeting him, I'd had two days' worth of teasing by most of the station telling me I was going to be humping my partner by sundown. They could be such assholes. And I'd let them get to me. Hank had no idea what he was walking into.

When I questioned his ability to do his job and made a not-so-nice comment about his looks, he'd challenged me with an arrogant smirk that had me steaming. We'd stomped down to the gym, removed our weapons, set them by the mat, and went at it. The thing that had surprised me about Hank was that he didn't take it easy on me, and my impression of him immediately rose.

But when he got me on my belly in a chokehold and threatened to take off his voice-mod and make me get on the police radio and tell everyone on duty how I wouldn't be able to concentrate because he was so "awesome," I flipped him over, kicked him off, grabbed my gun, and tagged him in the belly. I knew I'd get an earful for it, but I also knew it wouldn't kill him.

Hell, we humans had to stand there and go through Hefty and Nitro-gun training, where we had to take low-level shots to our bodies, just like we used to do in the past with Tasers. Off-world officers did the same with bullets and their opposing world's weapons. All part of the training.

The thing I hadn't really considered at the time was how the whole thing had affected Hank. He'd acted like it was all a joke and that it didn't bother him, but when I look back now, I know the other officers' teasing bothered him just as much as it did me. He was there to do a job just like I was.

When the sound of the shot drew the chief and much of the station, Hank had stood up for me and said it was a training mishap. I still got a three-day suspension without pay. He apologized for the threat he made, and I apologized for shooting him. And I learned very quickly that Hank's threats and teasing were all in good fun and no small amount of male bluster.

I suppose when one gets off on such a foot, the whole enchanted-by-siren thing kind of takes a back-seat.

"Charlie?" Bryn said, bringing me out of my thoughts. She bit her lip and toyed with the hem of her skirt again. "Can you do me a favor?"

"Anything."

"Ask Aaron if he would . . . you know . . . drop by. Well, I mean don't *ask*. Maybe just suggest."

Her vulnerability made my eyes burn, but I smiled. "I'm sure he's planning to already."

Her look said she didn't believe that at all, but she leaned forward and hugged me. I squeezed her tightly, breathing in the faint scent of fresh herbs and citrus. "I'll be back to visit you later."

We broke apart. I stood and pushed the stool back beneath the table and nodded to the guard to come open the door. Bryn resumed her former position on the cot along with her solemn expression. "Where are you going now, up to your office?"

"I don't know. Think I might head home and get something to eat. Check on Em, see what kind of trouble Rex has gotten himself into . . . The usual," I said with a shrug and a wry smile.

She let her head fall back against the plastic wall and her eyes closed. "Well"—a crooked smile that seemed out of place appeared on her face—"have fun."

I slipped through the open door, my chest going tight and uncomfortable. Bryn was in another world, it seemed, so I shook the odd feeling away and left the cell quietly.

My boots echoed loud and slow in the stairwell as I climbed one flight to the ground level of Station One. Seeing Bryn sitting in that cell made me tired, weary of this whole thing, and, to be honest, a little hopeless.

Mynogan, Tennin, the Sons of Dawn . . . their push to start a war and regain control of Charbydon had set in motion a bundle of obstacles that continued to ripple across the city's inhabitants as well as my professional and private life. If I could end this somehow, stop the insanity, then maybe my life, my family's life, and the entire city could return to normal.

Instead of going up to the office, I texted Hank to let him know I was headed home for a bite to eat and then I'd be back. With our *ash* victims secure, and before the fire sylph leapt out from around the next corner, I wanted just a moment of quiet time in my own environment to think and regroup and feed my crazy metabolism.

12

⁓⧫⧫⧫⁓

After I hung up my jacket and secured my weapons in the closet, leaving my sidearm on, since it didn't bother me as much as the shoulder harness, I went into the kitchen and grabbed Rex's leftover soup from the fridge and a clean bowl from the dishwasher.

As I filled my bowl, I heard the low voices of my child and Rex coming from the backyard. From the window above the sink I could see that the floodlights were on, but not where they stood.

I placed the bowl in the microwave, hit the timer, and then stepped out back to say hello. As soon as I crossed the brick patio, Emma jogged over, her face lighting with excitement. "Oh my God, Mom! You have to see this!"

She grabbed my hand and tugged me into the grass. "Slow down," I said as she dragged me, chattering so fast I couldn't understand a word she said, my main focus on trying not to trip.

Then she stopped in the middle of the yard. I looked up.

Oh.

Her hand slipped out of mine as goose bumps sprouted all over my legs and arms. For a moment I couldn't wrap my head around what I was seeing. I gaped, knowing in the lucid part of my brain that surely I was facing something most people, off-worlders included, had never or would never see in their lifetimes.

Warhound.

The floodlights beamed off polished armor plating. Red eyes glowed through holes of the skull plate, which had spikes running down the center. Brimstone stood in a wash of bright white light. In full battle gear. Looking like he'd just stepped out of the ancient past.

A loud whoosh of air finally breezed through my open mouth. I gulped and recovered enough to say, "Wow."

"Gives you goose bumps, doesn't it?" Rex came up behind us.

"Uh-huh." I couldn't take my eyes off Brim. He stood there strong and tall, balanced and ready, like a warhorse waiting for the command to surge into battle. "This is really how they used to look?"

"From what I can remember." Rex's voice held a quiet kind of reverence. "Hellhounds accompanied the jinn in every battle. The armor is really light, made of typanum and something else—can't remember . . . Once the nobles came and started taking over, they killed entire bloodlines, ancient ones. And after we lost the Great War, the jinn weren't allowed to train hell-hounds for battle or protection; weren't allowed to have them at all. The jinn set them free. The young ones and the pups stayed away, but the trained ones kept coming back. The nobles slaughtered so many . . ."

There was a time when I feared hellhounds, when I believed they were mindless, vicious beasts intent on killing anything in their path. I stood there ashamed of myself for being so narrow-minded. As an officer I'd been taught to either kill them on sight, depend-ing on the danger, or leave them to Animal Control. Same as if a lion or bear got loose from the local zoo. I'd believed the hype and the fear, until Brimstone came into our lives. "Where did you find all this stuff?" I asked.

"eBay."

"It's my Christmas present from Rex," Emma said, removing herself from my side to go stand next to Rex, putting him between us.

"Had to wait for the final piece," he explained. "So that's why she's getting it late. It's just a replica, of course—nothing from that age would've survived this long—from one of those stores that make repro-duction weapons and armor."

That *age* being thousands of years in the Charby-don past.

Emma nudged Rex; he nudged her back. They erupted into a jabbing session and an under-the-breath argument, which consisted of: "*You* ask her." "No, *you* ask her."

"Fine, you little tyrant," Rex huffed and then turned to me. "I hereby ask permission, O Great and Powerful Mother, to teach this child hellhound battle tactics. There. I asked."

Emma leaned over with an encouraging nod. "Every Warhound had a trainer. They worked together in pairs on the field. They knew all kinds of stuff, all kinds of commands, and ways to—" *Kill*. Rex elbowed her. "To fight. So, what do you think? Is it okay?"

The beast stood there looking so damn . . . *badass*. It spoke to all my protection instincts, to my love of the good fight, and all things noble and strong. My kid walking around with this at her side—no one would mess with her.

Well, that was if we could get a special permit from the city to permanently keep him. As it was, we were on borrowed time. My neighbor had reported an illegal hellhound living in our backyard. But thanks to the chief and some strings, we were able to get permission to keep him under an ITF Weapons Research Permit. Meaning we lied and said we were researching ways to utilize the hellhound for law enforcement purposes.

But standing here now—how cool would it be to patrol Underground with an armored tank with fangs and claws? With a daughter who could direct entire packs of them with a thought? The first true War-hound in thousands of years . . .

Okay, getting way ahead of yourself, Charlie.

"Mom." I looked over at Emma. She was leaning past Rex, clasping her hands together in prayer, smiling at me, and mouthing, "Please, please, please."

"There will need to be some ground rules . . . But I guess"—Emma's monstrous, high-pitched squeal made me cringe—"it would be okay."

"C'mon, kid, let's get the armor off him."

"Right." Emma ran to Brim and began unlacing the armor plates. She looked so tiny and exposed next to him—a giant Warhound looming above a kneeling eleven-year-old with a ponytail, jeans, and a faded Mickey Mouse T-shirt.

And there were days when you didn't think it could get any more bizarre.

"Hey," I said to Rex before he could take off after her. "Can we talk a minute?"

After giving Em some instructions, Rex followed me into the kitchen, where I removed my soup, which had gone lukewarm, from the microwave, set it on the table, and then opened the fridge. I grabbed two beers and handed one to Rex. It was ice-cold, and stung my throat, and I welcomed it with several eager gulps. My eyes watered from the sting. "I so needed that."

He toasted the air with his bottle. "Not every day you see a Warhound." Then he took a long swig.

"So basics for now, okay? Protection only." Rex

agreed with a nod. I took another gulp before setting the bottle on the counter, leaning back against it to cross one ankle over the other and my arms over my chest. "You were really in the Great War . . . It's hard to imagine."

"Not hard if you saw my original form. A bit taller than Tennin. Leaner. Meaner. To be honest, Charlie, I still can't believe it, either. I spent thousands of years roaming as a disembodied spirit, losing my memories, forgetting how I came to be a Revenant . . . And I lived so long ago that now when I do remember, it doesn't matter because there is no one left."

"I'm sorry, Rex." That had to be difficult, to finally remember and realize everyone you knew, everyone you ever loved, was long gone. Tennin's words came back to taunt me. "Do you want to be a jinn again?"

Rex weighed his answer, appearing conflicted either way. He took another drink. "Sometimes, I guess. Other times, no. I remember who I was, but I've also changed. I like who I am now. Not sure my personality would fit well in a jinn body." He shrugged, still looking undecided. "I don't know . . ."

He did have a point. I couldn't imagine a hulking jinn standing in my kitchen wearing a cherry-print apron and stirring a pot of soup. "Have you had any luck remembering that day?" I asked, changing the subject. "That day" was when Rex's jinn body had died. The day he'd been exposed to the biological warfare the nobles had concocted to win the Great War.

"Bits and pieces. It's coming back slowly. I remember the sensation of leaving my body and watching it die on the battlefield. Of watching so many others drop like stones and the nobles celebrating their victory. I wanted to kill them, tried to get back into my body, but it was already too late. There was nothing I could do."

The solemn tone in Rex's voice struck a deep nerve in me. I'd never thought I'd have compassion for a jinn, and here I was sympathizing with an ancient warrior who'd fought in the legendary war against the nobles for control of Charbydon.

The war was ancient history to the nobles and the jinn, but it had created the Revenants and Wraiths, those lost jinn spirits able to roam all three planes, casualties of war, slowly losing their identities until they had no idea who or what they once were, only that they craved a body to live in once again. And eventually they'd found a way to have what they wanted. One by force. The other by contract.

"So the nobles put this formula into vials, right?" I asked, remembering an earlier conversation I'd had with Rex over Christmas.

"Yeah, they threw them like grenades."

"So no peculiar smells or tastes when the vials exploded in battle?"

"No. Just a cloud of white and the honeysuckle smell."

The same as *ash*. The formula the nobles used to win the war had been derived from the rare, bioluminescent flower *Sangurne N'ashu*, a Bleeding Soul. They'd found a way to use it to rip the spirit from a jinn body. There was no way the jinn could fight *that*. After the war, as the years passed, the Bleeding Soul became legend, just a myth. But it was very real. Mynogan and Tennin had rediscovered it, cultivated it, and used its properties to create a new formula that wouldn't rip a spirit out, but could subdue a human's will, leaving them vulnerable and open to even the weakest of spirits. *Ash*.

Emma and Brim came inside. The hellhound was out of his armor, and the tap of his claws on the hardwoods was starting to become a welcome sound. "What are we talking about?" Em said, grabbing a yogurt from the fridge.

"The Bleeding Soul," Rex said. "How to get me out of your dad. The usual."

I rolled my eyes as Em pulled a clean spoon from the dishwasher. "Maybe all we need is straight Bleeding Soul," she said, pulling out a chair to sit. "If there's only a little bit of the flower in the *ash* for humans, then maybe the nobles needed all of it for the jinn. You know, like, full concentrate to yank a jinn spirit from his body."

"She gets the smarts from me," Rex said.

I gave him a twisted smile that told him exactly where she'd gotten her intelligence. Emma's words could, in fact, be right on the money; it was a thought both Rex and I had discussed in the last week.

Titus had identified the properties in *ash* in order

to make a synthetic replica for the victims to take in small, regulated doses. Without it they would die from withdrawal. But during this process, he'd discovered that just a small amount of the Bleeding Soul was actually in the drug. So it might stand to reason that a larger dose of the flower might do more than make a spirit docile—it might very well make it separate from the body entirely.

In order to get Rex's jinn spirit out of Will's body and restore my ex-husband to his former self, using the flower seemed like the only viable option.

"I need to get into Charbydon," Rex said.

With a mouth full of yogurt, Em said, "That's crazy."

"Not really. Think about it. The nobles must have that formula somewhere. It's not going to be here; it'll be somewhere in the City of Two Houses. You know, in their library, the arsenal, their hidden stash, whatever you call it. Heck, it's probably in with their crown jewels."

Emma's eyes grew round. "The nobles have crown jewels?"

"A double set, since they have two rulers."

She pointed her spoon at Rex. "It's called an oligarchy. Means a country ruled by two kings or queens. One is from the House of Abaddon and one is from the House of Astarot. They each contributed a ruler."

"Very good," Rex said, pleased. "And when disputes arise between the rulers, how are they settled?"

"Council of Elders, made up of old royal dudes from both houses."

My eyebrow lifted. "I hope you didn't answer like that on your last test."

Emma smirked playfully. Off-world Studies was obviously one of her better subjects in school, and Rex had taken it upon himself before Christmas break to help her with midterm exams. I'd been relegated to mere math and science.

"Have you been to the City of Two Houses? It's supposed to be thousands of years old," Emma asked.

"Not inside, but I've been to the gates. The nobles built their city above Telmath during their siege of the city."

"So all their valuables are there."

"The formula being one of the most valuable. It's the only reason they've ruled for so long without contention from the jinn again. The jinn know they have this formula; they know the nobles can use it again and wipe the jinn out for good."

"So fat chance of us getting it, then," she said, glumly.

Emma spent a lot of time thinking about her father being trapped inside of his own body, of a Revenant being in control. She was determined to save him and find a way to make everything right. She had the unrelenting optimism of a child, and it worried me because I knew better than anyone that things didn't always turn out the way we hoped.

"Well," I said. "It's not like we know for sure that

the formula would work anyway. We'd have to be sure it would only pull Rex out and not Dad."

"I don't think it would pull Will," Rex said. "I'm the dominant one, and it was designed to work on the jinn. Theoretically, it should yank me right out."

No one spoke after that. I tossed my bottle into the recycling bin and reheated the soup again. Sure, we all loved Will. We all wanted him back. He'd made a terrible mistake by contracting with a Revenant to begin with.

Getting around the issue of reversing this possession was going to be tough. Once a Revenant was in, he couldn't get out unless the host body died. If Rex wanted out, he could commit suicide or stop healing and regenerating his host body and let it die naturally. Only then was his spirit able to leave. And, of course, losing Will was not an option. The only reason my daughter had not had a major break was because her dad was still here where she could see him. If we lost Will, she'd be devastated.

But losing Rex was not something she wanted, either.

Emma wanted to fix things. She wanted her father back, and she wanted Rex to stay in her life. She might not have said that last part out loud, but she didn't need to.

The microwave beeped. I returned to the table with my soup.

"Before I forget," Rex said. "Em and I were invited to help decorate the League for the New Year's Eve party and help with last-minute stuff. We can go the day of and just change there for the party."

"Yeah, Bryn told me. I told her it was fine with me."

"Have you gotten your dress yet?" Emma asked, knowing I hadn't.

"I *will*. Don't worry . . ."

"Mom. The party is in two days."

Rex pushed away from the table, grabbing Em's yogurt and tossing it into the trash.

"Hey!"

"Bah on the good-for-you crap. Let's go get milk shakes."

And this would be just one of the many reasons why Emma loved Rex.

After eating my soup, I drove us to Blue Barry's Ice Cream Shop.

I was just walking back to the truck with our order when my cell rang from inside the vehicle. I saw Rex through the windshield pick it up and answer. By the time I got to the window, he was staring at me, his face pale.

I set the milk shakes on the hood. "What? What happened?"

He handed me my cell. "That was Hank. Bryn's gone."

"What do you mean, Bryn's *gone*?"

"Gone. Like escaped. Broke out. Got the hell out of—"

My hand flew up. "I understand what *gone* means, Rex." I jumped in the car and sped out of the parking lot, the milk shakes flying off the roof and landing somewhere in the lot.

My hands trembled on the wheel. There was no doubt in my mind now. If Bryn had been in control, she would have stayed. My eyes stung, and I prayed all the way to the station.

I told Emma to wait in the car with Brim, and I raced inside and down to the holding cell area.

13

Rex followed me down to the cell block. Every single *ash* victim was where they were supposed to be except one. Bryn's cell was empty, her door open. The guard stood by the door, another in her room searching through the bag of clothes and books Bryn had brought with her.

"What the hell happened?" I barked.

One of the guys shook his head as the other came out of the room. "Look, we were doing our job—"

"Don't feed me that bullshit. If you'd been doing your job, she'd still be here!"

"Calm down, Madigan," the chief ordered from behind me.

I spun on my heel. The chief and Hank marched down the hall. I wanted to hit something. Scream. Casey and Mike were dead. Amanda had tried to commit suicide, and Bryn was gone. Christ, she could on the roof right now, stepping off . . . *Oh God.*

My eyes caught Kyle's as he sat on the cot, watching us. Silent wasn't his style. I ran to his door. "How did she get out?"

Power stirred in my gut, so hot and angry that my limbs tingled.

He shrugged, not bothering to hide the smug light in his eyes. "Said some words. Door popped open. You know how mages are." He made a motion with his hands and said, smiling, "Poof. Gone."

My blood pressure rose, and I had to force myself not to pound the plastic. "Did she say anything?"

A female voice piped up, two cells down. "Yeah. She said, see you in hell." Her chuckle grated on my composure.

Kyle shot to his feet. "Shut up, Grace."

"Fuck you, Kyle," Grace responded. "I'm not one of her flunkies like you. I'm not going to leap off some building because she fucking tells me to."

Fear-fueled adrenaline shot through my limbs. I walked closer on numb legs. "Wait a second. She told Mike and Casey to jump? Bryn? Bryn told them?"

Grace gave a nonchalant shrug. Her hands were flat against the plastic. She looked the same as every other time I'd seen her, always in and out of the station on drug and prostitution charges—thin, strungout, and pale. But now her dull eyes burned. "We've got a second chance at life, and all he wants to do is kill us off and go have his revenge."

"'He'? Who are you talking about? Who is inside of my sister?"

"Let me out and I'll tell you."

Ah. So this was the game. Whoever was inside of Grace wanted freedom, wanted to take her body, steal her life, and live it for her. Fat chance.

I shook my head. "Can't do that."

"I'm not one of them," came another voice opposite Grace's cell. I spun around. A young woman stood at the plastic. I couldn't place her. "I'll tell you. I sit and I listen to them; they don't think I can hear but I do." A small part of me acknowledged how odd her calmness seemed, but in that moment all that mattered was finding my sister. I approached, my heart pounding hard, mouth dry in fear. I stood in front of her cell and waited.

"Your sister is going to Charbydon, to Telmath, to kill the Abaddon Father."

The others shot to their feet and yelled at once, a cacophony of curses and threats erupting throughout the holding area, but they all sounded far away as I reached for the wall to steady myself, the hallway turning like a fun house ride.

My mark oozed warmth as Hank placed his hand on my shoulder. "Hey," he said softly, "we can get to her, Charlie. We can stop her before she goes through the gate."

"I'm calling the gate officials now," the chief said from behind us.

Deep breath. Okay. Focus. "Who's controlling her?" I asked the woman.

"I don't know. They never use names other than the host body's."

"Why the Abaddon Father?"

"Revenge. Your sister said the Father would pay. Said the winter solstice plan was a failure, and the Sons of Dawn were finished, and this would be the final act. You know, like Plan B basically. Can't start a war, then go straight to revenge. She said she was going to kill the one who killed Malek Murr, her father. Or his. Who knows who's inside of her . . ."

Malek Murr. My thoughts churned. Malek Murr. He'd been the jinn High Chief who'd come to our world during biblical times to escape the oppressive rule of the nobles. His tribe and a few others had left Charbydon to make a new home in our world. And while Malek had several sons, there was only one that mattered here.

The answer struck me like a thunderbolt, slammed into my chest, and stole my breath. I stepped back. Blood drained from my face as all the pieces slid neatly into place.

"Solomon."

The others started screaming about revenge, about justice, but it all melted into the background. The biblical King Solomon. The Father of Crafting. The son of Malek Murr and the human woman Bathsheba. A hybrid, like Sian. He had started the Sons of Dawn cult, had learned about the First Ones and that the nobles once ruled in Elysia. His cult had planned to gather the proof they needed to share with the nobles—and once the nobles found out where they truly belonged, they'd start a war with Elysia to take back what was once theirs, and leave Charbydon to the jinn.

And that's all the jinn and Solomon ever wanted: to regain their world.

But Solomon's father and the other jinn tribes had been called back to Charbydon, the nobles afraid that Malek Murr was planning to raise an army on Earth.

"Who was king?" I asked, looking around at the faces staring back at me. "Who was the Abaddon king when Malek Murr and the tribes were called back to Charbydon?"

No one answered. They didn't have to. The Abaddon Father had to have been one of the kings back then. He'd given the order to bring back Malek Murr and have him executed. No wonder Solomon had created the spirit jars. No wonder he had devised a way to continue on after his death so that one day his cult could exact revenge and do what his father could not, free the jinn from noble rule—and, for Solomon personally, exact revenge for the man who had murdered his father.

Llyran and the Sons of Dawn had stood atop Helios Tower and claimed that I'd be host to Solomon's spirit, that with Solomon's knowledge and my power, they'd raise the First One. But it had never been Solomon in the spirit jar next to Llyran.

Solomon had gone quietly into my *ash*-addicted sister to run the show from the background.

No wonder we hadn't been able to detect another presence in her. She had the Father of Crafting inside of her—and with his knowledge, he could do just about anything.

And his last act was going to be killing the Abaddon Father.

Christ. It was like saying someone was after the Queen Mother in England. And no one would care that Bryn was possessed. This was a suicide mission after all.

"Bryn has a passport," I said numbly, "so she won't have a problem going through the gate, but I know she doesn't keep it in her purse. She'll have to go back to the League or her apartment to get it."

Then again, Solomon might have the ability to cross planes without using legal means of transportation . . .

"We need a team to go to her apartment," I said to the chief. "See who's in Underground right now and have them go over. I'm going to the League." I turned to Rex. "Can you take Emma back home?"

"Sure."

I tossed him the keys and he took off.

"The gate is on alert," the chief said. "No one, no matter who they are, will pass until we give them the green light."

"Thanks, Chief."

I didn't know where Bryn was headed, to be honest. Didn't know if I should go to the gate and assume she'd try to go through or if she'd head back to the

League for her ID. Hell, she could already be in Charbydon by now.

"Charlie," Hank said. "What do you want to do?"

I bit my lip hard. I had to be faster, had to cut her off. "Never mind about the League. We're going to Charbydon."

"What?" he and the chief echoed.

I turned to them. "Running around here, trying to find her is waste of time. It could put her farther and farther away from us. I guarantee you Solomon knows a way to get into Charbydon without using the gate. If we go now, we can head her off, be there before she gets there. Let her walk right into us."

"Sounds good," Hank said at length. "Let's load up and get to the terminal."

We raced to the weapons depot for additional ammo and weapons. Hank grabbed a thigh harness and strapped it to his leg. The familiar clicks and sounds of weapons checks and loading up filled the room.

"Solomon has had all this time inside of Bryn," Hank said, slipping a spare Nitro-gun into the holster at his thigh. "Why wait until now?"

"Maybe he was still hoping for war and waiting to see if Bryn could find out what we did with Ahkneri." I stilled, my eyes going wide. "I told Bryn about the sylphs. I told her I found a way to see inside of her and help her."

Hank straightened. "And he realized it was now or never. If he wanted revenge, he'd have to do it now before you saw the truth."

"Right," I said, grabbing two thigh harnesses for the two extra Nitro-guns I was taking. "Otherwise, he had time to wait, to see how things unfolded. I bet you Tennin convinced him to wait it out after they lost Ahkneri. And Solomon had other ideas. He started issuing the suicide orders, Tennin went ballistic . . ."

I walked to the wall, grabbed a black cloak, and tossed it to him. "If we're going into Charbydon, you'll need this. The less attention we attract, the better."

"How the hell do we find her once we get there?" Hank asked, tossing me some extra nitro clips. "Aaron has been to Charbydon . . ."

"No. He's too involved personally. And he hasn't recovered from dying." I flipped open my cell and dialed. "Rex. Change of plans. You ready to take a trip back home?"

As Hank and I hurried from the depot, I spoke to Emma after Rex, and told her to pack a bag and her party dress because she'd be staying at the League until we got back. For once, my kid didn't argue with me. Actually, if she had a choice, she'd have chosen the League herself. She loved it there. Her only words were, "Find Aunt Bryn and bring her back." And to be careful, and that she loved me.

I called the League next and spoke to Aaron. There were only a handful of people I'd entrust with my child and he was one of them. I told him as little as possible about Bryn and asked him to put Emma under his protection. I had no doubts he'd agree.

Then we were in Hank's car speeding toward Hartsfield-Jackson International Airport.

I was about to see hell for the first time.

14

It took ten minutes to get to the terminal near Harts-field-Jackson. Ever since the darkness, the airport had become dead space. No planes in or out due to fears of the darkness clogging engines and causing a crash. It had been a logistical nightmare of epic proportions, one of the worst casualties of the darkness—billions in revenue gone, planes rerouted, terminals around the country—the South especially—taking the over-load of redirected travel; even smaller airports were being used. People lost their jobs, their livelihoods—though, thankfully with the help of the government, union, and airlines, many were able to temporarily relocate to other terminals.

For two months one of the world's busiest airports had been closed and there was nothing anyone could do about it except deal with it until the darkness was gone. *Deal with it* being an extremely casual term, but in the end that's just what it came down to. The FAA, the government, the airlines, workers, the unions, everyone had to find a way to cope until the darkness was gone.

The place had taken on a dark visual silence. The only traffic led to and from the new off-world terminal, which—lit up as it was—looked like a beacon in a sea of dark buildings and shapes.

We drove around to the employee deck. After flashing his badge, Hank parked in an area reserved for security and law enforcement. One more checkpoint, and then we were striding down the long service tunnel. We came out into the long rectangular terminal at the midway point between the gates.

The gates had been built at each end of the terminal and offered continuous passage to and from Elysia and Charbydon. Departures and arrivals had been allotted special time periods throughout the day and night—half the day for those leaving, half the day for those incoming, and the same for the nighttime hours.

We veered right and headed down the terminal with its clean white tiled floor, glass walls, exposed steel beams, terminal seating, ticket counters, luggage checkpoints. In many ways, it was like any other travel terminal with clerks, gate patrol officers, stores, cafes . . . But that's where the similarities ended. Once you got a look at the glowing spheres at each end of the terminal it was an entirely different story.

Several uniformed ITF officers were standing by the Charbydon gateway, which had been closed off, much to the chagrin of the irate departing travelers loitering in the waiting areas of the terminal.

I flashed my badge at the gate agent behind the desk, knowing she was no typical agent; I was well aware she had three loaded weapons beneath her desk and was highly trained to protect the gate and oversee travel. As she read my credentials and then Hank's, my gaze lifted a notch to the copper alloy platform behind her. And, of course, hovering just a hair above the platform, the Charbydon gate—a large, glowing sphere colored with shifting shades of blue.

A low drone emanated from the sphere, a contained frequency which I knew to be the "music" of Charbydon—its individual signature, an electromagnetic frequency that not only manifested in sound but in light as well. The Elysian gate, on the other hand, was a pinkish-orange ball with a slightly different drone.

Above the entranceway to the Charbydon gate was a quote by Pythagoras:

There is geometry in the humming of the strings . . . there is music in the spacing of the spheres.

Titus Mott's passion had been the mathematics of music, the harmony of geometry, of the universe and its electromagnetic vibrations. He was inspired by Pythagoras and Kepler's "music of the spheres." His experimentation in sound and light waves and electromagnetic fields had led him to the discovery of the other worlds almost fourteen years earlier and then the subsequent building of the gates in Atlanta first and then in other cities around the country and world.

Like Earth, Elysia and Charbydon possessed unique electromagnetic vibrations that, once identified and then manipulated, could be *heard* and *seen* as color. And once enhanced by Mott's patented "harmonic resonance generator," a rift from our dimension to theirs appeared. A doorway.

So went the simple explanation anyway.

The biblical stories of trumpets signaling the arrival of "angels," for instance, came from the Adonai's sound wave instrument that allowed them to jump between Elysia and Earth. Some off-worlders had long ago created their own means of travel between worlds and they meddled in our civilizations long before we knew they existed. There were, apparently, more ways than one to open a portal. But after their existence became common knowledge, and laws, policies, and peace treaties were put into place, off-worlders adhered to travel laws just like everyone else. And if an illegal immigrant was caught here without the proper paperwork or visa, well, there were laws for that, too.

And that's why I was heading to Telmath without wasting time searching for Bryn in Atlanta. If Solomon, the Father of Crafting, was truly inside of her, he'd know how to get into Charbydon without needing to use the terminal.

I paced the tile floor in front of the gate, waiting for Rex, letting my thoughts and worries run wild.

My blood pressure was high, causing me to chew on the inside of my cheek. Mentally, I wasn't prepared to go into Charbydon. I wasn't like a lot of other humans who found adventure in inter-dimensional travel. I liked my city. I stayed put. Yet I was about to go into a fucking rift in space/time—whatever the hell *that* meant.

The sudden gasps and shouting and the fact that every single officer in the terminal had drawn his weapon kind of clued me in to the fact that *someone* had arrived.

I turned slowly, pretty sure I'd know who'd be standing there.

Rex.

In the center of the terminal with a battle-axe strapped to his back and Brimstone standing beside him. Now, that surprised me.

Christ, he was going to get shot—

"Stand down!" I yelled, running toward them. "Stand down!" I went immediately to the officer closest, the one with the best line of sight. "Stand down. They're with me."

The officer didn't lower his gun or take his eyes off Brim. "Hellhounds . . . or whatever the *fuck* that thing is . . . are license to kill."

"Not this one." *And not anymore.* Once this was over, I was going to see what could be done about that license-to-kill policy. "That *thing* has a name. And he's under special permit 6673 of the ITF Weapons Research Allowance." I leaned in closer, my voice dropping into a tight threat. "Lower your goddamn weapon or I'll do it for you."

The barrel of his gun dropped a half inch off target. "Permit." He swallowed, his eyes flicking from me to Brim.

I pulled the small card I kept in the leather case behind my badge and handed it over. After a detailed read, he lowered his weapon, called the stand-down order, and handed me back the card.

The relief that washed over me was so great it left me dizzy for a second. I re-clipped my badge and headed for the center of attention.

"What do you think?" Rex pulled down the edge of one of Will's old black T-shirts. "The shirt's a little tight. Probably from all that pasta I've been making. Found these black cargo pants. And how do you like the leather jacket? Bought it off eBay a few weeks ago. Says badass, doesn't it?"

Rex was one of only a few people who could make my mind go temporarily blank in utter astonishment. I literally didn't know what to say or how to even respond to that. Finally I shook the cobwebs from my brain and grabbed his arm, propelling him down the terminal. "What the hell were you thinking, Rex? And I don't remember telling you to bring Brim! If anything happens to him, Emma will be devastated."

"*She's* the one who told me to bring him! Besides, we'll need him. Trust me."

"I have a cell phone. A little warning next time might

be good. You know, so you don't get him *shot* on sight."

We approached the gate agent, who remained un-affected by the sight of a hellhound stalking toward her. "Ready to go, Detectives?" She eyed Brimstone with one quirked eyebrow, but other than that she didn't seem impressed. I liked her. I scanned her name tag. Officer Finley Holbrook.

I turned to Rex. "You sure you remember how to get there?"

He tapped his temple. "It's all up here."

Gee. That was comforting.

"And besides," he said with a shrug, his inter-ested gaze caught on the gate agent, "I'm caught up to speed on history and geography in Charbydon, thanks to Em's Off-world Studies class."

"Ear protection," Holbrook said, ignoring Rex's un-abashed ogling and handing us each a pair of disposable earplugs in plastic. "Walk into the sphere. Don't stop. You'll come out on the other side in the terminal at Telmath. Your boss called in for your permits . . ." She pulled out a stamp and pressed an ITF notary seal onto three permits and then handed them to us. "The Inter-Dimensional Bounty Hunter Act allows you to retain your weapons. You have seventy-two hours to retrieve your fugitive before you must reapply at the Telmath ITF station." I took the permit, shoved it into my pocket, and then opened the plastic bag.

We stuck the earplugs in as Officer Holbrook opened the gate and said, "Have a safe trip."

I drew in a deep breath, gave Hank a glance, and

then the four of us walked past the agent and up the three steps to the platform. I was just about to step on when I noticed Hank had stopped and was staring over his shoulder, frowning.

At the far end of the terminal, a group of sirens had come through the Elysian gate. One of them was trying to rush past the gate agent, pointing at us . . . No, I realized, pointing at Hank.

Hank's profile went tight. The muscles in his jaw flexed once. Then he slowly pulled the hood over his head, turned, and walked into the sphere.

I had no idea what the siren was shouting because of the earplugs, but there was no time to waste and the last thing we needed was to get embroiled in something we couldn't get out of. We had to cut Bryn off before she made it to the City of Two Houses. I followed the others into the sphere.

Keep walking, I told myself as I stepped inside the large ball of light. *Just keep walking and you'll make it to the other side.*

Every hair on my body lifted. Even with the eaplugs, I could *feel* the sound, the frequency inside the sphere pulsating into my bones and chattering my teeth. I'd once heard an audible recording of Jupiter and this droning beat was very similar, though amplified to an enormous degree.

Keep walking.

Six steps and I was out of the sphere and onto the copper alloy platform in the terminal in Telmath, feeling just a twinge of disorientation and nausea.

Shaking it off, I went down the steps, through the gateway, and tossed the plugs into a trash can nearby. The terminal was smaller, only one gate that went between Earth and Charbydon. It was darker here, the sphere casting a blue glow onto everything.

After we presented our permits and got some strange and appreciative looks at our hellhound, we left the terminal, pushing through the tall wooden doors outfitted with dark metal. I braced for the impact, my Charbydon genes already responding to the familiar power here.

If I'd thought the darkness covering Atlanta gave me energizing vibes, this place was off the charts. But my human and Elysian genes counterbalanced and allowed me to handle the jacked-up, live-wire sensation without bouncing off the walls.

Rex, Hank, and Brim were ahead of me, coming to a rest at a railing that looked out over the city below. I glanced over my shoulder and saw that the terminal was built into the side of a jagged rock wall that shot up to dizzying heights.

I approached the railing, surprised at the vastness of the city. Homes made from mud and brick and stone. All gray, all linear and grid-like with small, straight lanes and wide main roads separating areas. The buildings clung to the floor, the walls, the ledges, and even atop the massive rocks that jutted up from the cavern floor. Telmath was spread out over several acres.

To my right and far into the distance was a gaping, oval-shaped opening at ground level leading to the outside world, and the wilds of Charbydon lay beyond.

By my estimation, we had to be four stories up on the ledge, yet the cavern's ceiling rose another ten stories at least. Raw typanum ran in thick, jagged veins through the rock ceiling and down through the walls and outcroppings, casting a strange violet glow over everything.

"Telmath," Rex breathed, grabbing the railing. "Much bigger than I remember, but the landscape is the same . . ."

My gaze travelled over some beautifully crafted gray stone buildings, walls, squares, bridges over a black river below—so many bridges, spanning the sides of the cavern, linking one massive rock to the next, and the entire thing lit by the veins of typanum above us. It was breathtaking.

Moving in and out of the terminal were beings I was quite familiar with—ghouls, goblins, darkling fae, a few humans, nobles, jinn . . .

So far Hank was the only Elysian to be found. The two worlds rarely mixed. Seeing a blond-headed, angel-like being walking around in what basically amounted to hell would've been downright astonishing and not the kind of exposure we needed. The deep hood of the cloak hid him well, and he was smart enough to put a secure lock on his aura. But despite this, I was pretty sure some here could *feel* that his presence was . . . different.

Two roads led from the terminal, one winding down toward the city below and the other wrapping around the terminal and going up the rock in a zigzag fashion. The air was humid and warm, much like the deep southern states, but heavy with the scents of tar, damp rock, and muddy water. Sweat was already forming at the small of my back.

"Well," Rex said in a clipped voice, "there's our destination."

I followed his gaze upward and far across the cavern to a gargantuan spear of a rock that jutted at a slight angle from the floor below. It rose several stories into the air. The top of the rock was flat and several acres in size from the look of it. Palaces with thick columns and straight sides and balconies populated the space and clung to the very edges of the rock.

The small city was lit by open fires in massive stone basins and by the glow of violet typanum in the cavern ceiling above. The entire plateau seemed to shine. A winding road had been cut into the rock, appearing and then disappearing on the other side or hidden within the clumping of dwellings, like tiny villages clinging and cut into the massive gray stone. Bridges spanned where the road couldn't be supported.

"The City of Two Houses." Hank's voice broke the awestruck reaction I was having. I cleared my throat, narrowed my gaze, and looked at the city from an invader's perspective instead of a tourist's.

The Abaddon Father was within those thick

walls. Now we just had to get to him before Bryn/ Solomon did.

Rex snorted. "It's like some dark-ass version of Mount Olympus, isn't it?"

A reluctant sigh blew through my lips as I noted the steep, winding stairs that wound up the rock toward the city. "And I'm *so* not a fan of heights." Hank grunted in agreement. Not surprising after we'd taken a tumble together off the ledge of a forty-six-story penthouse . . .

"Looks like that road of steps is the only way in," I said.

"Unless you're escorted by one of the nobles," Rex said. "And we all know who we're thinking of, don't we?"

My hands flexed on the warm railing as I weighed our options. The only person we knew who lived in that city was Carreg. A royal. A Lord Lieutenant from the House of Astarot. Two and a half months ago, I'd met him in the back of Mynogan's limousine. He'd given me aid when I needed it most, helped take my daughter to safety while I faced Mynogan, but he'd been very clear—his assistance hadn't been out of kindness or honor or anything of the sort. He helped me because it suited his own agenda, whatever that was.

Question was, would aiding me now suit the Charbydon noble?

Hank shifted. I glanced up to see him gazing down at me, his face lost in the dark shadow of the hood.

"Carreg is our only way in," he said, echoing my thoughts.

"He could stall us in our tracks, though."

"I think he'll listen. He might be the only one who will."

"Well, I say you go for it," Rex said, turning to rest his back against the railing. "Beats walking and then being turned away at the gate. Might as well save some time and get our answer right here."

I swallowed and made my decision. "Okay, so how do we get in touch with him?"

Rex shrugged, eyes on the terminal doors. "We can always ask at the Info Desk."

"State your business."

We stood at the Info Desk as the receptionist, a lithe darkling fae female, returned from an Employees Only hallway with a dark-haired noble dressed in a robe of deep black lined with gold embroidery. He paused at the corner of the long counter and regarded us imperiously, taking in our strange group and the hellhound standing between me and Rex.

Nobles had meddled in Earth's affairs in ancient times, their presence inspiring the Sumerian pantheon, along with some early Egyptian and Greek mythologies. They had predominantly olive skin and dark hair, and were tall and very powerful. The one before us certainly fit the mold.

Brim growled. Rex made a soft command and the beast relaxed.

"You are aware training or housing a hellhound is not permitted in Charbydon? They are creatures for the wilds."

"Under the Bounty Hunter Act, we have the right to search for our suspect while being armed." An eyebrow shot up and he opened his mouth to argue. I cut him off. "As long as we have a permit for our weapons of choice, you have no grounds to detain him." I pulled out my permit.

He took it and read. "Humans are training hellhounds now? I should think the Federation will have something to say about that."

I leaned forward and snatched my permit back. "We'd like to request an audience with Carreg, Lord Lieutenant of the House of—"

"I know who he is."

And apparently this particular noble wasn't a fan. My heart pounded, though, and fear that we wouldn't even get past the terminal had a firm grip on me. "This is federal business and part of a criminal investigation," Hank spoke up in a clear, commanding tone. "We must speak with him immediately."

The noble's eyes went blacker than they already were, and his lips pursed together, making dark shadows beneath his sharp cheekbones. "A siren in Telmath. How . . . original." He paused for a long moment. "Stay here. I will return shortly with an answer."

We waited. And waited. And waited . . .

I knew we should've walked. We'd be halfway there by now.

I leaned my side against the counter and drummed my fingers on the hard surface. Rex sat on the floor, back propped against the wall. Brim was lying next to him, his head resting on Rex's thigh. Hank stood, arms crossed over his chest, one shoulder holding up the wall.

Finally the noble returned. I straightened, holding my breath.

"Come with me."

Rex and Brim scrambled up as Hank pushed off the wall. We followed the noble down the hallway, out an exit, and onto the ledge overlooking Telmath.

"Step into the circle," the noble said.

I glanced down to see the shape of a large circle had been carved deeply into the smooth gray stone and within it were intricate symbols placed in a circular pattern. I recognized a few Charbydon symbols, but not enough to decipher what they meant. Crafting and symbology weren't exactly my fortes . . .

We stepped into the circle as the noble took a spot in the very center, which was free of any design. He closed his eyes, opened his palms, and the symbols around his feet began to glow. He lifted his hands, pulling the light from the symbols higher and higher until it covered us. The ends of my hair lifted. Every fine hair on my body rose as though we were standing in the middle of a flat field in a lightning storm. The light grew so bright, I shielded my eyes, experienced a second of weightlessness, and then the light dimmed and the hum of power diminished.

The first thing I noticed was the air. It was cooler and cleaner, smelling less of tar and dirt. The sounds of Telmath were but an echo, a dim reminder in this quiet place. I opened my eyes to see we were no longer on the ledge at the terminal but standing in an enormous stone plaza flanked by colossal stone buildings.

The City of Two Houses.

The circle was just inside of the main gate. Twelve feet thick, three stories high, and built from one enormous slab of rock. The noble ushered us out of the circle. The plaza was several blocks in size and four main roads branched off from this centralized area. Regal, official-looking buildings claimed the prime real estate around us, and off the far end of the courtyard was a ramp that led to a building of black marble with a pair of thick pylons framing a tall rectangular opening. Like a temple straight out of ancient Mesopotamia.

There were palaces, temples, and beautiful outdoor spaces all crammed onto the plateau. The size, scope, and grandeur caused a shiver to scatter down my spine. The insignificance it inspired was nothing short of severe.

I drew in a deep breath, focusing on my purpose rather than feeling like the fish out of water that I was.

"Wait here."

I turned to see the noble once again close his eyes, open his palms, pull the light from the ground.

Then in a bright flash he was gone—no doubt back to the terminal—leaving us alone.

A few figures crossed the plaza and came and went from buildings.

"How long do we have to wait this time?" Rex said with a groan.

"Not long at all," came a voice embedded in my memory.

A slight tingle crept down my spine.

She is one child . . . You can have others.

Oh yes, two months might have passed, but I remembered that voice well. The raven-haired noble who had lit a fire under my ass, made me angry enough with those words to fight back, one who had taken my kid to safety while I killed his political opponent and brought darkness to the city of Atlanta.

Charlie.

His voice breezed through my head, amused . . . intrigued. I turned, slamming a hard block over my mind and putting a smart look on my face. "Carreg."

He leaned casually against the rock wall behind us, arms folded over his chest, in a crisp white shirt and loose black pants that pooled at his feet. Some sort of medallion hung from a chain around his neck, no doubt exclaiming his station as a royal and Lord Lieutenant of the House of Astarot. It looked official anyway.

His full lips curled with a hint of amusement, and his classic, angular features were wrapped in smooth olive skin and a deceptively calm demeanor. A satin-black eyebrow lifted. I caught sight of those unique irises—midnight blue shot with silver flecks, like stars in an inky night sky.

"To what do I owe the pleasure of your visit . . . Detective?" He pushed off the wall as his words slid through his lips like the purr of a predatory cat. The calm he exuded was not the easygoing, friendly type—it was of one who knows his power, his strength, the pull he has over others. One who knows his abilities are without question.

"We need to get inside, to see the Abaddon Father. Look, I know this is going to sound insane, but his life is in danger and my sister, Bryn . . ." Oh hell, the whole thing sounded crazy to me, so I could only imagine how this was going to sound to Carreg. But I drew in a deep breath and continued. "She's being controlled by the spirit of a jinn hybrid who wants to assassinate the Abaddon Father. If we can get inside, into his room, we can stop her before she can." I paused, surprised I could talk amid the hammering of my pulse. "Please, Carreg. I swear to you this is real."

His eyes narrowed, sharp and calculating. If Carreg had political reason to wish the Father dead, then there was no way in hell he'd let us inside. He'd simply let things play out and refuse us. But if it worked in his favor, or if he thought it might in the future, then he'd help us.

Carreg took a step closer to me, gazing down at me with such intensity that I wanted to step back.

Subtle notes of sage and cedar wafted around me. I could feel a light push at my mind, but I kept him blocked. He smiled at that.

"You are changing," he said quietly, as though we didn't have an audience. "And the Abaddon curse for blood . . ."

I drew back. It wasn't something I'd thought on for quite some time, certainly not now. But if this was what he wanted to know, I'd play. Anything to get inside and stop my sister. "If you're asking me if I've been going around drinking blood . . . not happening and don't have the urge to . . . Looks like that nasty trait didn't pass to me. Anything else you want to know?"

Carreg had been curious before, when he found out that I'd been injected with not only the DNA of an Elysian Adonai but that of an Abaddon as well. The House of Abaddon was cursed with the need for blood to sustain them. Astarot, however, was cursed with a need for, as Carreg had put it: *Life. That spark inside every spirit, that light that makes a being want to live. A fulfilled spirit, an excited spirit, has enough life force in it to share with those of us unfortunate enough not to have any at all . . .*

"Interesting indeed," he remarked, stepping back as another noble approached, hands tucked behind his back, dressed in a flowing robe of black and gold.

"I see you have off-world visitors, my lord."

"Hmm," Carreg said by way of an answer. "They claim the Father is in danger, Matsul . . ."

Matsul blinked. Then he threw back his head and laughed. My hope dropped like a stone. Shit. They weren't going to listen. Panic had me glancing around the plaza, wondering where the Father slept, wondering how to get to him on our own. I looked at those who passed by and wondered if Bryn was already here, or if she'd come barging through the gate at any second.

"You're not seriously thinking . . ." Matsul said, drawing my attention back to him and Carreg.

Matsul scowled down his aquiline nose, looking from Carreg to us. "The Father has no enemies. He is too old and has remained in a state of sleep for centuries. His very existence is a miracle and I can assure you, there is no one who wishes him harm. He is loved by all."

"You forget," Rex spoke up. "He made enemies while he was alive. He killed hundreds of jinn, slaughtered those he thought might rebel against him. Without trial, without evidence . . ."

Matsul went to reply, but Carreg stopped him. "Perhaps there is merit in what they say. Come with me."

Matsul gasped. "This is an Abaddon matter, not dependent on Astarot commands."

A silky chuckle breezed through Carreg's lips. "I believe the Father's life is at risk. Houses do not matter in this. Now, you may accompany us, or you may stay here gaping."

Red filtered through Matsul's skin as Carreg strode

away. But the noble followed us across the plaza and toward the black marble temple in the distance.

Thank God we were finally moving.

Carreg led us up the wide ramp to the temple. The black marble pylons loomed above us, the marble so smooth and polished, it looked like glass. The rectangular opening that led inside, however, was flat and dark and intimidating as hell. Statues of winged creatures similar to griffins lined the ramp on each side and were carved from gray stone with flecks that reflected the violet glow in the high cavern ceiling above. I craned my neck up to see more soaring columns and balconies with sheer curtains waving gently.

The walls of the temple were so thick that we walked for several steps in total blackness before the space opened up into a large chamber lit with strange bluish fires in wall sconces. The floor was also made of black marble, flawless and polished to a mirror shine. The columns inside were painted in bold colors, scenes of battles, heroes, and animal-headed, winged gods.

Matsul caught up with Carreg as we slowed, and together they led us down a long corridor. It was a maze, the temple leading into courtyards and other buildings, down long, echoing halls, through chambers, past the curious stares of nobles and the stoic faces of guards.

It all passed by in a blur. Until finally we stopped in front of a wide door with two guards—nobles; not the typical jinn bodyguards—on either side. Gone were the robes, and in their place was thin armor plating in polished black, swords at their belts, helmets, and a spear in one hand. I'd never seen nobles in war regalia before and the effect was nothing short of menacing, especially against a backdrop of black marble.

Apparently, the Abaddon Father was far too important for the usual form of protection. Though, after Matsul's comments, I was pretty sure the guards were more for pomp and circumstance, and honoring the Father rather than actual protection.

We beat Bryn. All we had to do was get inside, protect the Father, and then apprehend my sister.

Carreg pushed the doors open. I hurried inside, scanning the main chamber quickly, eyes going over the wall reliefs of battles and warriors. Round columns rose up from the floor, making a gallery of stylized carved symbols, writing, and sculptures. There was furniture and lush fabrics in bold colors, weapons on display, a fountain. And . . . no Abaddon Father.

"Where?" I asked. "Where is he?"

Carreg led us through the main chamber and into a smaller one, though it was still large in comparison to anything I was used to. My eyes went immediately to the far wall, or the absence thereof. Not good. White, linen-like curtains moved in a gentle breeze around the columns that supported the roof and led the eye out onto a wide balcony. Lights twinkled in the distance beyond, coming from other balconies, gardens, and palaces.

Dread gripped me tightly. I couldn't breathe as I turned my head to look at the rest of the room.

To my left. The bed on a raised platform.

My heart dropped to my feet. Matsul gasped in horror. And Rex said simply, "Oh. Shit."

On the bed, straddled over the resting form of the Abaddon Father, was my sister. Blood splayed across her white shirt, neck, and one side of her face. She sat up and turned her head in our direction. "The death of Malek Murr, my father, has been avenged. I am no longer for this world!"

She raised her bloody dagger. Christ. She was going to stab herself.

15

"NO!" Horror struck me with the speed of a locomotive.

I'd never make it to her before the dagger pierced her stomach, but I took off anyway. *Have to try. Have to stop—*

I gasped as I was jerked back by the collar, held still by a vise-like hand that wrapped tightly around the back of my neck. As I whipped my gaze around, I saw Hank yank off his voice-mod with his free hand.

A short but undeniable command burst from Hank's lips, laced with power and energy that made the hairs on my arms rise. It halted Bryn's hand, the dagger tip only a hairsbreadth from her belly.

Her eyes went wide and unfocused. Her hand shook. She blinked. Fat tears slipped down her cheeks.

Oh God. She was in there. Aware. And she was fighting.

I ran to the bed, grabbed the dagger from her hand, and flung it across the room. "Bryn!" I went to pull her to me, to hug her, just going on instinct, but she leapt off the bed, tackling me to the marble floor, her bloody hands sliding around my neck and squeezing.

The shock of being attacked by my sister wore off *real* fast. It wasn't difficult to break her hold, twist, and then flip on top of her back, pinning her face-down on the floor. I reached for the cold cell cuffs on my belt and slapped them onto her wrists. They worked great on most Charbydons, the cold subduing their power, but Solomon was only half jinn and a spirit at that. Probably wouldn't restrain his power at all. But at least they'd keep her from any more suicide or murder attempts.

"It doesn't matter," she muttered, one side of her mouth squished against the floor. "It's over. Whether I go now or later. They will kill this body for what it has done and either way I am free. I have won." She drew in a deep breath to scream, but I slapped my hand over her mouth. The last thing we needed was for the guards to appear.

"You know, Solomon, you're really starting to piss me off. Rex, give me something to gag her with."

Matsul inched closer to the Father as Carreg walked calmly over to the wall, bent down, picked up the bloody dagger, examined it, and then whispered. It disappeared.

A low keening began in Matsul's throat and built in volume. Rex leapt over us, grabbed the official from behind, and covered his mouth to cut off the wail.

Matsul could've fought, could've easily overpowered Rex. He was a noble, the strongest of the Charbydon off-worlders, but he was in shock. His eyes grew wider and wider.

Rex whipped his gaze to mine, his hand still firmly over Matsul's mouth. "What the hell do we do now?"

"Is the Father really dead?" I asked, still on the ground with Bryn and unable to see for myself if Solomon had been successful.

Hank tore the thin curtain and handed me a strip. I gagged my sister as Carreg strode to the bed and gazed down at the Father's frail body without a flicker of emotion on his dark face. "Quite dead," he answered evenly.

I hauled Bryn to her feet and handed her over to Hank, then faced Matsul, heart pounding, adrenaline making my entire body shaky and numb. "You heard what she said. The thing inside of her . . . it's not her. His father was Malek Murr. You do know who that was, right?"

Matsul nodded in acknowledgement.

"He was avenging his father's death. *He* is Solomon. The son of Malek Murr. You understand? He's taken over my sister."

He nodded again, eyes still bugging out.

"This wasn't her fault." My throat thickened, making it hard to talk. "She wasn't in control. That's what you're going to tell them."

Rex slowly removed his hand. Matsul had gone a very odd shade of white. He glanced to Bryn and back to me. "She killed him, I saw her . . . The Father is dead . . ."

He darted from Rex's hold, past me, and straight into Carreg's immovable form.

He stumbled one step backward and Carreg used the momentum to turn Matsul away from him, grabbed his head, and snapped his neck, wrenching the head free from the body in a blur of speed that left me stunned, the sound of breaking bone echoing in my ears.

"Oh God." I turned away and grabbed my stomach, forcing the bile back down my throat. "What the hell are you doing?" I gasped. "He was our witness!"

Carreg turned to me. "You believe the truth will matter to the House of Abaddon, Charlie?"

Panic and frustration formed a combustible mix inside me. I didn't know what to do next, how to fix this, how to explain, how to— A hand landed on my shoulder. Warmth spread from my mark through my torso, dimming some of the panic.

"He's right," Hank said, as though somehow understanding Carreg's sudden and gruesome action.

A lump welled in my throat as I turned on him. "I don't— What just— How am I supposed to fix this?" I asked in a high, hopeless voice. Totally rhetorical question on my part. We were screwed.

"How *you* fix it isn't important," Carreg said

evenly, totally unaffected by having just decapitated someone with his bare hands.

I spun on him with a disbelieving laugh. "Oh, it's not? We've got two bodies— Brim, no!" Oh God. The hellhound was sniffing the headless neck of Matsul. Rex groaned sickly and managed to whistle him off. My stomach did a nasty roll. I turned away as quickly as possible, back to Carreg. "Everyone saw us come in here . . ."

"And they won't see you leave." Carreg crossed the distance until we were face-to-face.

I froze. "What are you saying?" I asked slowly.

The sardonic tilt of his mouth deepened. "I'm saying that I will be a hero." Before I could blink, his hand shot out, delved into my jacket, and snatched my Nitro-gun.

Then the Astarot noble shot himself in the gut.

Immediately the nitro went to work, spreading through his organs and freezing everything in its path quicker than my ability to process what he'd just done.

Carreg's jaw tightened. His nostrils flared. Pain swept across his face. "I will say that your bounty was in the room, but as a weak human, she did not have the power to kill the Father. The spirit of Solomon jumped into Matsul for the kill. Matsul killed the Father. I, in turn, killed him, but not before Solomon was able to jump back into your human and fled, shooting me in the process. And you went after him . . ."

Carreg fell to his knees. He grimaced and let out a long, controlled breath of pain. "After the shock wears off, they will question it, but with me as their only witness and corroborating Solomon's possession, they will accept it long enough for you to escape and get back to your city. Be prepared, as they will come to you all for questioning. Make sure your story never wavers . . . or I will kill you myself."

He tipped forward, palms bracing against the marble floor. His head hung low between his arms.

I bent down. "All this to be a hero?"

He lifted his gaze, black hair falling over his brow. Intensity brightened the silver flecks in his eyes. "All this . . . to be . . . *king*." His head dropped. He gasped. "Main chamber. Wall relief. Warrior. Press the jewel in the hilt . . ."

Carreg fell onto his side.

I couldn't move.

"Go!" Carreg hissed.

Spurred, I swiped my gun from the floor, took Bryn's shackled hands, and pushed her quickly toward the main chamber. Solomon couldn't jump from person to person. He was stuck inside of Bryn until she died, or an exorcist pulled him out, but the nobles didn't know that, and they didn't know what he was capable of. Carreg's story might actually hold water for a little while. But not long.

We hurried into the main chamber to the wall reliefs I'd seen earlier. The black marble was covered in identical warriors, line after line of them. Way too many of them. Shit. "Start pressing hilts."

I forced Bryn to the wall and started pushing on

the small marble jewels of sword hilts. My hands were shaking. I repeated this several times, my desperation building until I thought I might scream.

"I got it!" Rex whispered loudly.

A slight hiss of air sounded. I scanned the chamber and saw a small, narrow opening in the marble. Hank snagged two ceremonial short swords from one of the walls and shoved them through his belt loop, one at each hip.

"Let's go," I said.

We filed into the tunnel. Once inside I searched for a mechanism to close the door, knowing there had to be one. I found a small, round knob nearby and pushed it in. The door slid closed, leaving us in pitch black, surrounded by black marble.

Rex cursed. Our movements were quick but careful as we started at a fast clip through the narrow tunnel. At least the floor was smooth and the walls kept us going in one direction. Our footsteps, heavy breaths, and Brim's claws echoed in the space.

I lost all sense of time, so focused was I on moving, getting away.

We didn't stop until Rex's face came into contact with a door, his whispered curses filling the passageway. I put out my hand to steady Bryn as she bumped up against Rex's back.

"I'll feel for a lever or a button," Hank spoke up from behind me, so close my hair moved with his words. "Be ready. We don't know what this will open up to."

Or if Carreg had set us up.

I pulled my gun.

The sound of stone cracking told me Hank had found the release mechanism. Rex whispered a command to Brim. "Brim goes first," he whispered. Light filled the tunnel, blinding us for a moment, but it didn't take long to acclimate and see that the light was actually dim and gray.

Brim stepped out slowly, alert for signs of danger. Rex went next. Then me with Bryn, and Hank behind us.

"Holy shit," Rex breathed. "Is this going to hold us?"

We'd come out on a small ledge in the rock that supported the nobles' city above. I glanced up and saw the sheer walls of palaces shooting into the air. Below us was Telmath, but just a very small edge of it, since we were facing away from the city and toward one of the rock walls of the cavernous city. Hank searched for a way to shut the door, found the depression, and pushed. The door slid closed.

Rex inched closer to one side, his back flat against the rock, and glanced down. "Looks like . . . some steps . . . oh, hell no . . ." He straightened, eyes wide, turning his head toward us. After a steadying breath, he attempted a nonchalant shrug. "Well, if we were a bunch of Munchkins going down the yellow brick road, this would be a piece of cake."

"Tiny steps or not," I said, trying not to look straight down, "we need to keep going and I don't see another way down. Let's move and try to be careful."

I gripped Bryn tighter lest Solomon try to throw her off the rock and "release" himself that way. She'd been oddly compliant so far and it made me wonder if Solomon had exhausted his strength escaping from the cold cell, traveling—however the hell he'd done it—to Telmath, and getting inside of the nobles' city . . . Or he could be lulling us into a false sense of security or resting up for another suicide attempt later.

Whatever the case, we needed to get as far away from the city as possible.

We started moving, falling back into our focused silence, going one by one down the small footholds carved into the rock.

Step after step, story after story. And I knew far above us, they had to know by now. Carreg was probably being healed and telling his tale. Sweat trickled down the sides of my face. My clothes were damp, and I longed to take off my jacket. I would've given anything for a gust of cool air or a drink of cold water. But we were close to the bottom. The scents and sounds of the city grew heavier and heavier.

Finally we reached the end and took a path which curved around the enormous base of the rock toward the dark streets of Telmath.

"If I never see another step in my lifetime, I'll be happy," Rex muttered.

"Me, too." I stopped before the path led us behind a house and into what looked liked the dead end of a street. "So I think it's safe to say they know by now."

"And the terminal is out," Hank said, echoing my own thoughts. Going back to the terminal meant the possibility of being detained. If I didn't have the sylph timeline breathing down my neck, it might be a different story. But as it was, I needed to get home ASAP.

"All right, Rex," I said, turning to him. "Time to put your jinn memories to work. How do we get back home?" The gates might be the current and law-abiding mode of travel, but in ancient times it was well-known that the jinn had ways of travelling to our world.

He frowned and then scratched his stubbly jaw. "Let me think . . ." After a long moment he said, "There used to be a jinn temple outside of Tel-math. The Temple of the Moon. There was a portal there . . ."

"You're talking thousands of years ago," Hank said.

"Well, I don't see you offering anything," Rex shot back.

"Could you find it again?" I asked.

He nodded. "Yeah, it was a couple hours east of Telmath, through the sand flats. The portal was underground and was kept secret from the nobles . . . If the temple is still there, the portal might be, too. Those things, once they're created, are near impossible to destroy."

I bit the inside of my cheek. "Okay, so first we need to find out if the temple still exists. We'll find out along the way. If it does, then we'll try it. Agreed? And as soon as we can, we steal a cloak for Bryn to cover the blood and the gag."

Rex shrugged and readjusted the axe strapped to his back.

I turned to Hank to find he was staring at me. He pulled the hood over his head. The stark intensity in his gaze had darkened the color of his eyes until they appeared nearly black in the dim light. "Hank?"

"We only have one day. If we're not back in one day, the sylphs' 'gifts' . . ."

"Will kill me," I finished for him quietly. "I know."

16

It wasn't hard to lift a cloak from one of the houses near the dead-end street. It was dark, quiet, and Hank had taken five minutes tops between the time he drifted into the shadows until he returned with something to cover Bryn. Once that was done, we started toward the mouth of Telmath's cavern.

The smoky, shadowed streets of the city reminded me of the congested atmosphere on Solomon Street back home in Atlanta, only on a grander, darker, otherworldly scale that stretched for miles.

I could easily imagine that I was walking through the crowded streets of some ancient civilization—the sunlight replaced with the dim violet glow of typanum running through the "sky," the sunbaked houses replaced with gray stone and timbers, and the humans replaced with hulking jinn warriors strutting around, cloaked ghouls peering beneath their hoods, darkling fae weaving effortlessly through the narrow streets . . .

As we moved through narrow alleys and busy marketplaces, over bridges that spanned rivers and gaping black chasms in the ground, our passage was either ignored or met with curious frowns that passed over us quickly and then were forgotten. I saw humans—more than I'd expected to see—shopping, touring, engaged in dark pursuits. Black crafting was allowed here. So were gambling and prostitution . . .

In one of the busiest corners we passed, Rex ducked into a storefront that sold what looked to be antiques and artifacts and came back out with a nod. "The temple is still there. In ruins. But there."

I had no idea what was happening far up on the plateau or if guards had begun searching. But if they were, they were slowed by the vastness of the city, the crowds, and the darkness. Still, I turned and glanced up even though the plateau was too high to see anything.

"Charlie," Hank said, making me jump.

He stepped aside. I gripped Bryn's arm tighter and nudged her forward, following Rex and Brim through the dense streets of Telmath as Hank fell in behind us. All the sights, sounds, and scents filled in around us, but we moved as though we were in a bubble of silence. Isolated.

★   ★   ★

The closer we came to the gaping twenty-story-high mouth of the cavern, the scents slowly changed from tar and earth to dry wood and sand. The humidity disappeared, the air turning arid and hot. Several lonely-looking paths, carrying one or two dusty travelers, led into and out of the city.

All the action was behind us, and in front of us, framed by the massive cavern mouth, was wide-open Charbydon sky. Inky blue and lit with stars. As beautiful as it was, a shiver crept down my spine. Despite the danger back in Telmath, the cavern had provided a sense of insulation and protection. Out here, in the wild . . . God only knew what awaited us.

As we passed into open air, our strides lengthened and our pace increased, all of us wanting to get as far away from Telmath as possible. Several minutes passed before my fears of getting caught finally eased and I was able to really notice the environment.

A dim, moonlight-like glow bathed the landscape. Everyone called the giant orb hanging in the sky a moon, but it was really a white dwarf star, one that was slowly dying out. Once this "moon" set below the horizon it was blacker than black, and when it rose again it was dim and not nearly—so I'd heard—as bright as in older days. Ahead of us stretched a barren land of shrubs, rocky outcroppings, clumps of stubborn trees, and patches of small flowers in blues and whites.

The road was so soft that fine grains puffed up like smoke as we walked, and the edges were littered with petrified woods and loose rocks.

"We might be able to make it most of the way before the moon sets," Rex said. "Once it does, this place turns pitch-black, and we're screwed. And don't use those lights on your belts. The light draws the predators."

Great.

The only one who seemed happy to be out here in the wild was Brim. He trotted around us in large serpentine patterns, his nose trailing the ground, investigating, processing the scents, and then coming back in toward us to cross over to the other side. He never disappeared from view.

My feet burned inside of my socks and shoes, and my face felt sticky and grimy. We hiked at a fast clip for at least three miles before I slowed, turning around to check our progress. The mountain that rose up behind us was a jagged behemoth. My jaw dropped. It made the opening of the cavern look like the mouth of a sea bass. Behind the dark, jagged shape were more mountains, an entire range that shot up into the inky sky.

I turned back around and continued on, amazed at what I was seeing—at what I'd seen so far. Bryn muttered something through the gag and jerked her arm. I stopped her and removed the hood and then set to work untying the gag. We were far enough away that her screams wouldn't be heard. But I shoved the gag into my pocket in case the need arose. She bent over and spit. "God, it's hot," she gasped.

"Make any trouble," I said, "and it'll be back on."

She didn't respond. I couldn't help but wonder if Solomon was still pulling the strings, but right then I didn't want confirmation. I was tired, too tired to deal with the emotional onslaught that would come if my sister "appeared."

The image of my baby sister straddling the Abaddon Father, blood sprayed over her front, and that dagger making its way toward her belly, was enough to make me sob. But, right then, all that mattered was making it across the flats, through the portal, and back home.

Hank trailed behind us, the cloak off and thrown over his shoulder. "I don't suspect the nobles would think we'd be desperate enough to cross the sand flats." He glanced over his shoulder to the mountain range. His profile was grim and since we were out of the city he let down *some* of the blocks on his aura. I couldn't see much, but I could feel the vibe coming off him and it was . . . distracted.

I frowned at that revelation.

"Well," I said, "hopefully they think we're off chasing after Solomon like Carreg told them." I wanted to say more, but then thought better of it. Asking him now about the sirens in the terminal probably wasn't the time or the place. But I hadn't forgotten. It was pretty clear they recognized Hank, and just as clear that he wanted nothing to do with them. I bit the inside of my cheek to temper my curiosity and took Bryn's arm. "Let's keep moving."

A strange rattlesnake sound echoed around us. The

hairs on the back of my neck lifted and made me shudder. I glanced around at the unfamiliar landscape, my other hand going back to rest on the hilt of my Nitrogun. But Rex, I noticed, kept walking and Brim didn't seem alarmed. My anxiety remained, however, the place too foreign and strange for me to relax.

Eventually the rocky ground, trees, and bushes disappeared, giving way to a vast sea of the finest gray sand, which slowly made its way into my clothes and stuck to my exposed skin. In random patches, large outcroppings of rocks and jagged monoliths jutted up from the sand.

Despite the "moonlight," there were huge black shadows made by the dunes. Every time we crossed through one, the idea of stepping on something or being ambushed heightened my uneasiness.

After what felt like hours, Rex suddenly stopped. He went very still, face turning from side to side, staring out into the shadowy distance. Even though he was in the body of a human, one very familiar to me, Rex seemed more jinn than ever. The way he carried himself, the confidence, the sense of self . . . It was all very . . . strange.

"They're already following us," he said, and started walking again.

"Who's following us?" I struggled through the sand as I tried to catch up. The faster I stepped, the deeper my boots sank.

"We're being tracked by a pack of nithyn. And probably one or two sand lizards."

Was it too much to hope that a sand lizard was tiny and harmless? As it was, I was already aware that nithyn were dragon-like creatures that grew to the size of large goats. Moon snakes ate their eggs, but once grown, the nithyn turned the tables and ate snakes, lizards, and—if they were hungry enough—off-worlders too weak to defend themselves . . . or humans stupid enough to trek through the sand flats at night.

"What the hell is a sand lizard?" Bryn asked in a scratchy voice.

"A chameleon," said Rex. "Blends into the dunes and rocks to catch its prey. Travels beneath the sand. Its scales are like armor, impervious to nitro, bullets . . . You have to get in close to kill them, find their soft spots."

A far-off screech echoed through the air. "Was that a nithyn?" I asked as Rex slid his axe off his back.

"Probably ringing the dinner bell."

"Brilliant," Hank muttered.

"See those boulders?" Rex pointed with his weapon to a large outcropping of rocks along the ridge of the sand dunes. "We'll head for the rocks. Don't run, though."

"What about the sand lizards?" Bryn said.

"They can only move on and in the sand. They're rather . . . large. But once we hit the rocks, we should be fine. And if something should happen to me, the ruins lie east; the portal is beneath the altar stone in the temple. Feed it your power. Where you end up is subject to your ability to concentrate on your destination."

I stored his information, eyeing the rocks about a quarter of a mile away. A quarter of a mile of thinking every step would land me in the mouth of a damn reptile. And what did *large* mean anyway?

We never made it to the rocks.

One second I was walking on soft sand and the next, the ground was falling out from under me.

I fell with Bryn as the sand was sucked downward. A plume of fine, gritty dust rose up to envelop us. "BRYN!" With her hands bound, she fell face-first and rolled toward the deepening depression in the ground—a deepening depression that revealed the giant sand lizard rising up to greet us.

My heels dug into the sand. "You said it was a lizard!" I yelled.

Rex was sliding on his back down toward the creature. "It is! Just a really big one!"

Big as an elephant with a scaled body as thick as a California redwood, the sand lizard emerged. It resembled a gigantic salamander with a forked tongue that snaked out and tested the air.

Bryn smacked into its belly. Its tail whipped out of the sand and thankfully the ground stopped moving. I rolled down the sides of the depression, using my momentum to pop to my feet and run for her, directly beneath the sand lizard's gaze. I grabbed her arm as she stumbled to her feet, covered in sand.

"RUN!" I shouted, yanking her.

Running in sand was an exercise in futility. My heart pounded so loud through my ears that it muted the sound that came out of the creature's mouth—a shrieking hiss that crawled up my spine like lightning with a thousand feet.

The hunt was on.

"Get to the rocks!" Rex's voice was close. I searched, finding him scrambling up the beast's tail like some fucked-up version of Legolas, as Brim leapt onto the scaly thigh and clamped down with his massive jaws.

Hank withdrew both of the ceremonial swords he'd taken from the palace and stabbed both blades between the sand lizard's tocs.

It swung around, the tail hitting me and Bryn square in the back, sending us flying. I gulped a mouthful of sand. It flew into my nostrils and eyes. I couldn't scream her name or see where she ended up.

I landed on my belly with a soft thud.

"Get these bands off me!" Bryn shouted to my right.

I wiped at my eyes, crawling to her. But I couldn't risk setting her free, even if she *could* work magic to help us. Solomon had a death wish and I wasn't about to let my sister going running into the jaws of a sand lizard.

I could hardly see, could barely run in the sand. Couldn't do much of anything without my weapons. But I did have power. Power inside of me and all around me.

Sandy tears ran down my cheeks as my body tried to shed the hard grains from my eyes. I dove inside of myself, to the very core of my darkest power, to the energy I always tried to ignore and suppress.

Fuck. It hurt. It burned. It took over, swamping me. This power was in its element. Its home. And it was harsher and more vivid than anything I'd experienced so far.

A scream tore from my scratchy throat as it broke free of its chain like a savage dog, bursting through my chest and flying down both arms and into my hands. I cast my scorching hands toward the sounds of the creature.

I fell back onto Bryn. Drained and trembling.

Something landed with an *oomph* beside us.

"Jesus Christ, Charlie! Try hitting your target next time!" It was Rex.

"I can't *see*, you moron!"

"Here." He grabbed my hand and turned me in the right direction. "You might want to hurry because your partner is about to be lizard snack."

"I used it all," I cried, my vision clearing somewhat. "I'm tapped out."

"No you're not, Charlie," Bryn's voice came from behind me. Her arms came down over my head and shoulders to hug me, her wrists still shackled. "Use me, draw from me and Solomon." Her voice shook. Her body was trembling all over.

"But . . ."

"He's weak, Charlie. After opening the portal and

getting me to . . . kill." She shook her head and her voice went sharper. "Just do it!"

"Hurry!" Rex yelled, running away from us and toward the battle.

I closed my eyes and gathered again, from my core like I was used to, but also from the energy wrapping around me, linking me to another. I gathered, pulled like a thin, starving creature, sucking it all, taking it all. I had no idea how I was doing it. Instinct? Necessity? Desperation?

Bryn screamed, her shudders filtering into me, and I no longer knew where her screams ended and mine began. When I couldn't hold any more, my eyes opened, I threw out my palms, and gave it all to the mass in front of me.

A high-pitched screech. Sand falling like rain. Panting.

"You got it!" Rex called.

Bryn and I fell back. I had no idea what *got it* meant, but as long as the thing was down I didn't care.

"Where's Brim? Is he okay?" I shimmied from Bryn's hold and pushed my palms deep into the sand to rise.

Before Rex could answer, a loud screech filled the air above us. The nithyn. My vision cleared enough for me to see the dark shadows circling above us. My legs wobbled as I stood. I pulled my Nitro-gun as the ground began to rise up beneath me.

Another sand lizard emerged from the ground, lifting me off my feet and onto its back, coming between me and my sister. I lost my balance and rolled off the creature, landing on my side with a jarring thud. I struggled to rise; my only thought was my sister. "BRYN!"

I ran through the sand toward the sand lizard's tail. Brim shot from the side and leapt onto its back, a snarling, drooling mass of gray and flashing teeth. Where the hell was Hank? The creature turned after me, clearing my line of sight. Bryn was booking toward the rocks and Rex was running toward the lizard.

"No, Rex! Get Bryn to the portal!"

He slid to a stop, glanced behind me, and hesitated. "Go east!" he shouted. "Follow the ridge! We'll aim for the cell block at the station!" Then he turned and ran after Bryn.

A shadow fell. *Oh shit*. I turned slowly to see the lizard's large head poised over me.

And then I was tackled by Hank as the creature dove for me. We rolled, his hand grabbed mine, and we were up and running. Away from Bryn, toward another ridge of rocks.

Brim shot past us, running hard. The sand vibrated, and I knew the lizard had gone under again.

A nithyn dove for us. We dropped to our stomachs. It missed, angled its body, and flew back up to circle again. Another was hot on Brim's heels, flying low to the ground behind him, gaining. I fired my gun as Hank turned and fired into the sky. My shot missed the body but hit the wing. The nithyn screamed, turned, and slammed into the sand. As soon as it did, the others descended upon it, attacking. Christ. They were cannibals. As soon as one of theirs was injured, it was anything goes. From pack to prey in an instant.

We made it to the rocks in a simultaneous leap. My calves and thighs burned. My lungs were on fire. The sand lizard rose up and hissed. We sailed over the smaller rocks, leapt up a bigger one, and then hit unexpected air.

Oh God. My arms pinwheeled. Blackness enveloped us as we fell screaming into a black hole.

Seconds of dark, weightless panic passed.

I slammed into rock. The force caused my legs to buckle. My knee slammed into my face. Every bone hit and bruised and broke on rock as I tumbled. Wave after wave of blinding pain stole my breath. Amid it all, I heard grunts, bone breaking, thuds, and gasps. Brim's claws scraping . . . a cry.

My skull cracked on a rock. The force of the blow sent my body swinging around, airborne, and then I hit one last time on my side and slid into a hard barrier in a heap of broken bones.

A sob broke past my busted lips.

The only thing that reached me through the haze of excruciating pain was the sound of my gasping breaths, loud and echoing, in the darkness, and Hank's muttered "Fucking hell" before I sank into oblivion.

*   *   *

The dripping of water was the first thing my waking mind processed. Slowly my other senses kicked in. The air was cooler and damper here.

My head ached. My torso was on fire from what had to be several broken ribs. The left side of my body had taken the brunt—left arm and leg possibly fractured. Three fingers on my right hand were bent at an odd angle.

Hot tears leaked from my swollen eyes. My exposed skin was raw and scratched, clothing ripped in places. I had no idea how long I'd been out, but I did recognize the healing process had already begun.

A series of coughs gripped my sore throat, every push of muscle causing extraordinary pain.

After several minutes, I pushed up enough to lean my back against the wall I'd slammed into. I grabbed my fingers with my left hand and prepared to reset the dislocated ones.

I set them right one after the other, crying out each time I did. Nausea gripped me hard by the time I got to the last one, and I had to force down the urge to puke before shoving that final knuckle back into place.

I must've fallen back into a state of healing because the next thing I knew, Hank was kneeling beside me, speaking Elysian in a near whisper. His flashlight lay beside me, creating a soft glow in the pitch darkness. I ached. Everything was stiff, but the intense pain of earlier had receded.

Heat engulfed me. My nose was stuffy from crying. "You okay?" I asked.

"Yeah, kiddo, I'll live. Looks like we fell into some kind of cave or ravine. There's water nearby. Can you walk?"

"I don't know. Where's Brim?"

"He's by the water."

"Is he . . . dead?"

"No. He's not dead, Charlie."

My eyelids fell in relief. *Thank you, God.* I grabbed for his arm. "We have to get to that portal."

With Hank's help, I pushed to my feet inch by punishing inch. My vision wavered as angry pain screamed through my hip. The scent of blood reached my nose. My wounds were a nasty concoction of congealing blood and sand.

Hank's arm slid under mine. "This way." His touch set off my mark, and his deep voice bouncing around the cavern walls gave a little extra jolt to my system; though I felt it on the inside, it did little to help the scratch of sand through my wounds as I walked. It filled my boots, my clothes. It was everywhere.

I smelled the water before the flashlight beamed over the surface of the shallow pool. Beyond the pool the water trailed into a ravine, and moonlight filtered in at gaps in the rocks above. It looked as though, once upon a time, an underground river had cut out the caves beneath the ridge above, leaving deep grooves in the rocks.

Brim lay by the edge of the pool, panting. He lifted

his head when we approached, saw us, and then returned to his position.

The water was a godsend. My mouth watered for a taste as Hank led me to the edge of the pool and I noticed that his feet were bare and his hair was wet.

"The water is drinkable over there where it's coming in from the rock," he said. "I've already washed up in the pool and got most of the sand from my clothes. I healed you some while you were unconscious, but I'm wiped out and need to regenerate before I can do more. You need help?"

"No. I'm fine." I went to bend down, but pain shot through my torso so fast I swayed. Shit. My eyes burned and my dry throat grew thick. I wanted so badly to get to the water, but it hurt too much.

I blinked rapidly, not realizing until he spoke that Hank was kneeling in front of me. "Put your hand on my shoulder so you don't fall."

I frowned, but did as he asked. And then it became clear as he gently placed one hand on my calf while the other pulled off my boot. Sand rained onto the ground. It took all my willpower to stay on my feet as each movement threatened to buckle my legs.

After my feet were bare, he stood. "We're going to need to move soon, but you've got sand everywhere and you'll heal faster without it rubbing your wounds raw. You can't get in there with your clothes on. They'll never dry and will be hell to get back on."

"Take them off, I don't care," I said. Modesty didn't factor at that point. Neither did romance. We were battered and bruised, sweaty and ripe. And Hank had seen most of me before anyway, just recently after my visit with Nivian and then Emain. "This is becoming a habit," I mumbled as he removed my pants and I tensed in pain.

He chuckled softly. "No doubt. And a bad one at that. God forbid I ever get to do this when you're not wounded or half dead . . ."

I smiled.

Hank removed my belt, my sidearm, and then my pants, which I stepped out of very carefully while holding on to both of his shoulders.

He straightened, eyeing me with concern. "Can you manage lifting your arms?"

I winced, knowing it would hurt like hell. "Not really. But my jacket and shirt are full of sand. It's even in my armpits. Let's get it over with so we can catch up to Rex and Bryn."

He smiled. "Brave girl."

"If you say so."

Carefully Hank peeled off my jacket, my weapons harness, and then waited as I sucked in a readying breath, gritted my teeth, and lifted my arms. He made quick work of my shirt. Sweat was rolling off me, tears streamed down my face, and I was shaking. My arms fell limp at my sides, the action causing even more pain.

Hank leaned down and rolled his pants legs up and then held out his hand.

And I froze.

The way he stood there . . . hair wet, a busted lip, his cheek scraped raw, a bruise shadowing beneath his eyes, yet strength and power still radiated from him . . . And holding his hand out to me. The image seemed suspended as though my brain decided to pause and take a snapshot.

Then it was over almost as soon as it began. My chest ached and I wasn't all that sure it was because of my wounds. Feeling exhausted and foggy, I slid my hand into his. His fingers closed around mine, warm and strong, feeding me some of his healing power, though I knew he had very little left.

Once my foot hit the cool water, I sighed. The cold wrapped around my skin, easing the burn of scrapes and hurts. Hank walked me to a ledge where I could hold on while going deeper into the pool, then he left me alone so I could soak in the water and rub the grit, sweat, blood, and sand from my body. Bra and underwear were completely soaked through, but I didn't care.

Feeling better, I headed for the water coming in from the rock crevice, cupped my hands, and brought water to my lips. It was heaven.

After I drank my fill I turned. Brim had finally gotten to his feet and Hank was shaking out my clothing and had our weapons set out in a line on one of the rocks. No doubt having cleaned them of sand the best he could.

I guessed if I was going to be stranded in a hot desert world, he wasn't a bad guy to have on my side.

Brim walked into the water as I walked out. I patted his head and approached my clothes. Hank kept his eyes averted and worked on brushing sand from his thigh harness and then strapped it back on. He had his socks and shoes back on, too.

I dressed as quickly as I could and had more of an issue with the smell of my clothes and the blood than I did with the pain of getting back into them.

"If we keep walking beneath this ridge, we should be going parallel with our original track. Rex said to head east."

I grabbed my belt. "Thanks."

He glanced up, his hands still around his thigh.

"For the . . ." I threw a hand toward the water.

A smile that he tried to suppress drew across his lips and he shook his head. "Anytime, Madigan."

"So how good are you at directions?" I asked, easing into my shoulder harness.

"Compass." He held up a dagger that I hadn't seen him take from the station. It had a nice little sheath along with the firearm at his thigh. The end of it contained a dome.

"We're not exactly home," I pointed out.

"All three worlds have poles, different ones, sure, but this has a compass for each of them. See?" He turned a small lever and the dome rolled to reveal another one.

"Okay, survivor man, I'm impressed. You ready to go?"

He shoved the dagger into the sheath and grabbed

his jacket. "We'll just make sure we're on an easterly track. The ruins hopefully won't be hard to miss."

Despite the dim light, I didn't miss his look. It was iffy at best. We were out in the sand flats without our guide, neither one of us having been here before. Separated from my little sister . . . Another snapshot rose up in front of me.

Bryn as a kid, sitting on the living room floor in her nightgown watching Saturday morning cartoons, her stuffed turtle in her lap—Turdy.

What started out as "Turty" had quickly become "Turdy" . . . Connor and I always had a good laugh about that. My heart constricted with the memory of my brother.

And Bryn.

Seeing her as a cold-blooded murderer, blood on her hands. It was a sight I'd never forget.

"You know it wasn't Bryn," Hank said.

"She doesn't deserve this, Hank. On top of everything else . . . it's too much."

"You'd be surprised at what people can handle, Charlie. Look at you. All that's happened . . . and yet you continue on. You're one of the strongest people I have ever met here or in Elysia. And Bryn is cut from the same cloth. She'll get through this, too."

I nodded and wiped at the corner of one eye, watching Brim walk from the pool and then shake his big body. Water and slobber went flying in all directions. "You gonna tell me what those sirens were doing at the gate?"

For a second, I didn't think he'd answer.

"Well, I'd guess they were there to take me home."

"Back to Elysia? Why?"

He shrugged and picked up another pebble from the ledge, turning it over in his hands. He threw it into the water. "Because I am a traitor."

17

"What?" I turned to face him. "What do you mean, traitor?"

No. Maybe I wasn't conscious yet. Maybe I was still out cold and healing and this was just some weird-ass dream. I snorted a laugh and pinched the bridge of my nose, then rubbed a hand down my face, avoiding the tender spots.

"I don't . . . understand," I finally managed. How the hell could Hank be a traitor? There was no way in hell. I *knew* him. "Hank, you're no traitor. Even I kn—"

"No, you don't know, Charlie." He whistled for Brim, turned, and strode off with parting words. "You don't know anything about me."

Alessandra's words came back to haunt me then. *You never truly know another, what they're capable of.*

Did I ever think Will was capable of leading a double life? No. I also didn't think the same of Hank. But maybe he was right. I didn't know a damn thing about his past or why he'd come to Atlanta.

I finished arming myself, then grabbed my jacket and limped off after him, ignoring the soreness and the pain, determined that my instincts were right this time. "I know enough," I said, catching up to him. "You're not a traitor, Hank." I grabbed his arm. "And if someone thinks you are, then they don't know you like I do."

My touch drew him to a stop. He stared into the blackness ahead of us. I watched Brim for a few seconds and then asked, "Will we have another fight on our hands when we get back?"

That seemed to knock him out of his thoughts. "You'd fight?"

"Yes," I answered, confounded that he'd think otherwise.

"Not knowing the circumstances? Even if I was a traitor, a fugitive?"

"You've fought for Emma, for me, and now for Bryn . . . Of course I'd fight. Look, whatever happened . . . I bet you had a damn good reason for what you did or whatever those sirens *think* you did." I paused. "Why do they think you're a traitor?"

Part of me was cringing inside and hoping to hell he didn't say something I couldn't overlook. I wanted at least one hero in my life, one guy who had some honor and dignity. One guy who could open up and tell me the truth. That would be nice, too, I thought darkly as I waited for an explanation that obviously was not coming.

I shoved my stiff arms into my torn jacket and pushed past him. "We should get moving."

"Charlie."

Exasperated, I stopped. "Look, just forget it, okay? If you don't want to share, you don't want to share." I whistled to Brim and skirted the pool to follow the path of the running water down the ravine.

"You know what *Malakim* means?" he asked behind me, frustration hardening his tone, and not waiting for an answer. "It means *guardian*."

I climbed over a rock. "Great. Good for you."

"A long time ago it used to mean something. It was important. Now"—he paused as though searching for the right words—"it's a tradition, a title, an honor. Like you humans use the term *knight*. That word used to mean something a long time ago, too. Now it's just a title given by a king or queen."

Hank spoke as though *Malakim* was a death sentence, a horrible thing. "So you were a *Malakim*," I said over my shoulder when he didn't continue.

Brim dodged in front of me, disappearing beyond the shaft of moonlight shining down from a break above us.

"I was. Our king chose the first *Malakim* from four families. My family was and still is one of those. We are known for our guardianship and our power. We are—or were—respected in Fiallan."

Hank stopped talking to concentrate as we picked

our way down a steep drop in the ravine. Water fell in a loud stream into a pool below and then disappeared beneath rock. Brim waited for us at the bottom. Above us the ceiling had opened up again, bathing a wide path of smooth gray rock in moonlight.

I waited for Hank. He eased down beside me, brushed off his hands, and then we continued side by side.

"So what? You decided you didn't want the title?"

"I wish it were that simple. You have to understand what the word means. The first *Malakim* were chosen as young children because all the grown sirens were off fighting with the Adonai."

I gave him a surprised look.

"Just because our world inspired humanity's idea of heaven doesn't mean we didn't have our share of war and fighting. At some time or another every being in Elysia has warred with the other.

"Long before I was born, sirens went to war with the Adonai. It lasted several generations. And our territory was reduced to our oldest city, Fiallan. It was our last stronghold. In order to save the city and everyone in it, the king chose four children—sons of his strongest warriors—and placed them into towers made by the Circe—"

"A witch?" I said, immediately recognizing that famous name.

"No. A group of . . . well, I guess you could call them witches. They are our oldest, most powerful female sirens. Ancient. Heartless. Conniving. They created the towers." Hank's voice turned cold. "Prisons are what they really are."

A bad feeling began to brew in my gut. "What did they do to the four kids?"

"Put them inside the Circe's towers, where they were eventually drained of power. Their power ran in rings of protection around the city, protecting it and saving it from Adonai rule. This was hailed as our saving grace, these children in the towers. And they called them *Malakim*. Guardians. To this day Fiallan is surrounded by four towers and between them run four continuous rings of power."

"How does it work? Does it hurt?"

"It's . . . intense at first. In each tower the Circe created some kind of energy field. It's tuned to the energy in our bodies and into Elysia itself, I think. Once you step onto the platform, it . . . I'm not sure how to explain . . . it activates. It attacks. Joining. Drawing your energy out the openings in each side of the tower, and then linking each *Malakim*.

"To keep the Adonai from ever breaching our world again, they continued the practice. To this day the children are chosen from the four original families. It's the greatest honor in our culture. But there is no longer any need for the *Malakim* since peace has been achieved between us and the Adonai for the last thousand or so years. My people continue the practice out of tradition and honor."

I swallowed. "How long do they stay in the towers?"

"Longer than they want to. They say only seven

years. But it's a lie. It's difficult to explain. It's like . . . being plugged into a grid. Hurts at first but then you get sucked in. You forget there is a world outside of this constant state of power and energy flowing in and out of you. It pacifies you. And when they come to ask you if you're ready to step down, that your service is up, no one ever wants to leave. No one *can* leave. The *Malakim* stay their whole lives, and the Circe will have everyone believe that it is a choice, that they sacrifice their lives willingly. But there is no choice, Charlie. And no one knows it because no child has ever come out of the towers to say so.

"They stay until they are so old and drained, the Circe must forcibly remove them in order to keep the rings strong. And by then they are lost. They cannot communicate. They come out comatose and old and they die a short time later with our city's highest honor.

"I was six years old when they chose me," he said quietly, and my heart dropped into my feet. " I was so proud. My family was so proud . . . There was a great ceremony. The king himself told me I'd be a hero. And to a young boy, it seemed like a wonderful dream. Everyone loves you, celebrates you."

And he had gotten out. Somehow Hank had escaped this fate when no one else had before him.

"But if I had known," he went on, "if I'd had a real choice, I never would've gone willingly."

"But your mother," I said, "and your father—how could they have been okay with that?"

He shrugged. "They were saddened to have me go, but honored just the same. When it's part of your culture, part of your traditions for eons, you don't question it. You accept it. They didn't know the truth. No one but the Circe knows.

"I went into that tower gladly, not knowing that it sucks you in and keeps feeding from you. *That* is the true meaning of *Malakim*. You give up living; you give up your life. Those who say they will wait for you don't; they move on, they mate, they have children. But none of it matters anyway, because you wouldn't leave even if you could."

"But you did."

A long sigh breezed through his lips. We passed through another darkened section of the ravine and clicked on our flashlights.

"How long were you guarding Fiallan, Hank?"

"A couple hundred years. I went in as a boy. I came out as a full-grown siren with no clue how to socialize, how to act, no understanding of the rules of my society. How to read and write, to care for myself. I didn't understand the simplest things: how to find food, what foods to eat . . . The grid keeps you sustained and strong. You feed it, it feeds you . . ."

"How did you get out of the grid?" I asked him.

He paused, a silence that stretched before he finally spoke. "Lidi. She was five. I was six. Our families were close. She was the only one who fought against me going into the grid. They had to subdue her during the ceremony. She was a small child, and no one thought she'd start sneaking into the tower to talk to me, to read to me. Every day before she snuck back out, she promised to wait for me. She did this until she was full grown. For many years, she read to me, talked to me, told me about life. The life I was missing . . .

"And then, one day, she stopped coming. But during her visits, I heard her. Every word, I clung to. And when she was gone, it started a seed in me to practice remembering her visits—I think it helped me to remember the outside world. I grew in body and in power, but I never lost myself. The memories . . . are hazy, but part of me stayed disconnected from the grid, and in time that disconnect grew until I was able to break free. I'm not sure exactly how it all happened."

I bit my lip, wondering what had happened to her, this siren who had given him the strength and purpose to break free.

"She didn't wait for me, if that's what's making you bite your lip," he said with a small smile.

"I'm sorry, Hank."

"I'd been gone for a long time; couldn't expect her to wait forever."

But he would have. I could tell in his voice. He would have waited for her if the roles had been reversed. I knew it down to the very marrow of my bones.

"So you broke free," I moved on, not wanting to think about it. "Wouldn't they know immediately? The rings around the city would've failed, right?"

"Yes. My ring simply stopped working. Disappeared. I remember coming to on the floor of the tower. The Circe and the king were there. I was weak. My speech was unintelligible at first, but memory brought it back. I found enough words to tell them the truth, what the tower does to you. They refused to believe. But I think even the king had suspected as much. And they didn't want anyone else to know the truth. They told me I was a traitor, a weakling, and as punishment they tried to force me back into the grid . . ."

Hank stopped talking, and the ravine filled with the sound of running water and the shuffling of our footsteps.

"I fought," he said quietly, though his tone was deep and echoing in the confines of the ravine. "I fought for my life. I was crazed and angry, and it gave me more strength than I should have had. I felt hurt, confused, and betrayed—a six-year-old in heart and mind, but with the body and power of a full-grown siren. And they didn't care. They never had . . ." His voice took an almost embarrassed quality. "There were no guards. I think because the Circe didn't want anyone but them and the king knowing the truth. They let the king deal with me. And I guess they thought I was too weak for them to bother with using their great power. It all happened so fast. We struggled and somehow I managed to throw the king into the grid. It attacked him at once and there was no way to fight it off." He said it like he was ashamed.

"Good for you. The bastard deserved it."

He glanced over at me with an odd mixture of bewilderment, humor, and regret. "Well, it wasn't an accident. I meant to prove my words. I told him if it was simply a matter of choice, then he could leave as he wished. While the Circe were distracted with the king in the grid, I ran. It's a blur. My memories of Fiallan were that of a child, but I knew my home, remembered it. But I knew if went there, they'd find me."

My throat thickened, but I forced down my emotion with a hard swallow. "So where did you go?"

"Outside of the city. That part was easy enough. The rest was . . . not so easy. I spent years roaming, living like a scavenger, eventually making my way into the woods of Gorsedd—fae territory—where a sidhé fae Elder took me in. Edan taught me the basics, how to care for myself, to bathe, to shave, how to eat properly, read and write, how to defend myself both physically and mentally.

"And eventually he told me the story of the king of Fiallan. How a traitor, a *Malakim*, had killed the king." Hank shook his head, staring off into the darkness ahead of us. "I wasn't thinking about murder or that he'd die. I wanted them to know, to hear me . . . I guess if I'd been thinking straight I would've realized no one comes out of those towers alive."

Except Hank, I thought. "Is that what happened, you think? He was trapped in there like the others until he grew old?"

"No. Edan said the king died shortly after I escaped. I guess the Circe removed him too quickly and it killed him. They put another child in my place, the king's son took over the throne, and a bounty was placed on my head. Nearly a hundred years had passed from the time I'd fled until Edan told me the truth. I guess he finally thought I was ready to hear it."

"And, of course, he'd figured out your part in the story."

Hank smiled. "From the very beginning, I'm sure."

"You loved him," I said, seeing it in his smile, in the admiration and softness in his voice.

Hank shrugged, a muscle in his jaw flexing. "I was with him for almost two hundred years before he died. He made me promise to never go back to Fiallan. He knew I wanted to return, to tell everyone the truth of what *Malakim* really means, but he feared my death even though so much time had passed. He wanted me to leave Gorsedd and make a new life somewhere far away. So I went to Murias—a siren city far from Fiallan. That was . . . an eye-opener . . ."

"How so?"

He turned and cocked an eyebrow. "I wasn't like other sirens, Charlie. I learned everything I could from Edan except for the one thing sirens are known for besides their voice."

Oh.

He chuckled softly at me, and then gave a nonchalant shrug. "I was a dedicated student."

"Ha. I bet you were," I muttered, concentrating on the path. "So how did you wind up in Atlanta?"

"I was only in Murias for a year when the existence

of our world and Charbydon was revealed, and I saw my opportunity to leave Elysia and make good on my promise to Edan."

"You don't fear living out in the open? Even if it is in another world?"

He shook his head. "Who would know me? My family hasn't seen me since I was six. Only the Circe know me as a full-grown siren, and they never leave Fiallan. The only one who knows me is Pendaran."

"How does Pen know?"

"He was sent to Edan for study one season. Edan was a hermit, but one whose reputation preceded him. One only found his hut if he wanted them to. Apparently he thought the druid worthy and accepted him."

"You said you and Pen knew each other as children. I guess that wasn't entirely true, then."

"Well, I was still a child in a lot of ways, so maybe partially true."

"That's a stretch."

We settled into a comfortable silence as I mulled over Hank's story. I never would've guessed he'd had such a troubled past. He never let on, never walked around with a chip on his shoulder or a woe-is-me attitude.

He'd been through so much. So much betrayal, from his people, his king, even his family. And all the obstacles he'd had to overcome; learning how to function in society again, even learning how to read and write, to interact . . . I grew angry, so pissed on his behalf that I wanted to go to Elysia and stop this barbaric practice myself. How cruel—using children to protect a city that didn't even *need* protecting.

"Do you think your family or the people of Fiallan would listen to your story now?" I asked.

He shook his head. "No. My story has passed into something of a legend where I play the villain. My family was disgraced. They denounced me, lost their position of honor that the *Malakim* had always afforded them. I'm sure they'd kill me on sight, if they could," he said with a wry smile.

"And the sirens in the terminal? You think it was Llyran who told them who you are, what you look like?" Llyran had called Hank *Malakim*. Somehow he'd discovered the truth. And Llyran certainly had the psychopathic drive to find intense pleasure in seeing Hank suffer.

"Him or Nuallan Gow."

I blinked and my step faltered. "Nuallan Gow? How the hell would the Master Crafter of Atlanta know who you really are?" A mental image of her swam in my head. Black crafter extraordinaire, a ghoul in the guise of a beautiful human, and the bitch who had slept with my husband and tried to have me killed. Nuallan was a plague, a bad rash that kept coming back to haunt me.

"Probably figured it out from my ring. Every *Malakim* is given a ring. It's special. It grows with you, stays on you from the time you enter until the time you leave. It signifies my family's contribution to the *Malakim*."

My stomach knotted. "The ring you bribed Nuallan with to help us spell Aaron's body when he died." I stopped. My mouth fell open. "Un-fucking-believable. How could you give her something that could identify you? We could've bartered for something else, Hank! Given her another reason to help us . . ."

"She wanted my ring. There are only a handful of people who could have known what it meant. The writing on it is the sirens' ancient language, not even used today . . . The stone is where the value lies. I assumed that's why she wanted it."

"How could you be so blasé about it? Why? Why did you do that? Why did you even keep the thing if it could identify you?"

"I gave it to her because Aaron was dying," he said simply. He stopped, dragging a hand through his sweat-soaked hair, and then stared at me with conviction in those glittering sapphire eyes. "We were there on that porch with time running out. She was the only person who could've saved him and she wanted my ring in return. I made the only choice I could."

My mouth opened and closed. I wanted to rail at him, to fault him, but I couldn't. How could I? He'd saved Aaron's life. It was noble and right, and goddamn the sirens in Elysia for thinking him anything *but* honorable. Goddamn his king, the Circe, and his family for turning their backs on him. Damn them all.

I marched away, so angry that tears blurred my vision. He caught up with me and grabbed my arm. As soon as he saw the sheen in my eyes, he stiffened.

A curtain of iron fell over his features. "Don't you dare pity me, Charlie. I can handle most anything but that."

"How do you expect me to feel?" I jerked from his hold. "I can't help but feel sorry for that little boy who was robbed of a life. How can I not? As a human being, as a mother . . . I can't stand even hearing about a child being abused or abandoned, betrayed by those who are supposed to love him! How can I not feel for the child you were?"

His icy façade cracked. Anger flared around us. His fingers parked on his hips—a sign he was about to argue—but I shouted over him as he spoke. "I don't pity the person you are now! I'm proud to even say I know you, and I sure as hell don't want you going back now! So don't you yell at me!"

My chest was heaving. Power coiled in my gut. I realized I was the one yelling, not him, so my words didn't make a whole lot of sense, but . . . Tears slipped hot down my cheeks. Frustration built inside until I could do nothing else but make fists, growl, and march away.

He'd stepped up. He'd defied authority and he fought to rebuild his life and reinvent himself. He'd come to my world. Alone. In a foreign place. Without anyone. Damn right, I was proud of him. And he could go to hell if he thought that was pity.

I got five steps before he grabbed my arm and turned me around. Bleak thunderstorms gathered in his expression. His Adam's apple bobbed. His head shook slightly as though he didn't know quite what to do. His lips thinned in sudden determination as he reached out, hauled me close, and hugged me.

Surprise made me stiff as a board. His pulse beat hard through his neck. I felt it pumping against the side of my chin. We were sticky and sweaty and gritty, but it didn't matter. My hands slid around to the hard planes of his back. I relaxed. It felt . . . good. Safe. Comforting.

"You really piss me off," I muttered against his shirt.

He kissed the top of my head, tucked my dirty, sandy hair behind my ear, and then graced me with a crooked smile that dimpled his scruffy cheek. "A clear indication you like me, Madigan."

I rolled my eyes, not bothering to lift my head, but I couldn't stop the ridiculous laughter. "Oh my God," I breathed. "We are so screwed." In so many ways. "What will they do if they catch you?"

"They'd probably put me back in the grid and make sure I can't get out. That would be worse than death and the Circe know it."

And his life would basically be over. Time would pass, people would come and go, and Hank would be stuck again. But he could break free from it. He'd done so before.

"No, Charlie," he said, perceiving my thoughts. "It took me a long time to break free. You. Emma. Everyone I know would be gone by the time I'd manage it again—if I even could. And by then . . ." He shrugged. "What would be the point? Everyone I care about would be gone. I might as well stay there." His jaw flexed and I could see he was uncomfortable talking about the mortality of those he cared for. "We should get going."

He took the lead this time.

I stayed quiet, mulling over his words and everything he'd gone through. He never had a life until he came to Atlanta. All those times his humor was off or he seemed a little schizo, or he steered me away from his past however he could . . . Now it all made sense. He'd been in my world for many years now, but he was still learning how to interact in human terms, learning all the subtle sarcasms and ironies and meanings of my culture. In projecting certain attitudes and behaviors, learning how to joke and make me laugh. I'm sure he'd taken his time learning about women as well, and according to Zara, he must've learned pretty damn quick in *that* department.

But I was glad Hank wasn't the usual siren with a couple hundred years' worth of notches on his bedpost. I was glad he wasn't a jaded, narcissistic ass like a lot of male sirens I'd come into contact with. And despite all he'd been through, he brimmed with iron will, strength, confidence, determination . . . He'd certainly come into his own as a member of society, as a man—a damn good one, too.

18

Hank and I hiked for what had to be a few more hours at least. The stubborn grains of sand still lurking in my shoes had rubbed my heels raw. My aches and pains from the fall still lingered, but I was too tired to heal myself, too tired to care, and too emotionally exhausted to do anything except put one foot in front of the other.

Eventually, the ravine grew shallow. The direction turned north, so we climbed out to stay on an easterly track. The slant and the jagged rocks made it easy to grab footholds and handholds in the ravine walls. The sky remained clear of nithyn. Nevertheless, as soon as I made it out, I stayed down and turned to call for Brim, letting out a low whistle.

He circled below, whined, and then ran at the wall, his long claws digging in and propelling him up the rock.

"Good boy," I whispered, patting his head.

I crept over the rocky outcroppings to where Hank lay on his stomach and dropped down beside him. The low gray sand dunes that greeted me caused a shudder to rush down my spine.

Across the sand, the dunes rose to another ridge that fanned out into a plateau littered with ruins. Moonlight shone over gigantic slabs of broken stone. A few intact columns jutted into the sky and practically glowed in the light. Others had fallen or were broken in half. A large Throne Tree grew on one corner of the ruins.

"Look," Hank whispered, pointing up.

Three nithyn flew over the ruins, circling like vultures. One dove down and landed at a fresh nithyn carcass that looked like it had been torn apart. The handle of an axe jutted up from the dead animal. "Looks like Rex had his work cut out for him."

"The nithyn are still circling. Rex and Bryn must have made it inside the ruins. We need to get you inside and through the portal."

"Wait a minute." I stared at his profile. "What do you mean, *me*?"

"Meaning if anything goes wrong, you go through that portal with or without me. If you're not back in time to receive the sylph's gift of fire, the other gifts will kill you. So what I'm saying is, don't risk it."

I hated this kind of talk. I started to say something to that effect and he stopped me. "I'm serious. You have a family, Charlie. That trumps everything else, including saving or waiting for my ass. I want your word."

My family meant everything to me; he was right about that. But the fact that he didn't consider himself important as well truly annoyed me—that and the rocks poking my ribs. "I think you're failing to recognize one very important thing."

"Enlighten me, then."

"You're my family, too."

I meant it, but I couldn't help but smirk because the times were few and far between when I could make Hank Williams utterly and completely speechless.

His mouth actually fell open. His irises shifted from sapphire to topaz blue as though he had no idea how to feel. His lips snapped shut and he looked as though he was about to make a comeback, but then frowned when he realized he didn't actually have one.

I reached out and patted him on the shoulder. "Didn't think of that one, did you, siren?"

I belly-crawled closer to the edge of the rocks. After a moment he joined me, his face a bit redder than before.

"Hank?" I said, a thought occurring. "Rex said to concentrate on a specific place when you go through the portal. That's how you arrive at your destination. I want you to think of a place those sirens can't find you. Don't come back with me."

He was shaking his head before I even finished talking. "I ran the first time because I was vulnerable and weak. I didn't know how to defend myself. But that's in the past, Charlie. I'm done running."

"Oh, and then what? They take you and put you back in the grid? All because you're too proud to run?"

His eyes rolled. "Thanks for the vote of confidence."

"That's not what I meant."

"Isn't it?"

"No." I blinked, feeling confused. "I just mean it's a bunch of them against two of us. By now they'll know where you work, who your friends are, everything about your life. What's so wrong with laying low for a little while?"

"Because they will *always* have someone watching my old life, that's why. That means I can never come back. This time, I fight. For what's mine. For the life I've made. I know what I promised Edan, but there are *Malakim* in those towers who don't deserve to be there, and when they run out of steam, more children will fill their places. I kept that ring as a reminder. I've always known one day I'd go back and stop them. I'm not running away, Charlie. This time, I'm no child in a man's body."

I knew about making a stand. I'd done the same. I'd fought for my life. I'd fought to keep my daughter. I'd chosen to bring darkness to the city in order to save my kid. How could I lay there and convince him to not do what he thought was right?

"Fine," I finally said. "Let's just get back to the station. We'll figure out something from there."

He leaned slightly so he could reach out and flick the ends of my hair. He winked. "That's better."

I rolled my eyes. "Yeah, whatever."

He eyed the nithyn and the mile or so we had to run across the sand. "You ready?"

I let out a deep sigh "No. But when does that ever matter?"

"Before we go," he said as I turned to him, "I think this is the part where we're supposed to kiss before facing mortal danger."

I blinked, flustered for a second by the change in direction. I was starting to suspect Hank took great pleasure in keeping me off-balance like this. "Says the guy who's pretty much immortal," I pointed out.

A boyish white smile broadened his face and crinkled the corners of his eyes. "Just admit it, Madigan. You like me. And saying so before we get ourselves seriously injured would be good."

"Sure, what's not to like?" I said flatly, rolling my eyes.

He frowned. "I *am* a siren. There is a difference between being into *me* and being into the siren."

So which one was it? While I was the type of person who, no matter how gorgeous the guy, could be turned off by a shitty personality, a siren was a different story. Whether you wanted to or not you were lured in. So in that respect, Hank's question had merit. And unlike most sirens I knew, he actually cared about the answer.

But more importantly, I saw the vulnerability in his words.

He wanted to be liked, not because he was a siren, but as a person, one who wasn't as confident as he let on. One who never got a chance to grow his confidence naturally like the rest of us. One who'd been forsaken by his family, his race, and the girl who promised to wait for him.

Of course, he was completely confident in his virility, in his power and ability to attract and please. That was never in question. But under all that was a vulnerable soul who wanted someone to care about him—not because of *what* he was, but because of *who* he was.

"Charlie, when we get back . . . if they come for me, I don't want you to fight."

It was my turn to frown. "And you've known me how long?" I shook my head. I knew why he said the words, but they made me angry, too. "Forget it. If you think I'm going to let them take you back to Fiallan, think again."

He leaned in, slid a hand behind my neck, pulled me toward him, and kissed me hard. Then he leaned back and searched my face. "Thank you. You don't owe me. I didn't have anything to lose when I fought for you and Em. No children, no family, no one waiting for me back home. You have everything to lose, and those who came through the gate won't care."

I swallowed hard. "I'll do what I think is right. You don't even know what we'll face when we get back."

"Yeah. Unfortunately I do." He looked out over the sandy plain and sighed. "I'll take the one on the column." The biggest nithyn perched on the top of a broken column. The other two flew circles above. Waiting. Waiting. "Can you run and use your power at the same time?"

"I can try."

"I guess we run like hell." He was already surging to his feet.

I ran after him. Brim bolted past me in a blur of speed.

We made it halfway across the plain before the nithyn spotted us. Hank stopped and lured the one coming in fast.

He stood still, waiting and mumbling, luring, enticing the beast to dive faster and faster. Closer and closer. I stopped running and screamed his name. Hank dove at the very last second. The nithyn crashed into the ground. Hank rolled, leapt up, grabbed its neck before it could get its bearings, twisted, and broke it. Patient. Efficient. Deadly.

"Charlie, duck!"

I belly flopped immediately, not even looking at the incoming bird. Wind blew over my face. Sand pinged me. Claws dug into my back. I screamed. Air rushed down all around me as the nithyn lifted.

A shot of nitro hit the tip of its wing.

I flailed, reaching around to grab at the leathery ankle. After three tries I got a good hold, sending everything I had into my grip.

Cold, cold, cold, I chanted, I imagined, I felt . . .

It dropped me six feet above the ground and let out a wounded cry. I landed belly first in the sand, flipped over, finally able to pull my gun, only to see the largest nithyn crash into the wounded one.

They tumbled through the air, landing in a rolling ball. I looked away from the macabre scene and focused on getting back on my feet.

A few feet in front of me, Brim circled and whined. He lay down and rested his jaw between his front legs. Alarm crept up my spine. I went for Brim, but only made it one step before I came face-to-face with the shadow creature.

I drew up short and gasped. Brim whined again.

It hovered inches from the ground. A tall, black form without solid mass and as terrifying as before.

Had it jumped planes? Jesus. My mind raced. Had it sensed my use of power earlier and had come after me? Come this far? Sensed it from another world?

What the hell was this thing?

My fingers flexed on the grip of my gun.

I saw beyond it to Hank. He was running toward me. Sand kicked up and circled around me and this creature. It spoke and the ground under my feet trembled.

Shadowy tendrils reached out, wrapping around me. The main mass of the creature pulled toward me in a blink so fast it seemed like one minute it was a few feet from me and the next it was inches from my face.

I swallowed, poised and still, utterly at the mercy of this thing.

Darkness that went on forever is the only thing I saw on the inside of this creature. Yet somewhere inside of it was a voice, a mouth, some type of creature, I was sure of it. Maybe one that didn't *want* to be seen . . .

It spoke again, this time with an inflection that suggested a question had been posed. My body thrummed, the words ebbing deep into my bones. A question I had no idea how to answer.

Then it drew back, spun, drawing all of the shadows back into itself. It disappeared like a puff of wind, gone on a breeze. The sand tornado around me dropped. Brim lifted his head, stood, and shook off the sand as Hank came to a stop, heaving from the run. "That was it? That was the creature?"

I nodded, rubbing my arms as the nithyn's death cries drew goose bumps along my skin. It made me shiver, cold despite the heat of the hot, dry dunes. At least it hadn't gone *through* me this time.

Hank was staring oddly at me. "You realize it jumped planes."

Yeah. I did. And it scared the shit out of me. If that thing was lured by my power and had the ability to cross dimensions whenever I used it . . . Not good. It had probably felt the first time I used my power fighting off the sand lizards and it had just taken some time to get here. All it had to do was hang around and wait for me to use it again and voilà.

"Come on, they can't be far behind us." I took off toward the ruins.

The ruins of the Temple of the Moon were colossal. Stone blocks the size of city buses littered the ground. Yet another testament to the god-like structures of the off-worlders.

"Rex said the portal is under the altar." I climbed onto a fallen column where I stood to survey the complex, trying to envision it as it had once been, to get a better idea of where the main temple might be. A piece of Bryn's skirt had been wedged between two stones, a marker from Rex no doubt. "Hank! Over here!" I slid off the column and scrambled over the ruins.

Hank studied the narrow, slanted opening near the stones. "Footprints, too," he noted, looking around. Brim trotted over and began sniffing. He darted inside the dark passageway. I pulled out my flashlight.

The passage was only wide enough for us to go single file. Blocks of stones stuck out of the walls, making us twist and angle our bodies around to make way. Eventually the space opened up to a larger area filled with fallen stones. The floor was streaked with footsteps. Rex must've cleared enough stone away to make the small passage.

I climbed through. "Be careful. This leads down into steps."

Stone debris littered the way, but the going was

relatively simple and soon we came to a dark chamber deep beneath the temple complex. Our lights beamed over large stones, fitted perfectly together. Side reliefs of jinn warriors had been carved into the walls, enemies and creatures subdued beneath their feet. Two ancient fire basins of black marble sat at opposite sides of the room.

In the center of the floor ringed in smooth black stones was a circular pool. Very shallow and filled with a substance that looked like liquid mercury.

"What is that?"

Hank stopped beside me. "The portal; I don't see anything else down here that could be it."

"Well, they were here. Their footprints are all over the place." My light trailed over the dusty floor. "And look, there's a dusty handprint on the stones. They must've made it through . . ."

Hank knelt down, examining the stones.

"Rex said to feed my power and think of where we wanted to go. He said the station, to concentrate on the station. The cell block."

"Using your power draws that creature. I'll use mine."

"You think Elysian power is going to work in a Charbydon-created portal?" I asked dubiously.

"We can try." He placed his hands on the stones and closed his eyes. Instantly the energy in the place changed. A soft yellow glow began to form beneath his palms.

And nothing else happened.

Finally he opened his eyes, his brow furrowed. "Let me try this." This time he stuck his hands into the pool. The strange liquid seemed to conduct power and the entire thing shimmered in a golden light and then dimmed. Again, nothing.

"Here, let me try." I returned my flashlight to my belt. "If this works, we'll be gone before the Grim Reaper gets here. If he jumps planes behind us, we'll deal with it at the station." All that mattered was getting home. "You ready?" I asked.

Hank nodded. I shoved my dirty hands into the liquid. It closed around my skin, heavy and thick, the consistency of honey, but dry and cool. I closed my eyes and brought to mind the hum, the memory of the power—how it tingled through my body, set me alive . . .

"It's working." Hank said.

I peeked. The pool shimmered blue, very similar to the colors of the sphere back at the terminals in Telmath and Atlanta. It began to swirl, going around and around until it resembled a whirlpool, the middle a long, bottomless pit.

"Hook your arm in mine," I said. "Think of the station, the cell block . . ."

"Are you sure?"

"Yeah." I just hoped Bryn had been strong enough to think for herself and concentrate on the cell block, too.

"And the hellhound?"

I whistled Brim over. "I sure as hell hope he's

thinking about Emma, or his bed, or his ball . . ." But he was going in that portal with us. It was better than leaving him here. "You whistle for him when we go," I told Hank. "I'm going to put all my concentration on the cell. Ready?"

He nodded. I closed my eyes and focused on our destination, seeing it in my mind, the colors, the smells, the architecture . . . I remembered it until I felt as though I was standing there.

I let my body fall forward, one hand in the liquid, my other arm crooked around Hank's. He moved with me. I heard his soft whistle to Brim and then we were falling into the spinning pool of liquid.

It sucked me in, coated me, and squeezed me tightly; taking me away from everything I'd ever known until the only thing remaining was silence. A vast, black silence. Slowly I became aware of Hank, our elbows still locked together. I held on tightly, linking my fingers and clinging for dear life.

The cell, the cell, the cell . . .

19

Being weightless with no sense of place or time didn't prepare me for my face meeting the hard tile floor of Station One. I sucked in a shocked gasp as pain exploded. Blood, warm and thick, spilled from my nose and onto the floor. "Fuck," I slurred as the sense of physical weight settled into me and the coppery taste of my own blood hit the back of my throat.

Hank cursed and groaned. "Note to self," he rasped. "Don't go in face-first."

My fingers curled. I swallowed. The veins in my head pounded. I pushed up—very slowly—more nauseous than when I'd stepped through the terminal portal. Blood ran down and along the crease of my lips. I wiped it away with the back of my hand and then gazed around, finding the light very bright.

"Whoa. That's some funky-ass shit right there," came Kyle's voice.

Kyle. Kyle was an *ash* victim. In the cell block.

We'd made it.

"You guys just appeared out of nowhere, man."

I struggled to my feet, falling once before I got up and then grabbed the wall for support. My vision wavered. "Where's my sister? Was she here? Did she come here?"

"Fuck you, Charlie Brown," Kyle said, snickering at his lame joke.

I shot him the middle finger. *Right back at ya, buddy.*

"She came out of nowhere just like you two," said the *ash* victim who'd helped me before, "with another guy. She ran out of here, and he ran after her."

"Shit." I shook my head, trying to clear the drunken-like haze. "How long?"

"Like a couple minutes ago. They were like you, though. Drugged or something. It took them a while to get up."

Yeah. Not drugged; screwed up by an ancient portal. There had probably been some kind of spell or pill the traveler took before jumping into that spinning pool. Or maybe you just had to be a jinn to go through without ill effects.

I sniffed in blood and coughed, wiping at my nose again as I staggered from the cell block.

Frustration ate at me as I struggled slowly up the steps to the main floor of Station One. *Brim wasn't in the cell block*. He hadn't come with us, and I could only hope he'd made it somewhere safe. Once I reached the main floor and staggered out of the back door and onto the landing, I pushed the worrisome thought from my mind and scanned the parking lot.

Bryn stumbled across the parking lot with Rex hot on her heels. Hank burst out behind me.

"BRYN!" I ran down the steps, missing the last one, and hit the pavement in a sprawl. My palms slid over the concrete, peeling skin as they went. I kept my fuzzy vision on my sister, though, determined to not lose her. Not again.

Surprisingly she heard me, stopped, and shouted, "I have to get to—"

Rex slammed into her and they went down.

I sucked in a breath with a single-minded purpose—get to my sister—and forced myself up. Hank's hand gripped my elbow, helping me to stand. We swayed together. He was pale. Sweat glistened on his face and his steps were more unbalanced than mine. Being Elysian, I bet he'd gotten a shittier dose of Charbydon travel sickness than me.

We were halfway across the lot when two sirens stepped out of shadows.

No.

"Don't *make* me hurt you," Rex's words echoed over the lot as he finally got the upper hand and sat on top of my sister, pinning her front to the ground. She screamed, kicking and flailing with drunken limbs.

"Let. Me. Go!" she wailed in a tired, desperate voice.

"So it is true," one of the sirens said as he moved to block our way to Bryn and Rex. He and his friend were as tall as Hank and their expressions held intense loathing and a gleam that said they'd just *love* to take him down right there.

"Traitor. Murderer," the other one growled, clenching and unclenching his fists.

"The king got the same punishment he inflicted on every *Malakim* who ever served him," Hank forced out. "He was a lia—"

The siren's fist shot out and connected with Hank's jaw with a sickening crack. The force sent him to his knees. The fact that he didn't lay flat-out cold was a testament to his strength. I grabbed his bicep and tried to help him to his feet.

"The others will be here soon and then we'll have a nice little . . . *talk* before we take you back to Fiallan. The Circe are eager to get their hands on you."

Rex cursed, drawing my attention. He was doubled over, holding his privates. Bryn struggled out from his hold, turned to glance over her shoulder. Her eyes went wide when she saw me. And then she started running, weaving drunkenly into the darkness.

"NO!" I surged forward, but the sirens blocked my path.

I shoved one of them. Hands grabbed me as Hank tackled the one in front of him. I fought like a maniac. It wasn't pretty or effective. I bit, pulled hair, fought as dirty as my drunken state allowed, but the only thing I managed to do was tire myself more and gain a few more bruises.

We were too weak to do anything. We couldn't outrun them, outthink them, or outfight them. Hot tears ran down my cheeks. I screamed at them, struggling, telling them they couldn't take him. One of them shoved me to the ground. My elbows hit the pavement hard. My eyes met Hank's. The siren had him stomach-down on the pavement, pinning the back of his neck with a knee.

"Go, Charlie," he ground out. "Find Bryn. Before she—"

I sat up and swiped a hand across my wet face. "I . . . I'll fix this, I—"

His eyes hardened, filling up with resignation and a warning. "Don't . . ." The siren jerked Hank up.

Don't make a promise you can't keep, he might as well have said. Don't be that girl who had promised to wait.

One of the sirens laughed as I pushed to my feet. "Consorting with humans?" The other siren chuckled. "That is beneath even a traitor."

Hank spun out of the hold, elbowed the siren's nose, cracking the bone, and then used the last of his strength to slug the siren in front of me with a hard right to the jaw. *Payback is a bitch*. It was a brilliant hit. The guy flew back and landed hard on his back.

Hank swayed on his feet. "Go, Charlie. Hurry!"

I froze.

"DAMN IT, GO!"

I jumped.

By the corner of the station, I saw three more sirens appear. Shit, shit, shit. They ran for us. I glanced from them to Hank. "Goddammit, Charlie," he muttered and threw himself in their path, fists flying.

"Hank." I meant it as a shout, but it came out as a whisper. My stomach rolled. The parking lot went fuzzy.

Move, Charlie. Keep going.

Tears streamed down my face. I ran. In the opposite direction, feeling as though my heart was tearing in two. Running away went against everything I was. But I was running toward something else—my sister. Hank was giving me a chance to save her. I grabbed Rex's elbow on my way and we hurried after Bryn.

As I ran, my strength returned with each step, each beat of my pounding heart, pushing the effects of the portal out of my system.

"Where the hell is she going?!" Rex yelled as Bryn ran ahead of us, dodging drunkenly into traffic, across streets, through pedestrians.

Christ. I had no idea who was in charge of her body, but with the cuffs on her wrists, and the travel sickness obviously hindering her, we had to catch her before she got herself killed. Accidentally or on purpose.

Block after block, street after street . . .

I was gaining on her. I'd always been the faster runner.

And then it hit me as we darted through a line of limos, down a familiar street, past the League's school. Holy hell. She was going to the Mordecai House.

The League of Mages mansion shone like a beacon, lit up with festive white lights for the New Year's Eve Party. Cars were lined up along the street and around the corner. Guests in tuxedoes and sequined gowns walked down the sidewalk and mingled within the grounds. Music poured from the house.

Bryn darted between cars, sliding over the hood of one, tumbling and popping right back up and racing for the mansion, hair dirty, blood caking her front, torn skirt flying out behind her.

She bounded up the wide front stairs, shoving people aside, broke through the line, and disappeared into the house.

I was right behind her, mimicking every step, screaming for people to move out the way. I called out my law enforcement status, leaping over potted plants, adrenaline driving me closer and closer.

I made it through the open double doors right after her and leapt.

Gotcha!

We went down in the packed foyer. People screamed. Glasses broke. The floor cleared as we tumbled down the hall, sliding into the ballroom, taking out two waiters and two trays full of champagne.

"Charlie, stop! Aaron! Help me!" Bryn screamed and cried so loud, I almost loosened my hold on her. "Get these cuffs off me, please! Aaron!"

Before we even came to a stop, her foot connected with my gut and she got free. I grabbed her ankle, tripping her up. She yelled. I yelled back. And to anyone watching, it probably seemed like the catfight of the century with two wild women caked with blood, dust, sand, and sweat.

I crawled over her, finally getting a hand on the side of her face and shoving her down and holding her there, breathing heavily.

"Mom?!"

I glanced up, dazed. "Emma?" I blew a strand of matted hair from my eyes and used my bicep to wipe the sweat from my forehead. She wore a cute knee-length sequined dress and her hand rested on Brim's back. A sudden sob of relief burst from my mouth. My shoulders slumped. The portal had dumped him where he wanted to be. With Em.

Bryn used the distraction, rolling out from under me, twisting her body as she sat up, slid behind me, and draped her linked arms over my head, putting me in a headlock and choking with her forearm.

Emma screamed.

The pressure widened my eyes. My windpipe closed. I threw out my hand to stop Emma from helping. If she hurt Bryn or Bryn hurt her, neither one would forgive herself.

"BRYN MADIGAN!!!!" The booming voice radiated through the ballroom. The massive chandelier shook, the crystals tinkling together like rain in the ensuing silence.

Bryn eased up, but only slightly. I could feel her head turn in the direction of the familiar, powerful voice.

Aaron strode across the ballroom floor, his emerald eyes burning with intensity. His dark Celtic looks bordered on barbaric, his face frightening and stark. Gone was the scholar and in his place was a pissed-off warlock who had had *enough*.

I pulled at Bryn's arm, flailing with my feet, trying to catch my heels on the floor to push back against her, needing desperately to breathe, but my heels kept slipping.

"I'm the one you really want to fight," he said, taunting her in a deep, challenging tone. "I'm the one who hasn't forgiven you for killing me. I'm the one who holds back, who might . . . not . . . *love* you anymore."

"STOP IT!" she shrieked so loudly, her voice broke, the words forced from a place so raw and broken.

I knew what he was doing: pulling her out, making her angry, making her strong enough to fight against Solomon's hold. But even I wanted him to stop. She was hurt enough.

Her hold lessened. Her entire body trembled. "I came back here for you!" she cried and I could hear the rejection and the heartbreak Aaron's words had caused her.

"Fight, Bryn," I rasped, tears falling for her. "Please fight . . ."

"Oh crap," a feminine voice I didn't recognize

rang out over the ballroom. "Did the party start without me?"

A slim female sauntered into my line of sight, stopping at my feet and staring down at me with a pout. Her face was tiny like her sisters'. She was dressed in a black mini, black leather thigh-high boots, and a tight tank that bared her midriff. A small, dangling belly button ring of a bejeweled flame flashed in the light. Her hair was long and wavy and the most intense red I'd ever seen. Her slanted eyes were framed by long lashes beneath yellow irises flecked with copper. A light splattering of freckles crossed her nose.

The last sylph. And her timing couldn't have been worse.

20

"You ready to receive my gift, Charlie Madigan?" Aaron and Rex stepped forward, but the fire sylph turned on them, eyeing them both boldly. "I suggest you take a step back, fellas. It's about to get very hot in here."

She turned to me, cocked her hip, and tilted her head.

"Let them take her," I forced out, nodding toward Aaron and Rex. My hands were wrapped around Bryn's arm as she choked me. Her strength had waned and I could feel her surrender as she shook uncontrollably, still in a battle of wills with Solomon. The sylph snapped her fingers.

Aaron stepped forward and placed an amulet over Bryn's head. She stiffened, her eyes went wide, and she screamed at him in a piercing string of curses. I ducked down, out of her hold, gasping.

Once Aaron and Rex drug Bryn away, I started sweating.

"Name's Melki. Do you accept my gift?"

"Yes." I flicked a glance to Emma. "It's okay."

Melki followed my gaze. "That your kid?" she asked without taking her eyes off Emma. "Nice dress."

"Thank you," Emma responded politely. "And if you hurt my mom"—her tone went flat, completely devoid of emotion—"I will kill you." Her big brown eyes stayed on the sylph, harder than I'd ever seen. My chest grew tight with emotion.

Melki chuckled. "Kid's got a little fire in her."

She turned her attention back to me and lost the smile.

I tensed as energy built around her. The temperature increased. Her hand lifted, palm up. A flame burst from the skin. Her irises glowed fire. Her hand went higher, making a swirling motion with her wrist, which her body followed, turning her into a spinning flame—one that shot toward me before I could even blink.

It hit me square in the chest, tunneling into my body and burning a path straight to my heart. My back hit the floor. A gasp froze on my lips as the familiar pain/shock of a sudden burn seared a path through every limb, every vein, blood vessel, cell . . . My eyes stayed open but my vision was lost to a glaze of orange fuzz.

Accept my gift.

I'd become my beating heart. I could see it as

though I stared outside of myself. Pumping. Contracting. Expanding. A muscle that frantically worked, that burned, fueled by fear and pain, causing it to speed up at a wild, dizzying rate.

The muscle burst.

There was nothing but silence. No heartbeat. No pain. Nothing.

Water. Air. Earth. Fire. They exist in their purest forms inside of you.

I saw into the dead husk of my body where four tiny lights began to shine.

They are the very essence of Earth, the gifts of this world, and together they create power, that which cannot be seen, but exists all around you. The true power of this world. Nwyvre. The Hidden Element.

As Melki spoke in my subconscious, I watched as the lights came together from different parts of my body and met in my brain, bursting into a rainbow of color, intensifying until a ball of white glowed in my head directly behind the center of my forehead.

Now you see. Open your mind, Charlie Madigan, and see the truth.

I sat up, pulled like a puppet on a string, and opened my eyes. No. That wasn't quite accurate. My eyes didn't physically open, yet I saw the ballroom through the white glow in my mind. My vision was filtered through this hidden eye and everything was ringed in white, ringed with the truth.

I searched the wall, finding Bryn as she stood wrapped in Aaron's hold. Poor Bryn. Inside of her was a haze, the gray shadow of a man—a seething, angry soul lashing out against the barrier of Aaron's amulet.

Solomon's shadow stilled and I knew he saw me. He bared his teeth. He cursed. Then, beneath him, tired and worn, a shriveled light that was my sister's spirit stirred. Still there. Still hanging on. *Oh, Bryn . . .*

The people before me, the ballroom, everything seemed stuck in slow motion, the white of my vision moving dreamlike from one person to the next as I *saw* not only into them but also what they were made of, their characters or the true nature of their spirits.

Emma: Purity. Hope. Strength.

Brimstone: Devotion. Loyalty. Sacrifice.

Aaron: Determination. Honor. Conflict.

The white flared as I came to Rex. Rex with the indomitable jinn spirit. A big personality. I saw him as he used to be thousands of years ago: large, powerful, confident, but now shaped by time and circumstance. Changed so that creativity and vitality glowed around him. How he loved life.

My breath caught. *Oh God*. Will!

Beyond the spirit of Rex was my ex-husband, his dormant soul stirring, as though waking up from a long slumber. His form so thin, like a wisp of smoke. But it was him. It swirled and turned and saw me like Solomon had. He had become a shadow of his old self.

Charlie. His voice. In my head. *I'm sorry.*

I was crying, though I felt no tears sliding down

my face in the strange state I was in, but I knew my body was shedding tears. It hurt too much not to.

Set me free, Charlie.

No, Will.

I've seen beyond. I'm not meant to be here. Please. Please give me peace. Rest. Freedom.

But . . . Emma.

Emma will understand. I'm not meant for this world. Not anymore.

I don't know how.

He lifted a hand, and smiled gently. *Yes, you do, wife.*

A sob stuck in my throat. Eleven years I'd been his wife. And I'd loved him, had been happy for so many years and envisioned growing old together. I still loved him, just not in the same way as before.

And now he was asking me to set him free. I wasn't sure I could.

Take my hand. Please.

At the edge of my vision, I saw my hand ringed in white lifting; saw it moving toward him. Our fingers touched and white glowed brighter from the tips.

And then my hand slid into his. He smiled; the old Will Garrity smile that could melt snow.

Tell Emma I love her and will be watching over her always. She must understand I cannot come back whole and full like I was before. No matter if Rex leaves, I will not come back . . . right. Tell her this, Charlie. Make her understand. I never meant to hurt her. Never meant to hurt you.

I nodded, pulling back slightly. He slid gently and effortlessly from his physical body. I didn't want to let go, but I found myself releasing him anyway. His form grew dimmer and dimmer, though his smile remained until he simply vanished.

Pain squeezed a heart I no longer had.

Grief wafted through my subconscious. So much regret, so much lost . . . He was gone. Will Garrity, the man I married at nineteen, the father of my child, the one with whom I'd made so many memories, was gone.

I watched with heartbreak and fascination as Rex's spirit filled out Will's body, settling into every part of him, making links, forming new connections. Tiny sparks flew from these new links as though Rex's jinn spirit was finally free to extend *all* of what he was . . .

With a sudden thought, I turned back to Bryn. Again, I reached out my hand. *Take it. Take my hand and I can set you free.* Solomon glared at me. *It's over. You had your revenge. Release my sister.*

The glow around my vision dimmed. I understood immediately that the gift of Nwyvre was fleeting, that it was already leaving me.

Hurry! Take my hand!

Solomon cursed me, the stubborn fool. It was there, the desire to be free, I could see it clearly, and yet he wouldn't take my hand, wouldn't reach out to me.

Solomon!

Finally he lifted his hand, but I was moving backward, away from him. I reached anyway. *No!*

Goddammit! I hadn't gone through all of this to

fail now. I was not moving another inch. With sheer, stubborn determination, I went deep into my mind, into this beautiful white glow in my head, and I forced it to remain, holding the elements together just a little bit longer.

I lost all sensation in my body. Everything in me sharpened in complete and utter focus. I *became* light. No longer did I look through it. No longer did my subconscious work outside of it. This light, this beautiful, white, healing, truthful light, encompassed all of me. Or I encompassed it. I wasn't sure.

Nwyvre I understood now. It existed all around us, more in some places than in others, like in ley lines, convergences, and earthen structures designed to heighten its energy. Very few knew how to access it, how to identify it, how to join with it. Being in this light was like sitting in the classroom of Mother Earth. I understood so much. I understood where my sister got her power.

My sister.

I moved closer, a gliding ball of light. Solomon shrunk back, but I didn't stop. I went into her and enveloped him in light, jerking him out and flinging his shadowy spirit into the air. He didn't fight, didn't say anything. He seemed stupefied, and perhaps a little humbled.

It is not meant to be held, Charlie.

Melki's voice invaded my wonderful ball of light. I ignored her. Bryn's spirit didn't fill out her body like Rex's had done. She was too weak. Too tired. Too broken by *ash* and its spirit-suppressing qualities.

Charlie, no.

But it was too late to stop. I had no real idea what I was doing, but if this power fueled my sister's abilities, then maybe it would wake her up, energize her, give her the strength to come back and be whole again. I took off, zinging around the room in an arc, gaining speed, using everything I had to hold it together, and coming back around, aiming for Bryn.

One giant dose of Nwyvre coming up.

I flew into her and released everything, dropping my concentration, my focus, letting the power explode out of me in a burst of white.

21

My chest collapsed in a great release of air. I sat up, eyes wide. Everyone in the ballroom was staring at me.

Melki was gone.

So was the power within me.

And Bryn was laid flat out on the floor, unconscious. Glowing. My sister was fucking *glowing*. I crawled over, not trusting my legs to support me. I shook, a billion tiny tremors vibrating at once.

Em dropped down beside me, hugging my shoulder as I sat next to Bryn and put my hand on her forehead, smoothing back the hair from her face. The glow enveloped my hand. Amazing. I looked up and found Aaron kneeling on the other side of Bryn, staring at me with an unreadable expression. After a long moment, he dipped his head. I returned the gesture.

"What happened?" I asked, unsure of what had been real and what had taken place in my mind.

"Momma," Emma said softly. "You're glowing, too."

I blinked, frowning. I lifted my shaky hand to see my skin ringed in white and my arm, my legs . . . Very dim, however. Not nearly as bright as Bryn's glow. My hair fell in my line of sight. I reached up and held out a strand—that, too, was glowing.

I started laughing. It was as if I'd been hit with pixie dust from Tinkerbell herself. And I knew now that it had all been real. It all had happened and everything would be okay.

"Bryn's just passed out," Aaron said. "She's breathing. Pulse is a little fast . . ."

"Momma?"

"Yeah, kiddo?"

"Are you okay?"

I stared at her for a long moment, and cocked my head as I realized that nothing ached or burned. I wasn't tired. And I was hungry—always a good sign. "I'm fine. I'm glowing like a lightbulb. And I'm okay."

She shook her head and smiled. "Except you *really* need a bath."

"Thank you, my darling child, for pointing that out."

"Well, you always say to tell the truth . . ." She stood and held out a small hand to help me up. "Can you stand?"

I took the help, gripping her small hand. Once I was up on my feet and balanced, I hugged her tightly, breathing in her scent and whispering into her hair. "Thank you."

She pulled back. "For what?"

I smiled and moved a strand of hair from her cheek. "For what you said to Melki. I never want you to put yourself in harm's way, but—" I cradled both of her cheeks in my palms—"Your courage makes me proud . . . And I love you."

"I love you, too. Your glow is fading," she said with tears in her eyes. "And I was hoping to take you to show-and-tell."

A half laugh broke through my lips. God, she was getting more like Rex every day. I glanced around the ballroom to get my bearings. The ballroom doors were closed and several warlocks guarded the entrance. The music was off, but the disco ball still spun. From beyond the doors and windows came the sounds of party horns and the sudden rise of voices as they started counting down to New Year's.

TEN! NINE! EIGHT!

I continued my perusal and found Rex.

SEVEN! SIX! FIVE!

He stood apart from the others. Tears of joy and sorrow ran down his face.

FOUR! THREE!

My heart sank. He knew. Will was gone.

TWO! ONE!

Sadness, grief, understanding, acceptance, it all passed between us in one moment, one look of pure understanding.

HAPPY NEW YEAR!

My daughter had lost her father. Forever.

Horns and clapping erupted with the crack of fire-works somewhere high overhead.

"Mom." Emma tugged at me. I was squeezing her hand too hard. I let go and turned. She grinned broadly at me. "Happy New Year."

I wrapped her in a hug, whispering against her neck as my heart broke. "Happy New Year, kid."

"I love you, Momma."

"I love you, too."

After clearing the ballroom, we took our small party upstairs to the room Bryn was using during her stay at the League.

Before I went into the room, I used the League phone in the hallway and called the chief—mine had gotten lost somewhere in Charbydon, if I had to guess. I told the chief what had happened to Hank in the parking lot, minus the details of his past—that was for him to tell, not me—and he was swift in his response.

"I'll put an immediate call in to the terminal. If they try to take him back through the gate, we'll detain them," the chief declared. "I'll get in touch with Washington and I'll put some serious pressure on the siren delegate here in town. I'll call as soon as I know anything. Get some rest, Madigan. You've been through hell. Literally. If we need to go in and take him back, I'll need you one hundred percent."

Easier said than done. Hank was a U.S. citizen. He had rights, and the sirens couldn't just come into our city and kidnap one of our own. Our big, bad bosses in Washington needed to step up to the plate and do something, anything, to get him back.

"Charlie," he said more gently than I'd ever heard him before. "There's nothing you can do at this point. Go home. Eat. Sleep. Let me do my thing. We'll find him and get him back."

"Thanks, Chief." I hung up the phone and stood there staring at the hall table until Emma poked her head around Bryn's door. "You coming in?"

"Yeah." I shook my head and went inside to stand by Bryn's bed side.

The glow on her was almost gone now, and her cuffs had been removed.

"And Solomon?" Aaron asked, staring down at her with his arms crossed over his chest.

"Gone." But that only solved one part of the problem. She was still addicted to *ash* and some of the others were still possessed. "Does she have any *ash* doses here?"

Aaron stepped into the bathroom and rooted in the medicine cabinet. "She has two here," he called, shut the cabinet, and came back into the room. "I'll see she gets it."

"Thanks. Why don't you and the guys"—I gestured to the two warlocks and Rex—"step out for a minute. I know she wouldn't want to sleep in those clothes."

Emma and I removed Bryn's soiled clothes, washed

her off the best we could with damp washcloths, and then dressed her in clean pajamas. After that was done, we pulled the comforter out from under her to cover her properly.

"Thank you, Char . . ." she mumbled.

I kissed her cheek. "You're welcome, little sis."

I straightened, gazing down at Bryn.

"What happened in Charbydon, Mom? Where's Hank?"

A tight sensation gripped my chest, making me wince. Hank was probably already back in Fiallan. "Let's just go home. I'll tell you all about it tomorrow." My Nwyvre buzz was wearing off and the exhaustion was starting to set in along with the beginnings of a monster headache.

In the hallway, I explained the situation in detail to Aaron, including Carreg's version of what had happened. The House of Abaddon would be coming for answers. I had no idea how long we had. "As soon as she wakes up, call me. Don't let them see her until Rex and I can talk to her."

"You have my word."

"Thank you, Aaron." Before he turned to go, I grabbed his arm. "She has paid enough. You need to move on or forgive her."

A muscle flexed in his shadowed jaw. I thought he might lay into me about sticking my nose where it didn't belong, but he just stared at me for a long moment before saying, "I already have. She just won't accept it."

He slipped quietly back into the room.

I gathered my kid and my Revenant and went home.

Rex and I took separate showers, washing blood and layers of Charbydon sand and grit down the drain. I sat in the tub, knees pulled to my chest, and cried. For Will. For Emma. And for Hank. I couldn't save him. I'd had to choose. And I knew in my heart I had done the right thing.

And the chief was right, too. I was spent. I didn't even have the strength to lift my firearm and focus on a target. Knowing this, though, didn't make the guilt go away.

Once clean, I dressed for bed, went downstairs, and rang in the New Year, albeit late, around the kitchen table with my family.

I smiled. I talked. I ate the ice cream drenched in hot fudge and whipped cream that Emma decided we should have since she couldn't drink the bottle of champagne Rex had apparently stolen from the Mordecai House.

But inside I mourned. Rex mourned, too; I could see it behind the stupid jokes and the goofy smiles. We made that moment special for Emma. Because she had lost something irreplaceable and soon her life would change and her heart would break . . .

The pall continued to hang over me as I tucked my sleepy kid into bed. "Night, kiddo." I kissed her forehead.

"You mean good morning," she said, smiling.

"Smarty pants." I shook my head, stepped over Brim snoozing on the carpet, and paused before closing her door. "Brim needs a bath first thing tomorrow. He reeks."

"Okay."

I shut the door and went tiredly down the stairs, every step carrying with it more weight and worry. The kitchen lights were already off, and the soft glow of the television led me down the hall to the living room where Rex sat on the couch.

I plopped down, pulling my feet in and snuggling into the cushy vee where the arm and the back of the couch met.

Rex turned down the volume and then angled his body to face me. "What the hell happened back there, Charlie?"

I didn't even know if the tale would come. It took a long time for me to answer, to find the right words, the right state of mind. I found neither. "He wanted to leave," I finally said.

Saying those quiet words out loud gave the whole thing a sense of finality. It felt like a fist squeezed my heart. "The sylphs' gifts . . . they allowed me to see him. I held his hand. Pulled him out. He wanted to go, said he wouldn't come back normal." I rubbed a hand down my face and let out a loud sigh. "I don't know if I did the right thing."

I glanced to the ceiling. Above. Where my kid slept happy and content. My throat thickened. I shook my head. "How am I going to tell her?"

I couldn't do it. How did I look her in the eye and tell her Dad was gone? A tear slipped out. Rex moved over the cushions and slipped an arm around me, pulling me into a hug. "I'm sorry."

My head fell against his shoulder. I turned into him, trying to hold out, but it was a losing battle. The floodgates opened. And I grieved for the loss of my ex-husband. He was gone. He was never coming back.

Rex held me, rubbing my back, kissing the top of my head, and giving me a supportive squeeze every now and again.

By the time I finally sat up, my face was swollen and hot. I couldn't breathe, my nasal passages were blocked, and my head pounded.

Rex reached over the couch and grabbed a tissue from the box on the sofa table. He handed it over, watching me for a while, a frown wrinkling his forehead.

"What?" I finally asked.

"I know you and Em wanted me to stay because Will was still here." He paused, gazing at the television without focus. "But now . . . Do you want me to leave?"

A half laugh, half sob escaped. I shook my head. "No. You definitely cannot leave us."

Frustration tightened his jaw. "Why? Because I look like him? It's just me now. He's gone. You have to understand. Em has to understand. I can never *be* him."

I glanced down at the ball of tissue in my hands, unwinding it to fold it over and over again until it was a tiny square. I drew in a deep inhale. "I know, Rex. Even when you tried to be him, you couldn't. Emma will understand. She loves you, you know. Not just because you look like him. She'll understand . . ."

His lips thinned. The muscles in his jaw flexed, and he ran a hand down his rugged face. Tension and emotions swirled around him. He scanned the room before settling his attention back on me. "And you?"

My sad grin widened a little. "I'm getting there. But," I pointed out, "*only* in a platonic way."

He rolled his eyes. "Don't have to kick me when I'm down." But I knew he wasn't serious. Rex was well aware I'd never have a thing for him, and I was pretty sure he was all bluster and would never have a thing for me either. "Speaking of . . . what the hell happened to Hank back at the station? I saw the sirens . . ."

I unwound the square and started working on folding it like the flag. "They came to take him home. Apparently they think he's a traitor. But he's not. They got it so wrong."

"You really like him."

I wasn't sure if that was a question or a statement, but I answered anyway. I was answering Rex when I should've answered Hank when he'd asked me in Charbydon. "Yes. I really like him." Him. Not what he was, but who he was. And now I wasn't sure if I'd ever get the chance to tell him.

A gleam appeared in Rex's eyes. "So when are we going into Elysia? We'll probably be banned for life from Charbydon, might as well make it two for two."

"*We* are not going anywhere."

"But you are going after him."

"Of course. I'll have to talk to the chief, make plans." And I desperately needed a few hours of sleep if I was going to be any help at all. "When I do go, I'll need you to stay here with Emma. I won't know how long it'll take. And I don't want to worry about her . . ." Rex's blinding grin made me pause. "What are you smiling for?"

"Nothing." He looked pleased as punch. "Just . . . you trust me."

I blinked. "Well, I thought we'd established that a long time ago. Where have you been the last few months? Look, nothing has changed, Rex, except that Will won't be coming back. I know what you're made of. You've been with us all this time, from the beginning of all this . . . craziness. I trust you. I know you love my kid."

Red rose through the scruffy jaw and up over his cheeks. "Blindsided me, that kid," he joked. "When did that happen?"

I shrugged, trying to be nonchalant even though I wanted to start crying again. "She's an easy kid to love." I released a heavy exhale, chuckling as I did. Making light. Trying to hold it together.

"That's one thing I haven't done, you know?" Rex parked his elbow on the back of the couch and rested his head on his hand. "In all my years. In all the bodies I've been in . . ." He stared off into nothing, his mood reflective, his voice quiet. "Didn't get the chance when I was a jinn either . . ."

"The chance for what?"

"To be a father."

Time seemed to stand still in that moment. We didn't speak. Just stared off into space, unable to look at each other.

I cleared my throat and drew in a stabilizing breath. "I don't know what to say to that."

"You don't have to say anything. I'm not looking to replace Will, not in that way. But I can still be a father figure. A male presence in her life. I've done just about everything I've ever wanted to and way more than I could've imagined. I'm tired. I want to settle down, be part of something, part of a family." His eyes narrowed. "And you tell anyone I said all this, I'll go Chuck Norris on your ass so fast, your head will spin."

I laughed. "Well, you *were* pretty quick with those chair legs . . ."

A deep smile brightened his face. Dimples. White teeth. Charming as hell. Just like Will. But never Will again. I sighed.

Get used to it, Charlie.

Rex leaned over and grabbed the afghan from the basket by the side of the couch. "Come on." He patted his chest and leaned back. "Come to Daddy."

Oh my God. I shook my head, laughing, crying, and beyond exhausted.

"Rest, Charlie. It's okay to lean on someone else, you know." He held out his arm. "Come, come."

I crawled forward and laid flat on top of him. He let out a suffocated *oomph* and I hugged him tightly. "Thank you," I whispered, kissed his cheek, and then rolled off of him and onto my feet. "Good night, Rex."

"Night, Charlie."

The next morning, Rex and I sat down at the kitchen table.

And we told Emma everything.

To say it was horrible was a severe understatement.

She just stared at us. Blank. Stunned. Unable to process what we told her. It was the longest moment of my life. I heard every bird chirp, every car pass, every tick of the clock in the living room.

It was as though time was suspended for this one cruel moment.

Emma had such an expressive face. Her big brown eyes were so wide, so round, so glassy. They latched onto me, desperate. So desperate. And I held them with my own, reaching across the table to grab her hand.

She didn't move. Her eyes said everything. Her face was a progression of disbelief, denial, panic, acceptance, and slow, agonizing grief. I watched each phase, feeling it all with her.

Never having done this before, I experienced a moment of uncertainty—more like panic—but I was trying to be calm and figure out how to comfort her and what to say. But when that first fat tear fell and her face turned red, I went down on my knees in front of her and gathered her into my arms as though she was a toddler, lifted her up, and carried her into the living room. I sat down with her in my lap and held her tightly.

Inside, my heart raced. I fought hard to suppress my emotions, to be there for her, to be strong, and not crack right along with her.

I smoothed her hair, kissed her forehead. My shoulder was already wet with her tears and her cries were loud and keening, like a young child with no inhibitions. The pain that came out of her was raw. I cried so hard that I only saw Rex as a blurry form that sat down beside us. His head rested on the back cushion. He put his hand on her back.

And we stayed like that for what seemed like forever.

I stood on the closed-in front porch, staring out at the soccer field across the street and biting the inside of my cheek. Supper was almost ready and the smells from the kitchen were warm and spicy.

Hank was gone. The chief had confirmed that the sirens passed through the terminal last night before the call went through to stop them. It appeared that Hank had gone willingly. With his badge and law enforcement credentials, he didn't need a visa or a permit. He could go wherever he wanted. And he did. He was gone. An entire world away, and no doubt in Fiallan.

I kept trying to convince myself that the Circe wouldn't put him back into the grid, but who was I kidding? To him, it was a punishment worse than death. To the people of Fiallan it was the best way to achieve their lame idea of justice. Tears pricked my eyes.

I'm sorry. I'm so sorry.

Sorry because I couldn't leave. Not when my kid was grieving, not when she needed me.

We'd stayed on the couch for hours. Then Emma had slept for several more. Now she was awake and in the shower. During her nap, I'd called to check in with Aaron, the chief, Sian, and then with Marti to see how Amanda was doing. The best bit of news, though, was the fact that Sian had been able to fly in an exorcist from Canada, and he'd already started interviewing the *ash* victims. No cure as of yet, but living with an addiction was far easier when you did it without a parasite pulling the strings.

The nobles had yet to show up. And during my conversation with the chief earlier, he said he'd notify me as soon as they came through the gate.

If we could convince the nobles that Bryn had gone into Telmath possessed by Solomon—and we had plenty of witnesses here to attest to that—and stuck to the story about Solomon jumping into the noble Carreg had killed, then my sister might actually come out of this okay.

I bit down harder on my cheek, crossing my arms over my chest as I watched a couple of teens tossing a football.

My thoughts turned to the shadow creature. After using Nwyvre in the ballroom, it was very clear the creature only showed up when I used my *own* power. Nwyvre was never mine. The last time I used my power had been at the portal in Charbydon. Wherever that thing was now, I knew it'd be back. Going into Fiallan to save Hank was going to require everything I had, and I'd be damned if that creature was going to stand in my way.

I bit the inside of my cheek, wondering if there was a way to thwart the creature's radar. Maybe I'd pay another visit to the Grove to see if Pendaran had learned anything new. I could pick his brain about his time in Gorsedd with Hank and maybe gain some insight into the sirens of Fiallan.

It wouldn't hurt to remind him to stay alert, too.

Grigori Tennin was not going to give up the search for the First One.

And with Solomon out of the way, Tennin would step up his plans. He'd continue to wage his battle for control over Charbydon. Or Atlanta. God only knew what his true goal was . . .

22

A week later, I walked into Bryn's shop in Underground. I needed a break after being on Solomon Street all morning, overseeing the search warrant for Darkling Properties and Rentals—it had *finally* come through. The search of property records and files was just one more link we were building in our case against Grigori Tennin.

It was slow and tedious work—countless files to go through, statement after statement from eyewitnesses putting Tennin at Helios Tower on the winter solstice, reports linking him with Mynogan and the drug *ash*, anything to pin down hard evidence of his involvement with the Sons of Dawn. It was like trying to build a case against a mob boss, one with serious connections, wealth, and power—we had one shot to get this right, to accumulate so much evidence that no judge, no lawyer, and no political envoy could dispute the charges.

The door jingled overhead as I entered and weaved my way around merchandise and stacked bookshelves, heading toward the back counter.

Bryn's back was to me, auburn hair pulled up in the usual sloppy-romantic twist. Soft murmurs came from her as she gently pruned dead leaves from a strange green plant.

"They're never going to talk back. You know that, right?"

She turned, suppressing her smile. "Shows how little you know about earth crafting. They *always* talk back."

God, she looked better. Standing before me was a vibrant, beautiful, feisty, softhearted person with a contagious smile and intelligent copper eyes. An earth mage with a gorgeous green aura layered with Caribbean blues. There was still the cloud of gray due to the *ash* addiction, but she was so much better now that the positives far outweighed the negatives. And she and Aaron had begun talking again. Talking was good. Those two were going to make it, I was sure.

"Why are you smiling?" she asked, reaching below to pull out her bowl of M&M's so I could have some.

"No reason. Anyone here yet?" We'd finally planned a meeting today—a sort of powwow to figure out our next move concerning Hank. "Where's Em?"

"I am in the back doing *inventory*," came a very bored voice from the open stockroom door, which then mumbled, "I'd rather pick up hellhound poop from the backyard."

I winced. "Wow. She must really hate inventory." Because she sure as hell hated cleaning up the backyard. I winked at Bryn and called, "Well, there's plenty of that left to do when you get home."

"Ha. Ha. Mother, you are *so* not funny."

Bryn laughed at me. "You're so mean."

I popped some candy in my mouth and smiled while I chewed. "How did the deposition go?"

Her eyes rolled. "Boring as usual. There are only so many times and ways the nobles can ask me what happened. I feel like if I have to tell that story one more time, I'll turn into a toad or something."

"Hey, I've had to sit there and repeat it, too. At least the nobles are accepting our story for now." And Carreg was being hailed as a hero.

Bryn's brow lifted in agreement, but a shadow settled over her—something I felt rather than saw. I knew thinking of the last few months really got her down.

I gestured toward the stockroom and lowered my voice. "How was she today?"

"Good. I think she really needed to get out of the house. I'm glad you let her come. The sadness will lift; you just have to give it time. I think you should consider putting her back in school soon. It might help. Be a distraction at least."

"Yeah. About that . . . Emma," I called in a stern voice, "can you come out here, please?"

"One sec!" After some shuffling and a bang, she stepped out of the stockroom and blew a strand of wavy brown bangs from her eyes with a huff. "What?"

I reached into my pocket and handed her a plain white envelope over the counter. Her eyes narrowed in suspicion as she opened it. "My birthday isn't until next week."

"It's not a birthday present."

She sighed and read the letter, her brow furrowing deep and then slowly easing the farther she read. Her big eyes lifted, utterly bewildered. "I don't get it. You said I couldn't go. You said we didn't have the money and—"

I leaned across the counter, grabbed her face with both hands, kissed her forehead, and then looked her in the eyes. "I know what I said. But I've thought about it a lot. If this is what you want, then it's what I want, too. And just so you know. I signed the papers before I went to Charbydon."

Before we lost Daddy. I wanted her to understand I wasn't doing this because she was sad, or because I thought it would cheer her up. I did it because it was the right decision, the right thing for my daughter at this stage in her life. She was ready. I believed in her. And I didn't want to hold her back.

One of the great things about being a mom is watching the range of emotions spread over your child's face when a wish comes true. When they've gotten something they've been begging for and never in a million years thought they'd get.

"Jeez, stop being all mysterious, will ya?" Bryn snatched the letter from Emma's hand and read. She let out a low, impressed whistle and then started grinning broadly. "I knew you were good enough to get in. And partial scholarship, too. Nice."

"Is this real?" Emma's gaze held mine. "Are you serious?"

"It's a done deal. You start on Monday. If you're cool with that. If not, they said you can start the following week."

I watched my kid smile for the first time in a week. My heart expanded with joy even as it broke—odd feeling, that.

Then she was the one leaning over the counter and grabbing my face, smashing my cheeks together. She put her forehead against mine. "Thank you, Momma."

"You're welcome."

"Oh, hell, you guys . . . You have to stop being so . . . mother-daughter-y. You're going to make me cry." We glanced over together to see Bryn already crying like a baby, her nose bright red.

Emma laughed. We held out our arms at the same time and Bryn stepped into our hug as we laughed.

"If you all start singing 'Kumbaya,' I'm *so* out of here."

Rex.

I hadn't heard the door jingle. Brim walked in beside him, immediately sniffing around for Gizmo,

Bryn's little gray gargoyle. The two had apparently taken a liking to each other, much to everyone's surprise.

"Rex, I'm going to school at the League!" Emma told him, waving the letter with excitement and then coming around the counter with her hand out. "Pay up. You owe me twenty bucks."

Rex glared at me and dug into his jeans. "I thought you'd never say yes."

I shook my head. Emma was bleeding him dry and he let her.

The door jingled again. This time Aaron appeared, and before anyone could say hello, the bell rang again. Marti and Amanda—free from her possession, thanks to the exorcist—looking more like her old self, which was basically a teenage version of her mother, walked in with Titus bringing up the rear. For once, he was out of his lab coat.

"Sorry we're a little late," Marti said, giving us a friendly smile as Emma told Amanda the good news. "We got sidetracked by the sale at Klein's on our way in." She glanced at Titus and her cheeks went a subtle pink color. I detected a bit of interest happening between those two. And if it bloomed into something, I couldn't be happier.

"Aunt Bryn," Emma said, "can I show Amanda the dead pixie in the back?"

Several stunned eyes fixed on Bryn. She bristled. "It's a *mummy*, people. Pixies are extinct. What? It's wrapped." She gave Emma a nod. "Go ahead."

Once they were gone, the adults chatted.

And then things turned serious . . .

"So your informant is sure he's in the tower?" Aaron asked, the only one standing straight with his arms crossed over his chest. Everyone else had found a chair, a chest, a counter, or a bookshelf to lean on.

They all knew now what had happened, what Hank had gone through, and what he faced back in Fiallan. A few months ago, I would've gone it alone, would've wanted to protect everyone and keep them in the dark—my heart was in the right place in doing that— but I realized that we were stronger as a unit than as one individual. And I needed them as much as they needed me. We were a family. All of us.

"Yes," I answered. "My guy was in Fiallan for three days, trying to get confirmation. The towers are guarded, Hank's especially. But he was finally able to get a visual during a guard change. Hank is definitely in the grid."

"Well, that's good, right?" Marti asked. "No one can hurt him there. In a way, he's safe at least."

"And perhaps there's a way to get him out safely," Titus offered, thoughtfully. "From what you've said, Charlie, I think there is a clear difference in being forcibly taken from the grid versus breaking free on your own. Before, Hank's mind was obviously not lost in the grid, it was a bit disconnected, right? That must've been what allowed him to retain his faculties and eventually escape the tower. But if Hank is completely connected and immersed, lost in the grid, if you will, we could be looking at the same kind of situation that happens to the other *Malakim*—"

"The only good thing is that the Circe are keeping Hank's capture a secret, which should make extracting him easier for us. The less guards and obstacles in our way, the better," I said.

"If the sirens of Fiallan knew the Circe had Hank; they'd definitely question his punishment, wouldn't they?" Bryn asked. "Going into the grid is supposed to be an honor, not a punishment fit for their traitor."

"Exactly. And we might be able to use that to shed light on the truth of those towers." The Circe were taking a huge risk by putting Hank back into the grid. If the sirens were to find out who he was and that the grid was being used as a punishment, it might make them rethink the *Malakim*.

"So whatever the case, we should probably plan to carry Hank out," Rex said. "Take a sling or something."

"Another consideration," Aaron began, "is causing a political incident. Relations between this world and the Elysians are good right now, but we must be careful of going in and thumbing our noses at their customs and laws. Not that I believe the *Malakim* practice is right by any stretch, but . . . we must get them to listen to us." The door jingled.

"It's more than simply rescuing him," Aaron continued. "To prevent the sirens from continually hunting him, Hank needs to be exonerated. We need to prove his case against the towers and the Circe."

"Well, maybe I can help with that." The chief strode down the narrow aisle, his wide shoulders taking up much of the space. "A group of civil rights attorneys are headed to Federation Headquarters along with ITF representatives from Washington. Hank's an ITF agent. A U.S. citizen. His record here speaks for itself. We might be able to get him released and sent back to us without having to step foot in Fiallan."

Liz stepped out from behind the chief's large form as he cleared the aisle. He'd completely hidden her from view. "Yeah," she said, giving me a wink through her glasses. "Flex our legal muscle and see what happens."

I tried to smile, but was pretty sure it came out as a wince. I wasn't as optimistic as the chief and Liz, and I didn't have the kind of patience Aaron was talking about. While they wrangled over Hank and the truth of the towers, he'd be fighting the grid, losing himself little by little . . .

"Point is," Bryn said to me, "we're all here. We're not going to accept what's happened. We will get Hank out, Charlie."

Faces smiled. Heads nodded. My throat thickened and I could only dip my head in thanks. The room grew quiet after that, minds turning and working . . .

"You know . . . this is just like that 'Dora Saves the Prince' episode."

All eyes went to Rex.

"What? A guy can't watch cartoons? You all try living as long as I have and see if you don't start watching Nick Jr. at some point."

I laughed, shaking my head. "What's your point, Rex?"

"Well," he grumbled, "it's usually the princess in the tower and the prince charges off on his white horse to rescue her. So, you know . . ." He glared at Bryn, who was laughing under her breath. "Never mind."

Bryn's laugh grew louder. "So what are you, Rex, like Boots or something?"

He shot her a sarcastic look as Emma and Amanda burst through the stockroom door, pale and frazzled. "Did you see it? Did it come out here?"

Bryn's expression went deadpan as the laughter died down. Her eyes narrowed. "Did *what* come out here?"

The guilt that slid over the girls' features had me straightening in alarm. A small knock sounded. Something fell from one of the bookshelves that lined the main aisle. We all turned in unison.

A thin, ten-inch-tall mummy wrapped in faded linen strips waddled down the aisle, bumping into everything.

"Emma Kate Garrity."

"Amanda Riley Mott."

Marti and I spoke at the same time.

Bryn hurried from behind the counter, her skirt flying out behind her, her ankle bracelets tinkling.

"You reanimated my pixie!" She dashed after the tiny thing.

Emma gave me a defensive look. "Well, I didn't *mean* to."

It only got worse as Brim and Gizmo appeared at the end of the aisle, eyes on the pixie. Drool dripped from Brim's mouth. Oh no. Emma yelled at Brim. Bryn yelled at Gizmo, and chaos erupted as the pixie darted to the left and everyone started chasing . . .

The door jingled again, and I heard Sian's yelp of surprise.

Aaron slid up next to me, leaning against the counter, humor glistening in those emerald eyes. "Never a dull moment with you Madigan women."

I sighed heavily, watching the chaos unfold, and letting out a small laugh. "Welcome to my world, warlock."

Acknowledgments

Many thanks to my family, friends, and readers. Your support and encouragement is nothing short of amazing and I appreciate it more than I can ever say.

I owe a huge debt of gratitude to Cynthia Cooke and Kris Kennedy, authors and friends who provided invaluable feedback in early drafts of this book and who helped me stay afloat when I felt like sinking. Thank you, ladies.

Thanks also to Miriam Kriss, Kameryn Long, my friends at Destination Debut, all the wonderful folks at Pocket Books, and my editor, Ed Schlesinger, for the guidance, the insight, and being an all-around fantastic person to work with. It's truly an honor.

And to Jonathan, Audrey, and James. For everything.

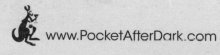